Camping Out

BOOKS BY ELEANOR CLARK

FICTION

The Bitter Box
Baldur's Gate
Dr. Heart, A Novella, and Other Stories
Gloria Mundi

OTHER

Rome and a Villa
The Oysters of Locmariaquer
Eyes, Etc., A Memoir
Tamrart: 13 Days in the Sahara

FOR CHILDREN

The Song of Roland

TRANSLATION

Dark Wedding by Ramón Sender

Eleanor Clark

CAMPING OUT

G. P. Putnam's Sons / New York

G. P. Putnam's Sons
Publishers Since 1838
200 Madison Avenue
New York, NY 10016

Portions of this novel originally appeared in the
New England Review, Winter 1979, as "A Man of Worth" and in
The Georgia Review, Spring 1982, as "The Fortress and Raggedy Ann."

Library of Congress Cataloging-in-Publication Data

Clark, Eleanor, date.
Camping out.

I. Title.
PS3505.L254C3   1986   813'.54   85-25772
ISBN 0-399-13122-1

Printed in the United States of America
2   3   4   5   6   7   8   9   10

TO
RED

I

"CAMPING! OVERNIGHT? in this weather? It's freezing! Marilyn, you're pulling my leg." Dennie's expatriate English was dotted with old-hat anglicisms, as it had taken her only three days in "the States," as she called her native land, to dimly realize. She just wasn't always sure what fell in that category. "You're joking." But Marilyn wasn't much of a jokester, and in a few minutes they were stuffing ski-time garments into a dufflebag and peculiar foodstuffs and fire-blackened utensils into two knapsacks and lashing the aluminum canoe to the roofrack of the car, to which it had miraculously gotten itself heaved. "I'm glad Carter isn't seeing this. He'd have a stroke."

The first mishap, right after their arrival the day before, had been Dennie's stepping in her myopia on a rusty nail, one sticking up through a board on the ground and that went clean through the sole of one of her borrowed sneakers, so having just driven two and a half hours from New Hampshire they had to drive another twenty-six miles round trip to a doctor for a tetanus shot and other appropriate measures. They were no sooner back from that jaunt than Marilyn's little terrier Corky tangled with a porcupine, and rather than drive another thirty-odd miles to the vet's the mistress of the house got out the chloroform and they operated themselves with an assortment of pliers and tweezers down the dog's gullet and over and under its tongue. Then probably from the fatigue of all this so soon after the funeral, Dennie in her fractured sleep mistook an owl's shriek close by the window for an Italian terrorist attack and bashed her head on a bureau, so she was now bandaged both hoof and brow.

However, this was another day, and sunny, only unnaturally cold for late June, and Marilyn's small red-shingled cottage on its sparsely traveled dirt road, sinister as it had all seemed the night before—and for a woman alone! really insane—had become quite charming. So Dennie had agreed to delay her flight back to Rome a day, needing the rest as she put it. But now this camping idea! She just didn't know her friend well enough to gauge how much and what kind of objection to raise, and in what tone, and her diplomatic hesitation gave the hostess all the edge needed to start pulling out the obviously much-used gear.

The two were old friends only in the sense of having first met some years before. Dennie, partly raised in Europe, was then a sophomore at Radcliffe, and Marilyn, with a reputation as both poet and lesbian already well established, the latter a little more, was a grad student nearby. They didn't hit it off at that time, to put it mildly. Dennie, though not exactly in love, was going around with the Harvard senior who was to become a sociologist and her first husband and a crashing bore in both departments. Marilyn sneered and jabbed; Dennie flushed and bridled. There were several such awkward encounters around Cambridge, then nothing more until they found themselves guests together, two years ago now, at a cosmopolitan composer's villa in the Dolomites. There, after the years of never quite forgotten umbrage, the genial tone of things got them better acquainted and they had parted on fairly amicable terms, in spite of some blatant rudeness by the older woman to Carter, Dennie's extremely handsome, cultivated and almost always well-liked husband number two. Marilyn, on that visit, was without her own longtime companion, soon afterwards dead of cancer, and there were rumors around the marble-floored halls of a rupture there. But the two or three people present who had ever met the female in question, usually spoken of with some sarcasm as Miss Beasley rather than Agnes, thought her thoroughly disagreeable and uninteresting and were only glad to be able to enjoy Marilyn's company without her. In that predominantly homosexual group, too multinational and sophisticated to be calling itself gay for another season or two, the Hensleys, Denise and Carter, didn't mind being warmly fêted as the token straight couple at the party. They were fond of their English host, had strongly disliked only one in his succession of bedmates, relished the wit and the music, and it was all a welcome change from the round of diplomatic proprieties or semblance of same.

As for Marilyn, good company she could certainly be when not riled by hostile forces real or fancied, and it had been on the whole quite a spirited weekend, even leading to an occasional exchange by mail of poems and critiques thereof between her and Dennie. It was a correspondence still short of friendship but on the warm side of civility, even if the criticisms were pretty harsh in the eastward direction. But Dennie knew that her stabs at verse, fewer and farther between every year, were lucky to get any criticism at all from such a quarter.

"And you say *we*'ll carry that canoe several hundred meters I mean yards to the water?"

By this time she was herself more or less joking, tumbled into the spirit of the thing, in spite of several kinds of misgivings. The younger by several years, and a born non-athlete, she found her friend's physical strength and competence amazing, but then she hadn't herself for ages been called on to do any heaving or strapping or think of cooking utensils even for a kitchen still less an open fire by some godforsaken little Vermont lake. Or pond as she was told it was called there. In Rome, and the other diplomatic posts before, they had people paid to do such things. The bombings and such hadn't come very close to her and Carter; their nine-year-old son Alan spoke English with a BBC accent while knowing the names of a number of drugs and people who peddled them; the parties and conferences summit and otherwise continued as usual and all looked suddenly now quite dull if not sunk into the earth for good. "It's fun to be crazy for a change." She was aware of Marilyn's silent putdown of that inane remark. "Carter's a darling but he *is* pretty conventional. You'd never think it when he gets one of his zany fits, the kind that used to make me think he had the makings of a poet. But he doesn't have those much any more, poor angel, he's so driven with reports and meetings and parties and everything."

It had been at one of those correct parties six days before, in their own lush garden off the Passeggiata Archeologica, that their flawlessly trained butler Mario, who later in the evening they knew would be railing against capitalist toadies of whatever nationality, careful to betray no feeling that might cause a stir among the guests, handed Carter the cable about Dennie's mother's death. Heart failure; on boat at Bar Harbor; funeral Tuesday at old family place in New Hampshire. Whoever thought of that last? It was ridiculous. Some such ancestral abode there had been for a time but the deceased herself had never lived there or even seen it as far as her daughter could remember, there having been something of a generational replay between them in the matter of early expatriatism. Little Evie Jones and her sister had also, though on a near-poverty level, had some school years in Europe, and the home base in Evie's youth had been not in New Hampshire but her mother's, Dennie's grandmother's, usually empty if much-loved country house in Connecticut. Evie's longest chunks of American life had been during World War II, when she made the mistake of marrying Dennie's already somewhat unbalanced classicist father, and in late years mostly in a string of marinas on her second husband's yacht. It was true they did keep apartments here and there in the interest of his "work"—some kind of lingering connection with chemical corporations and government agencies.

"You don't have to be comforting," Dennie had said to Carter on the way to the airport early the next morning, he having stolen time to drive her himself rather than send an embassy chauffeur. She spoke with the rough candor that had grown more pronounced in recent years, and that her husband rather admired in private but had come to be nervous about in public. "We haven't been close since, I don't know, I guess really since she married Stevie and stopped asking any questions for the rest of her life." Dennie and her twin brother had been nine then, in Italy, where their mother, determined to be a dancer, had hung on by financial fingernails after the break with the children's father. "Of him, the less said the better," was all Dennie would usually impart on that score, usually with the merry and husky, almost baritone spurt of laughter that men of all ages found so appealing. Indeed her father's story could have hurt the Hensleys in certain circles. In postwar Italy he had laced his classical studies with a newfound mania for black-marketeering, moved on to very lucrative smuggling of stolen antiquities and finally, after being expelled from Italy and buying his way back in several times, had gotten himself murdered by a cheated accomplice in an affair of a 2nd Century marble torso, in Damascus.

"Stevie's a good sort, though. I suppose it'll be hard on him." She hoped Carter would try to look in a few minutes on their son's birthday party. "And I'm afraid I'll miss that Nato banquet or whatever it is. I wouldn't have time to get my hair fixed or have a fitting for that new dress anyway." Probably she would stay on a few days and visit a friend or two. "I haven't been to the States in so long, except for that little time in Washington and you know what that was like."

Carter said to her surprise, with a rather whimsical little smile, that he hoped she wouldn't visit Marilyn Groves at least. Oh? What a peculiar idea, whatever made him think of that?

"I suppose just that her kind of thing is so in, nowadays. People would talk."

What an absurd locution, her kind of thing. He really hated to say lesbian and still tended to gag over gay too.

"If you mean she's been getting a lot of critical acclaim for that last volume of poems and the novel now too . . ."

But she'd been thinking, of course, of real friends, the so-and-so's on Long Island or the such-and-such's who were really more his friends, in Maine unless they were still in New York. Anyway she'd heard from somebody or other that Marilyn was living in some out of the way little place miles from anywhere, in Vermont she thought it was; she wouldn't be taking time for such an excursion as that, to see somebody she scarcely knew. For this assurance, as they waited for the flight gate to open, Dennie's mouth, hardly ever touched by lipstick and oddly full as against the tight, nearly classic strictness of her facial bone structure, went into her own brand of peculiar pout, that could make her look like a little girl playing grown-up or else a recent beauty aged overnight by obscure disappointments.

He kissed her goodbye with a special intensity, almost as though in tears, and she thought oh my God he loves me so. And where had her own love gone? where and when? She thought the sense of loss that engulfed her must be a belated one for her mother and truly hoped that was so—for at least one parent it was hateful not to be able to grieve, but honesty must prevail. He pressed her neat little head against his shoulder, a strong one by build but lately too unfleshed and at this moment positively quivering, and it was as if they were pressed together naked there in the pushing crowd, trying to make up for many nights of passionless sex or tired fondness short even of that. Their romance, not just in the beginning but for several years, had been wild, furious, dazzling to themselves and to all who knew of it. The sharp collarbone against her cheek vibrated and then seemed to snap like a breaking violin string, and her soul snapped too, in self-hatred and hatred of the scorn she could not quell, for the immensity of his longing. She smiled adorably and said don't worry, she'd almost certainly be back by Tuesday and not stay to visit anybody at all.

However, it happened that Marilyn Groves was doing a reading, or rather being the star at some kind of literary confab at the University of New Hampshire. She had read of Dennie's mother's death, turned up at the funeral, and soon after, the two were driving past lakes and around mountains that Dennie hadn't seen for many years. On her side, accepting the invitation was a way of dodging another evening on board the yacht, by then moored at Portsmouth, with her stepfather and two half-brothers. The younger of those was already bleary with cocaine and the other and his father, along with assorted cronies and more remote relatives, were getting ready to drown their sorrow in booze. The twin brother she still adored was trying to help rescue refugees somewhere in southeast Asia and hadn't yet been reached with the news, according to a consul's cable.

On the sex front, barring one puzzling recollection that Marilyn's detached behavior helped to bar, she wasn't worried, nor did she think Carter had been meaning anything like that. In the arts of rebuffing suitors she had long practice—most often if not invariably males, including a fair number rarely or even never before drawn to the opposite gender. A certain incongruity of physique had a role in that, visible even when formal floor-length dresses hid her rather heavy buttocks and lower quarters generally; her stride in spite of some efforts to practice the contrary was mannish; in shorts and bathing suits she looked ungainly, and that was when men tended to find her irresistible, in the contrast between that false picture of the big breeder and the equally false boyishness above, where no bra made could keep her quite ponderous breasts from looking like a mistake—snitched from a Calabrian mother of ten and stuck on the chest of some passing ganymede. She followed no current styles of coiffure, her very dark wavy hair remaining trimly short—"bobbed" as they used to say and she still did—as in her student days, around an olive-dark complexion and eyes nearly black, as over-large as the bosom was and in the common view enormously voluble, although that was actually due in part to quite severe ophthalmological trouble since early childhood. In any case the glance they could at times emit was apt to be called mysterious, or marvelous, for lack of a word to express its combination of appeal and reproach, merriment and melancholy, childishness and over-hasty disillusionment. There was in that glance, along with a quite knowledgeable, even risky or wicked come-on, the sense of a fruit picked too early for shipment and turned rotten before ripening, or of a human being who goes on surviving unspeakable emprisonment. It caused a number of people, disregarding verbal evidence, to think of her as more sensitive, and brainier, than her husband.

"Oh Lord where's the what do you call it, the bug juice? I'm being bitten to death." She giggled, however, and Marilyn, terribly efficient in such matters, had her hand at once on the spray-can, at the top of one of the knapsacks at their feet. Corky, recovered at last from yesterday's anesthesia, tore every which way over the strange terrain, yapping wildly at nothing in particular. "And how did you say we're to get the canoe down to the lake? I don't even see any lake—all right, pond. Are you sure we took the right road? Ouch, I forgot to limp."

The expedition leader meanwhile was hoisting knapsack straps over both pairs of shoulders; the huge dufflebag they would carry. Perfectly good path, look, right there. They would leave all this by the water and make a second trip for the canoe, which she had often carried that far alone, you just had to fix the paddles for a good grip on either side of your head, but it might be easier for the two of them to carry it right side up. "Even if it's not quite sporting. But it'll be something for you to wow them with in the palazzi." The touch of the caustic in this was just congenial, not meant to hurt. Marilyn's mood in general that day was as close to jolly as her somewhat snappish nature permitted, very different from the sharply probing tone, edging on accusation, that she had had in some of their talk the night before.

They had driven to the end of a broad, quite new and apparently senseless gravel road several miles off from an oldtime mountain traverse, much narrower and bumpier but which did at least lead, though only in summer, to a town of some sort. The incongruous branch-off, Marilyn reported, was part of a hugely expensive federal project designed to provide campsites for the motion-crazed and nature-starved populace, not local of course, but funds or enthusiasm seemed to have given out midway and the ambitious avenue into the wild was already reverting to that state. Still, the government-engineered path remained, as did a small wooden two-part outhouse—Dennie thought Marilyn might have used the women's section but didn't say so, besides in rural Italy there'd have been only one toilet or none—and the spacious circle at the end of the road could have held a large number of parked cars. And would soon; Marilyn wouldn't think of going there in July and August but now they could count on being absolutely alone. And was the canoe really necessary? It was. There was no path around to the good end, no way in except by water, "Unless you want to carry this stuff through about four miles of rather impenetrable underbrush and over a couple of swamps and a beaver pond." Might they see a beaver? Dennie would love that. "Though I expect we'd scare any wild animal off, the way we look." She went into a fit of girlish laughter, like a thirteen-year-old's, and in consequence had to cry for help to get the knapsack off so she could fiddle with her contact lenses.

Except for lace panties and bra, everything she had on was borrowed and more or less a duplicate of Marilyn's garb: long-johns, jeans, workshirt, sweatshirt, windbreaker, army surplus jungle cap of olive drab with ear flaps down against insects. Only she was several inches shorter than the owner of the clothes and had been fighting overweight lately for the first time since adolescence—"too much pasta," or too much dissatisfaction with life—so had a large safety-pin at her waist and the bottoms of the jeans rolled up, giving Corky the great pleasure of nipping at them most of the way down the steep path. The path, however costly to the taxpayer, was about a foot wide, gullied here and there by spring freshets and hidden from her view besides by her rear section of the enormous dufflebag. She puffed, groaned, squealed, at the end with relief and delight at the water's edge but that was where gnats, mosquitoes and deerflies were waiting to attack en masse. Never mind, the wind would carry them away from the camping place; Dennie had begun to wish it would carry her practically anywhere else too, or that at least they had a couple of strong men in the party to do the rest and worst of the carrying, but had the tact to keep her expression cheerful and her mouth shut. Life in the diplomatic corps did teach you a few things.

Not enough to deceive anyone as shrewd as Marilyn, who proposed to lug the canoe by herself after all, but of course the weaker vessel couldn't agree to that and with only a few minor, that is nearly but not quite catastrophic slips and stumbles, they made it once more to the lake, and strangely beautiful Dennie could see it was, in spite of the aerial horde sizzling at them without cease and a torment of resulting welts on face, hands, ankles. She didn't even overturn the heavily loaded and rather leaky canoe, just went overboard herself but at the shallowest point and partly over the rotten half-beached log they had used for a dock. The icy water didn't soak her through except in spots, they would soon have a fire and would dry things, the afternoon sun was glittering across a series of mountain shapes that seemed to encircle them almost totally, and though of course placed in the bow as the one of little if any competence, she got treated to an exclamation of surprise and praise for her paddling. It was in fact the one activity of the kind she had ever prided herself on or had any knack for at all and she had done quite a lot of it at one time and another.

She too knew how to twist the paddle Indian-fashion at the end of a stroke to avoid any telltale drip, and could plunge the blade back in as silently. She had learned this from her brother Rick and their grandfather on one of their times together in America, long ago, and wondered if Rick might be putting the skill to desperate use now, in some kind of oriental bark loaded with sick, starving escapees, amid jungle foliage and sounds of pursuit: rifle fire would it be? machine guns? But the lovely stillness of the Vermont scene and their motion through it, smooth as a marble rolling in a velvet crease, dulled the envy that often tore at her of Rick's courage and conviction, belated though they were, that could make her own life look so selfish and meaningless. The strong, even pulse of the paddle in the stern, oddly powerful from a woman, set up a rhythm of deep reassurance too, which seemed to extend beyond the immediate landscape and happenings to regions more difficult, including some rather prickly subjects of conversation the night before. Even the somewhat brittle (was that fair?)—anyway never understood mother so suddenly dead, seemed now no less suddenly about to be embraced, for the comfort of survivors at least, by the great Mothering principle that puts all creatures in their good and evil equally outside of time and blame.

Something like that. Swift, garbled images of Astarte and Cybele and the wolf of Rome scrambled the thought, such as it was, but the masterly throb of their propulsion through the still water, given mostly by the pair of arms behind her with the larger of the two paddles, went on conveying a very deep sense of reliability, and safety. The feeling survived even their having to back off from a tangle of water-lilies and farther on a bad scrape on a rock. Dennie's fault in a way, the one in the bow should be watching but after all her vision was quite poor, a fact that caused her husband to be over-protective at times, if not downright old-maidish about her. It had even figured greatly, she knew, in his passion for her in the first place; thoroughly masculine looks and behavior notwithstanding, there seemed to have been some little pocket of self-doubt in his psyche, which the need for a firm grip on her elbow in traffic or entering crowded restaurants did a lot to dispel.

"It's funny getting adjusted to such *low* mountains," she said when they had pushed off the rock. The canoe didn't seem to be leaking any more than before; it had been wrecked, Marilyn said, by a fool nephew of hers who took two friends running rapids where only the weight of one person could pass; the repair job hadn't been too good, but it would do, nothing to worry about. "I mean after the Alps. Or even the Dolomites. I suppose the Rockies too but I've never seen them. I wish I had. I *must* try to get Carter to take me out west some day." These last mountains, with the archaic marital note she blushed for at the end, she had tacked on hastily, to wipe out the Dolomites, though she was no doubt alone in that disturbance.

It was from the recollection she had mostly succeeded in putting down on the drive from New Hampshire, of a night in their friend's villa two years before. She had gone to bed, as had Marilyn in the adjoining room. Carter had stayed downstairs to listen to music a while longer with some of the other guests. The building was a made-over 18th Century monastery, with stuccoed stone walls enormously thick and more or less soundproof. She knew she must be imagining the little sounds of bedtime preparation in the next room, but she did imagine them, more and more intensely. Marilyn could never be called goodlooking, nor even particularly distinguished in appearance, when seen in a moment of idleness or inattention. Flat-chested, wiry, impulsive to the point of jerkiness in most of her movements on whatever scale, from walking onto a platform to reaching for the mustard at her own table. She had a long, slightly bent nose a little too splayed at the nostrils to be called aquiline, quite ordinary blue-grey eyes that at times could seem those of an ill-tempered saleslady at the end of a bad day, thin narrow lips always meticulously coated the same hue, a near-magenta, above a sharp little chin that positively cried out for a goatee. There was just enough of her drab and stringy hair to form a suggestion of spitcurls in front of the ears; her unmanicured hands were large and rough from such chores as log-splitting and even welding, in which she had once taken a course in the interest of independence. She wore pants and pants suits exclusively, seemed never to have owned a skirt since her middle school days when her mother was still in control. Her whitish skin tended to blotch and turn red instead of tanning in wind and sun.

Yet there was a profound trick, an actual reversal of the visible show in all this, and Dennie had once heard it described, in a tone verging on adulation—something the subject had a way of inspiring in the most unlikely quarters. The key fact of the matter was that idle or inattentive Marilyn hardly ever was. She didn't even have to guard against any such disfiguring state of mind. She was just naturally, vibrantly, and almost invariably on the ball. The male admirer in question, who had also been explicit in adoring her absolute lack of sexual existence in regard to males—"Such a perfection of a negative! and you can't tell me it's all innate, it's been *achieved!*"—said she always made him think of cosmic rays: such was the electric beautification at work in that common clay.

And such was the electricity Dennie had begun to feel and respond to that night through the thick villa, or monastery, wall. The head of the Hensleys' bed and the unseen one were both against it. She and Carter had slept in that other room on a previous visit. It was easy to visualize every motion being made, the posture over the wash basin in its little alcove, the trip to the toilet cubicle down the hall, the dabbing on of face lotion not in front of the mirror, the book picked up and pillows adjusted for a time of reading before the last light would be turned off. That would be soon, it had been a long full day, everyone was tired, but the charge of lust through the wall came on even sooner.

Shattering, it had been; amazing. Googly eyes from females Dennie had been the recipient of once or twice in her life but a real pass never; clearly she hadn't given off the right vibes to encourage that, nor had she ever dreamed of wanting to. It seemed to be the vision of tooth-brushing that swamped her, taking her right inside that unbeautiful mouth to explore fillings, match tongues, follow the little brush in every stroke up down and sideways, before drooling out and in ecstasy pressing her large bosom against the flatter yet mothering one, never before given the time of day in her thoughts and now so suddenly enrapturing. Her nipples rose hard; she clawed at them,

and at her crotch, writhing, fighting back a cry that was in part
one of desperate disbelief.

Never before or since had such a spasm seized her. Later she
cultivated a covering of incredulity like moss over it, but still at
times could be upset by the recollection. Luckily her husband
just at that time came down with a mysterious and bloody
genital infection that kept them chaste for some weeks: from
some sordid adventure perhaps? unimaginable from him and
he wouldn't have appreciated the joke if she had asked. Now in
the canoe it was refreshing to find that her own shame had
lightened almost to vanishing; the name Dolomites bothered
her fiercely for only a moment, whereupon the episode struck
her as quite understandable if not ordinary and certainly as
implying no threat for the night ahead, although Marilyn had
made it clear that they would have to share a double sleeping-
bag, to keep warm.

Some of the last evening's conversation had probably served
to defuse that old embarrassment. But then really, too, it was
time to admit that she and Carter weren't much of an ad for
sexual bliss, for all their long mutual hunger and infatuation.
Twice since their son Alan was born, leaving out a certain
earlier matter that didn't bear scrutiny, she had been violently
attracted by other men, not quite to the point of literal infidelity. In the case of the young American artist adrift in Rome
that was only because when they got to his sleazy room in
Trastevere he was too drugged to make it, and on the morning
before what was to be their next rendezvous he shot himself in
the head. The other idyll was with a Roman communist prince
of great wealth and charm, named Luigi, in whose arms, in the
front seat of his Alfa Romeo or in other people's hallways and
once a coat closet, she had thought for a week or two that she
would happily have died. In the crux, alone and with a couch
handy for the first time, he drew back with a howl of
"Mamma!" He had forgotten that he had promised to take that
lady somewhere at that hour, and for the next month he was
said to be dutifully keeping her company on the main family

estate, in Lombardy, preparatory to giving most of it to the Party.

Just now the only uneasy thought that came to Dennie's mind was about as lightweight and passing as a butterfly. It had to do with a snitch of their breakfast-time talk, before the idea of camping arose. She had asked Marilyn if there weren't ever any bad characters, housebreakers and so forth, in that isolated place. The reply was oh yes of course, in earlier years when she wasn't living there most of the time the cottage had been broken into any number of times, so had most of the vacation camps and cabins along the five miles between there and the pretty village where they had stopped for groceries, but the county sheriff had people patrolling the section now, at different times every day, and she also had put in an alarm system. It couldn't be hooked up to any police station, which would be forty miles away, but it made a hell of a racket. And didn't she ever get nervous at night, there by herself? Marilyn smiled, pointing to the rifle on its rack by the big bookshelf, and what she called her bowie knife, not that she'd ever needed either for any such reason. She kept a pistol by her bed too, which she'd had to "brandish, as they say," one winter night when a drunken hunter came in out of the snow and alarmed the friend who was with her: Miss Beasley presumably. Actually the poor dunce had seemed to be genuinely lost and just wanting shelter, to sleep off his condition; she'd felt a little contrite afterwards about scaring him out to bumble another five miles to the village, assuming he could stay on his feet and the road and didn't freeze to death first.

And then for rapists, Marilyn had added with a note of hilarity, there was another weapon. And what was that? Simple: just two or three good stout needles fixed in the end of a tampon. "Like this. I keep one around just in case." She went over to a small jewelry box and with a smile pulled out the ghastly little object. A friend of hers had learned about it years ago from a nun in Argentina, though the nun must have had to use a more primitive kind of wad. Dennie said that struck her as a good way to invite strangling but it seemed the shock and pain were supposed to be sufficient to let you get away or get the better of your assailant, for instance by biting the wounded member right off. With this, Marilyn had them both in stitches, her mirth could be so contagious. Actually, she said, she'd only had to use the contraption once in her life and that was with a highbrow acquaintance, "not a killer type at all," so she really didn't know what would happen under more ordinary circumstances.

However, for all the comedy, Dennie had noticed the weapon in question being transferred to a small tin box, together with matches and first-aid things. The hunter's knife hung in its leather sheath from Marilyn's belt; you always needed one, she had said, on a camping trip, if only to cut extra string for tent pegs, and it would be fine for carving the chicken they were going to broil over their campfire. She also had packed an elegant little folding saw from L.L. Bean's and a hatchet, for firewood. The rifle had been left in the house but hidden behind rags in a storeroom space over the woodshed; the hi-fi with its speakers had been whisked off under three other piles of trash; the alarm system was on.

———

All the above details appear in the handwritten, unfinished letter to Marilyn that was found among Dennie's papers in October of that year, after the helicopter crash in Africa for which credit was claimed by two rival terrorist groups, neither of them nationals of that country. In the list of ten fatalities, Mr. and Mrs. Carter Hensley, without their young son Alan, were the most prominent, as he had just assumed his first role with the rank of ambassador, in a small new nation badly needing a strong and skillful U.S. envoy to help steer, or quell, or understand certain popular disturbances. Among Carter Hensley's qualifications for the post, his political acumen and the social charm of both him and his wife had rated high. The boy was reported to be in a boarding school in Switzerland.

It seems likely, or quite possible, that the letter would never have been mailed. It is in the nature of an Apologia pro vita sua, is an attempt at least at some such piercing examination, but centered entirely on the night of the camping trip, which had cast a glaring light on certain ambiguities while perhaps creating new ones. Indeed she speaks of the adventure, by way of excuse for going on at such length—relating facts of course equally well known to the addressee—as the catalyst of her life and consciousness; and her tone at moments suggests that she is on the brink of drastic changes in her ways of being. But obviously, if any such had been made by October, she would not have been at the new post with her husband, who also might not have been appointed to it, or might not have accepted the appointment without her, and the crash would have had a somewhat different human configuration.

Or it may be that in writing the missive she was not groping toward pastures new but on the contrary, was opening her eyes and arms to what was. For all her contradictory traits, there was a streak of the stubbornly puritanical in her, no doubt reinforced by disgust at what she knew of her father; she had made her bed and her aim at that juncture may have been to lie in it, but with the grace of insight as far as possible, not in the blind faute de mieux that had caused her to gain twenty-five pounds in the preceding year. In any case, whether or not the document would ever have been mailed, she makes it clear that she and Marilyn had no plan ever to meet again and would aim to avoid chance encounters through mutual friends, such as the weekend gathering of the past in the Dolomites. This seems to have been not at all a question of animosity. The account breaks off before their parting the next day, we never learn from it how Dennie got to the return flight to Rome; perhaps Marilyn, too stricken to drive her anywhere or with her car still disabled as we learn of its becoming earlier, coaxed some neighbor in the village to take her to the nearest local airport. But there is no hint of hostility, no more than was latent beforehand and which, as is already plain, was one of the large ambiguities.

No, it was just that too much had been revealed all around and not of the stuff that bears sharing; and there were good reasons on both sides not to fear the other's gossiping, even if either had been the gossipy sort, which to an extent rare in women they were not and never had been.

Yet for all the grave underpinnings in what happened, and the crucial role of the interloper from across the lake, the pivotal point in the narrative and Dennie's mullings over it remains the death of the dog, Corky. She comes back and back to that, until by dint of repetition it takes on a note of fierce obsession, while plainly serving her to evade other questions, for example the true impact of her mother's funeral. The fright of the man's appearance in the motorless boat that was certainly stolen, his ravenous hunger, the thunderstorm, the sinking of the canoe, many such non-sexual points that might seem to claim priority, if the more intimate ones were too hard to face, are made incidental to the dog's story.

She does dwell on the precautions against robbery on leaving the house: how the rifle was hidden and so forth. These measures, along with the assumption that they were necessary, stayed as a vague backdrop to her growing feeling of refreshment and serenity, or rather came and went, much as the equivalent did at home, that is in Rome, where thoughts of crime petty or fanatical were never far below the surface and you just naturally carried your purse on the side away from the street, without thinking about it. Probably some such latent image of the enemy forces proliferating in society, the ignorant and unmoored, the drug-destroyed, the politically and/or sexually lunatic, had figured the night before too, in the dream that made her mistake an owl for that unknowable human threat. How far off and long ago it all put her mother's quaint erstwhile verbiage of "the workers," "the proletariat." As for the *canaille,* now in such different clothing, Dennie herself had always been partial to the French Revolution, at least up to Robespierre. The generation gap with her mother lay mainly in the latter's meandering pro-Russianism, originally straight party-line Stalinism, more absurd in the daughter's eyes considering that Mummy's two husbands had both been men of wealth. Not that that helped her or her infant twins much in the first instance.

Yes, she says she realized a month or so after the event, as she hadn't at all at the time, that Marilyn's little arsenal of weapons, the whole underlying acknowledgment of threat, were dimly in her mind when they heard the scuffle in the underbrush. This was not at or near their campground. They were on a little sightseeing detour before reaching it, to look at a curious area of floating land on the other side of the lake. ("Pond" she could not keep saying. Those Vermonters! anywhere else in the world it would be a lake.)

"And you too, I've come to feel that you had some suspicion of the truth then, some reason for apprehension, that you kept to yourself. Why, I wonder; unless I'm mistaken. Well, of course, so as not to alarm me, to the point of possibly canceling the whole expedition then and there, paddling back where we came from, spending the night once more in your house, comfortably; and with what recriminations? regrets? *Chissà*, as we say here. Who knows. I'm not as frail or timid as you thought in protecting me that way, if you did; you surely learned that before the night was out, unless you were too gone in grief and shock to see anything. Perhaps your own pride would have kept you, no matter what, from giving up at that point. Perhaps too—oh what a strange puzzle all this is—not all that much would be changed if we had done that. I mean if we'd had the simplicity to let ourselves be scared in time and not fret over whether the scare was imaginary. As God knows I wish it had been. If only for little Corky. Dear lost forever friend, forgive me for coming back to what hurts you so. I can't help it. I never forget it, never will. Sometimes I feel I could quite easily blank out everything that happened that night, as I have so many other dramas in my life—including the huge one you threw at me at the end—except for the way Corky was killed."

It wasn't just Marilyn's extreme attachment to the little creature that made the moment so searing. Dennie had been won over herself. The dog had slept most of the way over from New Hampshire, but once home had turned into an unholy little pest, a yapping mile-a-minute bugbear, not only in her escapade with the porcupine, which added strain to an evening ticklish enough anyway. She was a year old and decently housebroken but otherwise had outgrown none of the vices of puppyhood. An untoward sound of whatever sort, a passing car or chipmunk, a branch cracking, set her to barking and the bark was relentless and intolerable—a high-pitched rapid fire of staccato yelps, something between an angry parrot and a machine gun, except for the glissando howl at the end of a phrase or volley. She didn't walk or run, she whirled, now here now there with no sign of locomotion between, and in that manner landed for a snooze on the guest's pillow, which the guest had been glad to observe was up a flight of ladderlike stairs on a balcony over the living room, as far as possible from the bedroom occupied by the lady of the house. It was far from the bathroom too and she would probably break her neck getting there in the dark if she had to but that was a small price to pay.

Meanwhile the hairy devil had not just napped up there. She had chewed a chunk out of Dennie's Via Condotti suitcase and another, still more inconvenient for the traveler, at the back of a Ferragamo shoe. When apprehended, just before the porcupine episode, she was working on a translation of the Odyssey. A number of hand-hooked rugs and wicker scrap baskets, Marilyn cheerfully recounted, had ended the same way. Dennie, though not often hard-hearted, came to feel the quills had gone down the right throat; anything requiring a whiff of chloroform in that quarter seemed a public blessing. She had just come from a rather harrowing occasion, after all, and felt the need to make sense of it; in Corky's company she couldn't make sense of the next five minutes, let alone a whole human life and her own in relation to it. Humans, so her febrile thought went, had some rights too.

Yet she succumbed. It occurred at 7:15 A.M., when she was

jolted awake not by the Red Brigades of the night but what turned out to be a little pink tongue very delicately caressing her neck and chin. On the verge of hurling the intruder to the floor, if not down the ladder to the floor below, she found herself looking into the most irresistibly trusting, companionable and adorable little face she had ever seen. We're real friends, aren't we? the big black button-eyes were saying under their ledge of whisker, with another dainty tongue-swipe on the lady's cheek for perfect clarity, although the tongue must still be hurting and its owner was not yet quite over her grogginess. You could cup her whole tousled head in one hand, she was so small, and Dennie gently did so, with a hurt at the heart-strings from the swiftly passing awareness that her son had not since quite early babyhood looked at her that way. Then the right word came to her for the dog's color, not on the back where she was an off-black, between soot and gun-metal, but on head and legs and a patch of rump. Cocoanut-shell brown, that's what she was, and as rough in texture as one of those shells, whiskers included, nothing fluffy or furry anywhere. It was all a good stout announcement, in hair as in behavior, of energy and will and readiness to take on the universe, porcupines and all, with only the slick, nearly bald underbelly for a mark of vulnerability. Indeed her mistress said she did badly in snow because of that, would be raring to go when the snowshoes or cross-country skis came out but before long would be shivering and whimpering piteously and someone would have to carry her tucked inside a parka all the rest of the way.

She snuggled up against the visitor's armpit on the nice warm bed, got that almost hairless belly scratched a minute, paid with another drowsy kiss, and the two went back to sleep.

"And now I keep hearing the first thing that man said to us, from just offshore, where even I could see the miserable board he was using for a paddle, and I was thinking he was probably not as young as he looked. He said, 'Would you mind tying him up just a minute? I'm allergic to dogs.' He said it with a smile, very pleasantly. You said, 'It's not him, it's her,' and didn't put the leash on Corky, who was yapping her head off in your arms. We were both smiling then too."

A fact that may be of some peripheral interest is that Marilyn later raised no objection to Dennie's letter being made public in this modest way, just so her real name was not used, as it has not been. But she was bound to be recognized, as she can't have failed to know, and it seems surprising that she shouldn't have cared to veto such an invasion of her privacy. Some peculiar pride? perhaps a taste amounting to greed for publicity at any cost, acquired from her really rather limited literary triumphs? Or to give her more credit, a passion for truth? a quixotic sense even of debt, or posthumous reward due to that companion of little more than a day? She also may have seen it as a way of immortalizing her beloved Corky, as she would never be able to do herself. As the author would put it, *chissà*. No question mark. It is just an obeisance before the inscrutable, like the waning old custom in some Latin countries of making the sign of the cross when passing a cemetery.

The one criticism Marilyn was heard to voice was not of the sort calling for suppression or deletion. She was quoted as saying, in a small-town newspaper interview, that the phrase "Dear lost forever friend" was the kind of thing that had made poor Dennie's poetry so bad.

II

It was about 3 p.m. but the next day would be the longest of the year, there were hours of daylight left, and the clouds that had looked somewhat threatening earlier, over a mountain hump to the northwest, had slid away. A fish jumped, an excitement in that quiet; the breeze was enough to abate the insect horde, yet the water was scarcely ruffled and it was only some mysterious play of current that created a large dark area out from the farther shore. Birds of various kinds and sizes skimmed, squawked, chattered, and one, a veery Marilyn said, gave forth heavenly song from somewhere just back in the woods. Dennie was proficient in French, German and Italian, aside from what was supposed to be her native tongue, and was often admired for her smattering of Swedish and modern Greek too, and in something deeper than pride it hurt her to realize that she didn't know the name of a single one of those birds, or fish either, in any language. Perch; pickerel; that much swam to mind from the camping trips with her brother and grandfather ages ago, but she wouldn't have known one from the other now if she'd had them in her (ah, nice word, hang on to it) *kreel*. In one of her tart moments the night before, Marilyn had scoffed, "You career expatriates! No wonder you can't write; in conversation your only adjectives for people are 'tiresome' and 'amusing.'" However, there'd been at least one foreign scene that

Marilyn had been only too eager to have spelled out, for a special reason of her own.

Veery; related to the thrush; but then there were several kinds of thrush, with names. You didn't need them at embassy parties, and most other polyglots she'd known, like Luigi, didn't know them or miss them in their own language. Never mind, it was lovely to be applying this so different, non-verbal skill to gliding through the unsoiled water and air. That one dominant bird sang the urban-based exile's reprieve from long suffocation, and a very complicated aria it was, of many moods and phrases before a repeat of the main, full-throated theme. *Merci*, bird. Music at least had no passport.

Corky looked a moment toward the limpid voice too, and perked up more for another fish breaking water not far off their bow, but in general she was subdued, not to the point of curling up on the dufflebag; she stood on it, her forepaws on the gunnel, ready for surprises, needing to see the world go by, but there was no danger of her making trouble just then. Earlier, when they were loading the canoe, she had disappeared and given them a scare. Marilyn with her excellent far vision finally spotted her on a rocky point half a mile away; she must have gotten on a scent and arrived there at her usual furious clip by land, only land it was not, just swamp and waterlogged tangle of vegetation all the way. Marilyn called to her to stay, she would go for her, but before they could get the canoe pushed off, the little brown rumpled head was way out in the water, indomitably coming toward them. Dennie begged Marilyn to go anyway, but then at that distance she wasn't seeing the head at all, just thinking of the skinny, fragile-looking legs too long, as the tail was too, for a true terrier; she was just "mostly Yorkshire," and often looked as if her strength were not up to her enterprise. Her mistress, though hesitant, knew better; the dog would make it, was making it, shivering and contrite did reach them in just a few minutes, for a half-hearted scolding and a rubdown with a spare sweatshirt. She wasn't worn out either, only tired and chilled enough to let challenges go unmet for a while.

Their destination was a narrow wooded peninsula at the end, pointing south, but they agreed it would be fun to paddle a little farther and nose into an inlet over to the left where there were some botanical specimens of interest and the land itself, over about half an acre, with all its covering of marsh grasses and tall wildflowers, rested bargelike on water alone. Such a barge as in dreams you would set forth to sea on, only to find it is segmented, not trustworthy. The channel quickly narrowed, though it would widen again farther on. They laughed, in gentle pleasure and reflection, poking this swatch and that of the floating garden with their paddles to make them rock. To one side a steep little headland reared, topped by tall and dense conifers; along the water below it masses of wild iris were in bloom.

"Lovely. I've never seen so many. Oh, and look back there. Why, that's quite a high mountain, for here." Yes, the tallest in that part of the state, not visible from the other shore; a big ski area in late years but now at the turn to summer and in its blue distance gone back to its deeper dignity in time, savage and aloof, yet sheltering.

Then they heard the scuffling in the brush, to one side of the steep place and back a little from the shore. The dog sprang to alertness, quivering but silent. Marilyn with long-practiced balance stood up and after peering here and there said that was funny, old Jess Allen must be hiding his fishing boat farther from the road than she had imagined, at least she thought it was his, from the piece of bow she was seeing up by a bend where a secondary channel went off a short way; probably it was too much for him to lug the outboard back and forth each trip and he thought it would be safer there. Or even if he didn't risk leaving the motor, which she couldn't tell from that glimpse, the move from trailer to water might be easier. There must be a track she didn't know about, going over to the main mountain road, a walk of several miles at least. They'd met the old man yesterday at the store, which he owned and still ran together with his son; fishing was his big love, he knew all the tricks and characteristics of every pond and lake for a hundred miles around, but didn't feel like hauling the trailer as often as he used to, so had taken to hiding the boat somewhere for a week or two, until he saw fit to move on. Right now, he'd told them in the store with blistering profanity, the sciatica had him so bad he couldn't get out to fish at all, right in the best time of year for it, if the damn fool doctor didn't have him back out there in another week he was going to tell him something he wouldn't forget in a hurry.

What they'd heard must be a deer; or it could be a bear, there were some around; nothing to worry about, they'd keep their distance. No sense trying to push on for a closer look at the boat, too shallow and all a mess of weeds in there, better back out and get where they were going. They did at least see a mink scuttling under the bank. "You'll have to wait for your beaver. They're on the other side."

The breeze had stiffened and they were paddling against it now, but it was nothing to strain over and they had only a few hundred yards to go. Their talk of the previous evening drifted to Dennie's mind, in fragments, off and on, minus certain sharp edges she had felt at the time. In the mellowness of the present scene she even caught herself thinking it might be amusing, more than tiresome, if her companion were to try to seduce her, whatever that might mean unisexually. She had never given it much of a thought and really had no idea, unless it was with that Faulkner character's corncob or the upper-class dildo of Elizabethan and later times with its expensive variants, of glass and whatnot. Or was it all clitoral? That seemed poor pickings; maybe she should get around to asking, but her curiosity was less than burning and she probably wouldn't. At any rate Marilyn had shown no sign of interest in her of that sort and had only startled her with her offhand picture of the lesbian vogue in general, with some bits of autobiography along the way.

She had to make a living, didn't want a regular job but taught off and on at various colleges, a semester each, and of course on campuses now everybody was trying it, it was the in thing, often with a steady boyfriend on the side who was probably playing the same game; she practically had to fight the girls off. Actually, she said, she enjoyed male company, had several straight men friends, and she was damned if she was going to play feather in some callow co-ed's cap, just because she'd published a couple of books and they could boast about it afterwards. One campus beauty, though, and a brain too, three years ago, she'd really been in love with. It lasted two months and was marvelous, except that it broke up her marriage to Agnes Beasley—"You never knew her, did you? Such a warm, great person, but what can you do? Sometimes I blame myself for her death." But then the girl panicked, went home to Texas for Christmas and married a man who'd been her high school sweetheart. "A perfect dunce, a big rich oaf, with a pecker I suppose. She never even went back to college. Just sent me a goodbye telegram. That's the one time I've seriously thought of killing myself."

A couple of years before that, she'd had a yen—"Don't laugh!"—to have a baby, "if I could get it without the drek. My own, I mean. We looked into artificial insemination, Agnes and I. I'd have been the fall guy. She never could have stood nine months of nausea and swelling and farting and burping, and I don't know why, she had a horror of varicose veins, was sure she'd die of it if she ever got them. We thought it would be fun to raise a child together. But the thought of the genes you might get, out of some anonymous tube, was too blasting. And then when you look at friends' children and what's happening to them, you realize how lucky you are without." With a stab at courtesy she put in, "I suppose yours is different. You only have one, haven't you? A boy, is it?"

Dennie said yes and he was just fine. Oh of course there could be little things that upset you, but Alan was a good student, warm-hearted, really adorable, and so goodlooking.

"That's nice. You sound proud of him."

"Oh, absolutely."

Up to the last bit, a trifle edgy, this talk had all been quite casual, over a gin and tonic after the chloroform job. Later, when they finally got to her idea of a meal—hamburger rocks thawed in the pan, ready-mix mashed potatoes, a snitch of lettuce spared by the rabbits in her ill-tended garden patch, some juice-free, no-taste New Jersey cherries from Mr. Allen's store for the big treat—Marilyn grew more intense in probing certain aspects of her guest's European life. In particular, she was avid to hear about a semi-ruined fortress over the Mediterranean, where Dennie had spent a good many summers in her childhood and early teens; one afternoon by their friend's pool in the Dolomites she had told some stories about it which much later came to take a peculiar hold on Marilyn's imagination, for a reason that now came out. It was even this alone, Dennie quickly guessed, that had caused her to go to a funeral of so little significance for her and brought about the Vermont visit with all its consequences. The lady on the inviting end—and she had been quite urgent about it—wasn't, of course, saying anything that crude, but was not reticent about the nature of her curiosity.

She had spent several weeks in Paris the winter before and got so filled with the latest thing in critical theory, she hadn't been able to write a line since. Not just filled with it; bedazzled, swept away, enamored of it, head over heels; it had made her see everything in a new way, and in that condition one would naturally be stymied at the typewriter. She expounded some of the basic tenets to a by-then very sleepy guest who had a sore foot besides. All life and literature were contentless, meaningless. Like a little child's drawing in sand, on a beach? Well, more or less. All sense is given by the beholder; to analyze the intent or content or portent of any work of art is an absurdity. Michelangelo and Dante too? Don't be childish. A certain genius, a young or youngish professor of phoneyatrics, that is the new critical discipline replacing what used to be called linguistics, named Dolmecq or Draminck or something, was if not the fountainhead, a top-flight exponent of this inspired doctrine. Marilyn realized she had been on the wrong track from the beginning. She had to find a new approach to reality, not that there really was any, but a substitute, something to give a frame, or container, or armature to the play of illusion that used to be considered subject matter or the material of art.

Dennie had yawned, and apologized for it; yes, it was all fascinating, she could see how wrong she'd been to have felt quite a lot of reality in the Vermonters they'd met in the store, just in their turns of speech, for one thing; in fact, it had given her a sudden appetite for getting in touch with the U.S. again, a feeling that her and Carter's life abroad was somehow shallow, a skittering over the surface of things.

"It may be, but not for the reasons you think. And in their heads, these natives are flying around just as much as your jet-set friends, with TV and tourism and developers on all sides. But that's not the point anyway." She spoke so harshly, Dennie wondered if her sexual deviation might have raised some eyebrows, made her feel slighted and sore, whether or not the community was as old-fashioned as outsiders might think. But people had seemed friendly enough to her in the store; all the atmosphere the visitor could detect was of live and let live. No, the real trouble stemmed clearly from Paris and the scintillating Professor Drumblank, who had shown her so irrefutably that there was nothing for her to write about, for instance, in Vermont; for a person who knew nothing about it there might be, on the debatable assumption, the guest rather meanly reflected, that any art had any value, except in giving these supercritics the pleasure of dismembering it. A *verbal construct* was the only thing worth aspiring to and for that you needed an ambiance quite *un*familiar, so as not to get bogged down in the deceits of the actual, meaning of course reality, or cliché.

Another yawn, another apology; the diplomat's wife, veneer wearing thin, heartily wished herself home in Rome. She had read a good deal of French literature, contemporary and other, in spells off and on, had taken in vogueish ripples of existentialism with her baby bottles, gone straight from Babar to Robbe-Grillet, spent her teens stuffed with that decade's *nouveaux romans*—which her present companion could have known only in translation where such had been perpetrated, as her French was quite limited not to say lamentable. In fact, as slowly became clear, it had been from American friends and acquaintances living in Paris, or from Europeans of cultural interpreter status, not from the horse's mouth at all, except as a few grooms around the stable were fluent in English, that she had taken in all that grand illumination.

Very thin and boring stuff, Dennie had at last found the courage to call the whole craze and its several aftermaths; in fact in a recent conversation with a French journalist in Rome she had argued, in a rare fit of rudeness and irritation, that his country had theorized its novelistic genius into the ashcan for a good long time to come, through a form of artistic tyranny that no other bunch of intellectuals had ever exercised in that degree. Could the semantic unraveling that had so burst upon Marilyn be just one more elaboration on poor old neo-deconstruction? mis- or discreation? un- or antiverbiotics? Certainly not; those had been only tentative approaches to the problem and nothing was now more passé; in Paris they were screeching with laughter at all the American academics who were still falling even for old Deconstruction itself, and providing a lucrative living for its leading exponent, that smart cookie Professor Montrose or Montblanc or Montazur, some color of mountain, who knew how to play the gullibility circuit around U.S. institutions of higher learning.

The Drumbluch theory, in contrast—and here Marilyn waved toward a scattering of slips of paper tacked to her walls, scrawled over with what looked like mathematical graphs of a rather elementary sort mixed with dictionary definitions and equation signs—was far more sophisticated, although not entirely divorced from the same basic logometrics. It was commonly called *nihilogatry,* but its two cornerstone concepts, on which all other verbal refinements and interpretations must be based, were the triangle (not necessarily 90 degree) and the color grey, and the true name for this school of criticism was

TG 53, or in English GT, for Grey Triangle. The significance of the number was not for any neophyte to try to grasp; in this one's French diction, it came out as *sang cunt Troy*, and she reported, not altogether without merriment, that some loyal adherents—she didn't say of what nationality—generally referred to the movement as The Trojan Hearse.

At this juncture, somewhere into the demise of the previous decade's version of semiotics, Dennie must have dozed a minute. She had a blurred recollection of a stream of enormous words, among which only the smallest conveyed some vague meaning to her, from philosophy courses at Radcliffe years ago. Had she perhaps dreamed this outlandish vocabulary? But no, it had come laced in with an account of previous moves in the author's treasure hunt. It seemed Marilyn had acquaintances and family connections, cousins perhaps, or there might be a brother or two, in the international business world, and she had gone to some trouble to pick their memories of their months or years in Iran, Germany, Ceylon, Japan, wherever, but for some reason their observations were no more useful to her than her own quite extensive travels. After all, Dennie thought later, Marilyn herself, as well as all those corporation pilgrims, had seen plenty of 16th Century fortresses, a dime a dozen around Europe, and everybody has seen everything by now, even aside from the boom in U.S. emigration; she'd heard just the other day that there were 80,000 American residents in Rome alone, which left out dozens of such enclaves elsewhere in that one country, and hundreds in others not far behind in military architecture, poverty and bizarre characters. So what on earth could she supply that wasn't in the general kitty? Well, the kitty hadn't quite done the trick for Marilyn. Some essential depth, or juxtaposition, or perhaps just realistic detail though of course she wouldn't use that, had always been lacking.

But then idly glancing through the obits as she always did at breakfast to wake herself up, Marilyn happened to notice whose mother it was who had kicked the bucket, as she put it, and Dennie's tale had sprung to her mind. At that juncture in their talk she was forgetting her manners and made light of the death in question, perhaps because of a detestation of her own parents. At least she thought her father, an historian of science, an abominable tyrant, self-absorbed, demanding and oblivious; her mother she partly pitied but mainly scorned for sticking to such a mate.

Dennie had at last gotten the point, and laughed. "But how could you write about that? You've never seen the place, you don't speak Italian . . ."

Precisely; she hadn't gotten the point at all. What was needed was just such a sketchy armature for a structure of sufficient originality to get an accolade or at least a nod from Paris, and rescue the author from her creative dumps. Just a nuance, an adumbration, for the linguistic construct to take off from without the danger of any worn-out verisimilitude, any of the shabby old delusions about the nature of fiction. Dennie refrained from saying that one aspect of the story, which seemed to loom particularly in Marilyn's memory and quest, struck her as rather risky from that point of view, as involving to her more everyday mind quite a chunk of old hat or reprehensible reality, whatever the feminist pummeling it was going to get.

"It's the two main, antithetical varieties of female subjugation to the male, the romantic and the conjugal, and with the two main varieties of male louse. There's the little old lady, the owner, what did you call her?"

"The Signorina."

"Yes. And the not-quite servant one."

"Assunta."

"And your mother for the third, the alien lost soul between. That's the *human* matheme—a triangle, you see? and set in a hundred percent male stronghold. A fortress! Designed with an eye to nothing but war waged by men. Did you ever think of that?" Actually no, she hadn't, but then she had been just a child. "So there we get in that actual structure, a matheme in itself, we get all those literal stone triangles, of the outerworks I think it was. You drew some diagrams of them in the dirt that time. What a combination! what a graph!" Her sweeping gesture dismissed a dozen of the little graphs tacked to her living room walls, as now suddenly seedy and superseded. "Oh it's perfect. I've simply got to hear it again."

She must have grasped the doubt clouding the other end of the sofa.

"It's all in the treatment, my sweet dumbbell"—this was the nearest to intimacy she had come that evening—"can't you see? And that's where my not knowing *their* language, or the place, or the whole country outside some museums and restaurants, is just the ticket. Just exactly what I've been looking for." The magenta lips parted wide, in the first genuine smile of the day; her whole narrow face had suddenly blossomed, beatifically; she was seeing her way out of a killing impasse, and on to achievement as yet unknown, since it was no secret to either of them that so far this scintillating school of criticism had bred nothing but more and more abstruse criticism; it would be for her to apply its mind-splintering tenets in what was once called the creative sphere. And Dennie had no objection to telling the story again, whether it would help in the next great anti-novel or not. But it would have to wait. They were both much too tired by then, and thoughts of her mother in other locales, other times of her life, were making themselves unexpectedly vivid and pressing, so in the last minutes before the two went off to their widely separated beds, she told an anecdote of a different kind, to ease her own mind.

It was about the moment when her mother decided to leave her first husband, Dennie's father, and a single, precise moment it seemed to have been, with no conscious awareness of any preamble in the way of lost affection or disillusionment, in spite of his having beaten her once or twice in drunken fits of temper. When Dennie walked out on her own first spouse, the boring young sociologist, it was after harboring the idea through the whole eight months of their legal marriage, if not for a while before. Not Mummy, at least according to her account of it to a friend one night when the twins were about ten years old and eavesdropping as usual.

They had been four at the time of the episode she related, early spring 1948, and living in Rome where their father was a fellow in classics at the American Academy. The two parents planned to join a group of artists and architects at the same institution for a ski trip to Switzerland. Baby-sitters were acquired; both parents needed a change, they didn't quite know why; all was happy anticipation. The group would all travel together, a full night and day by train under what were still postwar travel conditions, except for her father who had to go a day ahead to attend some "business" in Zurich. It seemed he was a goodlooking, energetic and witty man, of superb academic credentials, fond of the children and good company most of the time. Their mother understood nothing of business and didn't inquire much into his; he was of a rich family, she knew that much, and that it made them unique among their associates in Rome; also, that he engaged in black market money-changing in a big way, for poorer fellow Americans as well as himself, which everybody said was the normal, accepted procedure at the time. It was only much later that she had any inkling of his smuggling operations, in currency that spring and art treasures soon after, and of the devouring obsession behind them, so that didn't really bear on what happened in Davos.

It was rather an exhausting trip, third class; nobody slept; they had to change trains with a long wait in Milan, and change and wait again in Zurich. Finally arriving tired and late for dinner at the hotel in Davos, they found her father exuberantly high at the bar, with some pickup acquaintance, or perhaps one of his business pals. He shouted profuse and profligate greetings all around, and insisted on everybody's joining him in a *pflümliwasser* immediately; they were not even to go to their rooms or a w.c. first, they absolutely must have some of that wonderful liquor that very minute, there was no eau-de-vie like it anywhere else; and he proceeded to demand, more than order, a round for the whole bedraggled company, who got it down with the best grace they could muster before escaping to wash up for dinner. His young wife was of course embarrassed, but she had seen him like that before, he would be forgiven. The stroke of lightning, the horrible illumination that would change her life, hit at breakfast the next morning, when he announced to the whole group of friends, in a loud voice, peremptory and dead serious, brooking no contradiction, that is, positively inviting some demurral so that he might proceed to crush it, "You all owe me four francs fifty for *pflümliwasser!*" And he went around the table collecting it.

"It happened in that one sentence," Dennie recalled her mother saying. "'You all owe me . . .' I wanted to go through the floor. But all over the floor, and the walls, and our friends' faces, and the beautiful snow rearing up to the sky out the big dining-room window where the joy we had come for was supposed to be waiting, I saw the word *divorce, divorce, divorce.*" So the decision, never before thought of still less discussed, was made. It was just a small postscript to it that after breakfast when they all went to get their photographs taken for the week's ski-lift pass, her husband slipped out of line at the photo booth, said he had to speak to somebody he knew, and turned up after a few minutes wearing another man's pass and picture. He got away with it too, as long as they stayed. Bought it at half-price. He'd heard the stranger telling somebody in the liftline that he had to leave suddenly and wouldn't be able to use the rest of his pass.

Marilyn sighed, her left arm raised to cushion her uptilted head at the back of the shabby Victorian sofa, legs masculinely crossed, eyes musing through her cigarette smoke at the frayed toe of the suspended and rhythmically dandling sneaker. "Oh God, it's all so drearily *common*place. But I can understand your having to talk about it just now. I suppose when my mother splits, I'll be thinking of a lot of crud like that too, for a day or two. Of all the locutions we still let ourselves be victimized by, I suppose 'death' is the worst." Smiling a trifle, Dennie murmured that "love" was pretty terrible too, but that got ignored.

"One of the most seminal French minds alive—I'd have given anything to meet him but he's rather a recluse—has called it 'excorporation into non-being.' You see how that clarifies the categories. There's the formula for it right up there over the stove. No, no, not that one; that's on the properties of grey— yes, the color grey, of course. That other one, with all the lower-case f's and m's. If you can't see that far go up closer. Tolstoy could have been a great writer if he'd had that on his wall." This last might have been half in jest, it was hard to tell.

She sighed again, kissed the still unconscious little dog on the forehead, began turning out lights. "I wish I hadn't always been so rotten at math. I'm going to take a course in it next year if I can manage. A little five-letter word like 'death' gets you all balled up without it. And then, what bothers me is, it only has four letters in French, so the formulae don't all work. Some people in Paris don't seem to have considered that."

III

THEY DID SEE a beaver, at least sharp-eyed Marilyn did. Dennie just heard the sharp slap of its tail, warning the others to scuttle home, and then that one must have dived for the entrance too; she could just barely make out the big scraggly mound of brush and branches of all sizes. Their dam across that far nook of the pond looked senseless but as usual some separate inflow, of rivulet and perhaps springs, had made it raise the water level enough to kill a few hundred conifers and birches and give that part of the scene an air of war-blasted desolation. It made her think once more of her brother in his far-off, dangerous enterprise. Once in a great while for a few seconds, usually after a fit of longing for his physical presence or a flash of reminiscence normally dormant, she would be aware of wishing him farther away than that, out of her hair, out of her mind and life for good, and the mortuary enclave wrought by the beavers brought on one of those horrid moments. The camping place, however, was on a slight rise and as delightful as Marilyn had promised.

Good; nobody there; there might conceivably have been other campers they hadn't spotted, with a boat tied up around a farther bend. Furthermore the previous occupants, or occupyers, had been the oldtime outdoor sort who respected the courtesy of the woods, a rarity nowadays, Dennie was told; they hadn't scattered the blackened rocks piled together for a fire-place, had left a neat stack of sawed wood for the next-comers and must have buried their garbage. The landing place was a bit awkward and unsheltered, alongside two jagged rocks offering little if any foothold before the jump up to a sloping hillock thick with brambles, but with some grunts and squeals and near-misses they got the heavy bags and themselves up and the canoe tied a few yards to one side, in the direction of the beavers, where they hoped it wouldn't be banged around if the wind rose.

The sun was still fairly high over the western ridge, the light brilliant, shadows everywhere a multitudinous scrawl of hard-edge, utter black. Hardly an insect; as predicted, the breeze was flapping them off somewhere else. "How exciting, to breathe! I'm so glad we came. It shakes me up, so deliciously. I suddenly realize I've been letting myself feel *old* the last year or two, I really have, and nothing seemed worth remembering, isn't that funny? I feel I've been sort of saying to myself without knowing it, 'All right, go ahead and get fat if you want to, the ship's sinking anyway, just give up and go down with it and stop trying to be young all over again,' as if being young had ever been that much fun to begin with. Something like that."

Dennie smiled, directly into her friend's eyes, feeling that they had indeed become friends in the last hour or two, no longer the cautious companions of the day before, when there had been something of the highwayman and his prospective but fully aware and wary victim as they moved along side by side. "You're about thirty-five, aren't you?" Marilyn said drily, being herself thirty-eight. But there was no stiletto in view; only the old-woman act made bad stagecraft, coming from a face almost childishly glowing at the moment, and in general abnormally unwrinkled for its age, as from a will to live held too long in abeyance.

They were squatting before the semicircle of rocks getting a fire started, their camping gear still not unpacked, Corky sniffing here and there in excited investigation but at no great distance. Memory and desire, mixed; that was supposed to be in April, but Eliot must have been thinking of a less northern climate. Dennie's weak eyes re-created the delicate purple, un-royal, more like a tint in the finest Venetian glass, of the wild iris over by the other shore. The birds, perhaps with fledglings still to care for, were at their busiest now, swooping with loud cries after thousands of specks of supper or in the case of the large predators a single butcher-job. The smell of balsam was very fresh and strong, mixed with the sweet woodsmoke smell from the fire that was at last beginning to catch. Memory and desire—of what? for what?—rushed in torrents through her. It was as if the beaver dam over there, product of who knew how many hundreds of hours of patient tooth-work plus transporta-tion of materials and all the wondrous builders' skill in fitting piece after piece into the edifice so there should be not the slightest leak, had been dynamited, as she'd been told they often had to be before roads or too much land were damaged.

She was one of those sharp-pointed pieces, swept away; or rather the torrent itself, too long held back by a contrivance alien to its nature. Her maternal grandfather, the glamorous old hunter and fisherman—such a failure in the business world!—strumming his battered guitar by the campfire in New Hampshire or Maine, whatever likely bit of wilderness they happened on in his ancient Ford or Chevy, just so there was a rowboat to rent, teaching her and Rick the parts to his enor-mous repertoire of old glee club songs, for the three of them to sing in harmony in the evening by their fire; that would be after their day's catch of perch, pickerel, bass, once a lake salmon, had been cleaned and eaten and the overflow, the still live fish, kept first in a bucket in the boat, secured in the makeshift pound Grandpa always rigged up if they were going to stay a few days. The taste of beans and molasses from the bean pot they would have buried on a bed of coals early in the morning to simmer all day, an Indian practice picked up in his wander-ings in the West; the wild yarns, out of an endless stock, that the twins would beg for so they could shriek with laughter, tales

of gargantuan humor and energy most often, out of his older,
perhaps already then vanished America: all this, and his sorrowful love for those semi-expatriate and fatherless children of
his own blood, came tossing forth in the flood. She had been
burying them deeper than any bean pot, but now scene after
scene burst into memory. One was of them setting the woods of
a small island on fire, with the coals for their beans, and how
desperately the three of them, the old man and the two children, raced about with pots and their one pail and blankets
hurriedly soaked in the lake, to stop the fire that was already
dreadfully creeping through the matted pine needles and beginning to jump in flame from bush to bush; they put it out,
burning themselves a little.

There were several such trips, and she had learned much
later that Grandpa had scraped the bottom of his barrel, had
even pawned his watch and most of his clothes once, to have the
children sent over from Europe, it grieved him so to have them
raised in a foreign land, knowing next to nothing of their own
heritage. And she remembered how supercilious they used to be
to him, for all their fondness and joy in his company, because
he had never been to Europe and hadn't the slightest interest in
going. Yet he had had some foreign experience of an "un-
cultural" sort. On short-term jobs as a mining engineer, having
never recouped from the enforced American exodus from the
gold mines of Mexico in 1910—before his own children were
born! it was hard for them to imagine anything that long ago—
he had had some rough trips to Central America. These provided him with another stock of narratives, of a boa constrictor
around his tent pole and other such, and a snake rope from
Guatemala, to coil around your cot or sleeping bag at night,
which he always brought along on their expeditions; it was
coated with horsehair bristles that no sensible snake would
cross, so he said. He had a freak memory, for the poetry of
Rudyard Kipling among other things, and his Spanish though
mostly unused remained usable.

"But Grandpa, it's just absolutely *barbarian* not to want to go to Europe, and see the opera and the cafés and the museums and everything." He said, "Well, maybe some barbarians are better off than some other people. At least I'm not a cannibal, you'll have to give me that." With the same twinkle he added that there was plenty of opera in his own country and he didn't intend to go to that either. They found this very mystifying from a man who had "perfect pitch," whatever that meant— they had heard it said of him, in a tone of awe, also that when he was young his singing voice had been so fine, certain musical bigwigs had tried to steer him toward "grand opera." That last was the gossips' phrase, meaning the Metropolitan as against anything so slight as *opéra comique* or still lower, what would develop in the U.S. as musical comedy. He was to have sung up there with the great ones, the gods of song, the wood-thrushes, the veeries of mankind. But he would choose instead to wow the Columbia School of Mines; it was without complaint, certainly with no bitterness or invidiousness, perhaps with little under-standing of how it happened either, that all his high gifts and promise would wind up in a series of abortive, second-string business positions and bad investments.

The children knew, this too from their inveterate eavesdrop-ping, that before they were born their pretty, blond and then furiously radical mother had had heated arguments with her father, trying to make him understand that he was a victim of the capitalist system and ought to be out with her on the picket lines; to which he would gently reply with such notions as rolling with the punch and not trying to lay blame for the breaks, there were bound to be some bad ones, you couldn't always have things your way. The twins themselves often enough heard him say that he'd had a good life, had done a lot of the things he loved to do—meaning mainly fishing and bird-hunting, but he'd won a few silver cups at the bridge table and had a zest for that too—and had built some things he could be proud of, such as thirty miles of railroad through a jungle in Ecuador. The mine that went sour in Kentucky, the dredge that sank in a storm off the Louisiana coast, and quite a few similar setbacks, were just the luck of the draw; he didn't even blame "the politicians," unless horse sense left no alternative.

Actually, his granddaughter had come to see, it wasn't so much either American capitalism or the Mexican Revolution that had done him in, as a so-called asthmatic heart, which had nearly carried him off at the age of thirty-odd and prevented his ever seriously qualifying as a mining engineer again. He couldn't stay underground long enough, had to walk very slowly and carry a spray in his pocket and would frighten them with choking fits that turned his face purple. At those times of course he couldn't have shot from the hip or in any fashion, and that in itself was vaguely alarming; they would never realize, except when he was so incapacitated for a few minutes, how much of their feeling of protection in his presence came from his extraordinary speed on the trigger and accuracy of eye. Once it was a rattlesnake he got that way, before they had even spotted the source of the sound. Another time, coming back after hours of fishing, he shot from way offshore in the rowboat, and just delicately blew the cap off an ugly-looking character who was making away with some of their camping equipment. "I guess *he* won't be back in a hurry," was all he said, and soon they were perfecting their three-part rendition of "Sweet and Low."

He would never even complain of loneliness, though there must have been some, between ladyfriends, or about his long-since ex-wife, their grandmother, except to remark once in a while, mildly, that she had a will of her own and was culture-crazy; if extremely goaded he might substitute "domineering" for the first half of the appraisal. Having known Grandmother only in her alcoholic old age, Dennie never could see how the two had gotten together in the first place, any more than she could in the case of her own parents, unless it was just that they were both handsome, witty and high-spirited, of similar genteel, professional family background, and Grandma mistook the brilliant young engineer's total recall of Kipling's verse for a devotion matching her own, which was really somewhat less to poetry than to the idea of it. She rarely turned to or discussed

Shakespeare and like most college graduates in her time, had probably never heard of John Donne or Gerard Manley Hopkins, but in the glow of young love seemed to have imagined that the two would spend their evenings reading Dante to one another; it was the kind of thing cultivated people did. Also she was emotionally, vehemently Franco- and Italophile, speaking both languages fairly well. So the separation was not long in coming, and Dennie's mother and aunt were soon being dropped off in the cheapest possible European convents or traipsing under the maternal wing through the most execrable pensions of those high-culture countries, with Papà scraping up a pittance to send them now and then when he wasn't on his uppers, and Maman taking teaching jobs in institutions for the well-bred, at home or abroad, as opportunity or necessity might dictate. "She always had guts," Dennie heard Grandpa say of her more than once. And although the erstwhile couple hadn't met in years, it came as a truly saddening blow to him to hear that toward the end, when she had come at last into an adequate income, she was boozing herself blotto on her lonely hillside in Connecticut, among the vellum-bound volumes of Dante, Racine et al.

To such a roost had the pursuit of European culture come home, and the elder daughter, Dennie's mother, only yesterday "laid to rest" as the minister expressed it—really it was just ashes in an urn that they had watched being lowered into the surely unwelcoming, because so inappropriate, New Hampshire ground—had taken one part of the lesson to heart, while still preferring to live in Europe when possible. For all her red-flag waving, she would not be poor; that above all was to be avoided, somehow, and a better somehow than a rich young classicist, headed for archaeological digs around the Mediterranean, there clearly could not be.

About that exploded pipedream, his elder daughter's first marriage, Grandpa by the campfire would be far too solicitous of the children's feelings ever to say a word, though they often poked and pried and fished for one, being ill-informed and

naturally curious about the parent they could scarcely remember, and strongly suspecting that the father of the bride
had held a dim view of him from the beginning, out of something more than his prejudice as a barbarian. But the old man
would just say, as he did of his own failure of a marriage if he
was forced to say anything, "Sometimes things just don't work
out, there's no point trying to say where the fault started and
whose it was," and it would all be deflected with another tall
story, of the Earp brothers, or some oldtime revival meeting, or
how Jesse James's brother came hunting a job at his mine in
Guanajuato; or they would get on once more with their little
musicale, Grandpa generally taking the bass, and she and Rick
taking turns in the air and tenor.

She was hearing all three parts now, of "Just a Song at
Twilight" and "The Road to Mandalay"—he was super on the
guitar in that one, it brought tears to their eyes sometimes, he
plucked such rollicking grandeur from the strings, along with a
sadness, a kind of yearning homesickness for the strange and
far-away—and "Drill Ye Tarriers Drill" and "Bring the
Wagon Home, John" with the snappy switch in the last verse to
"Bring the Hack Back, Jack," and a lot of hymns too, not just
"Rock of Ages" though they were extra good in that, or thought
they were. The grandfather's bass—still lovely in old age, never
a booming one but true and so subtly vibrant and of a carrying
power strange for its modest volume—was mingling in her ears
once more as it used to, with the wind in the pines and the wild
bird cries and the low, lulling caress of lake water on rocks. The
songs were filling her head and throat; it was almost more than
she could stand not to open her mouth and sing.

"Have you gone deaf? What on earth are you brooding
about?"

She smiled, giving herself a little shake. "I was thinking
about my grandfather. He used to take Rick and me camping,
in places like this."

"How deadly. No wonder you look down in the mouth. I
never could stand family excursions myself. Or could you mean

you did like them and are swooning with nostalgia? I was saying Get up! Come on!" They could unpack everything later; they must have their swim now, before the sun was too low.

"*Swim!* In this cold? Marilyn, you're pulling my . . . I mean, you can't be serious. Why, it's freezing . . ." That *was* where she had come in, and *in* she was. The same dialogue as that morning when the idea of camping was broached.

"You'll love it, we'll feel great afterwards and now we have a good fire to come back to . . ."

Memory. And desire. Oh, for what? Of what hue of iris-purple or pearl was her unknown, unspeakable desire? *Where the flying fishes play, and the dawn comes up like thunder, out of China cross the bay.* Why, for heaven's sake, she must look at a map when she could, Rick must be somewhere not too far from Mandalay right now, trying to get a leaky junk full of starving slant-eyed children to some safe harbor, and she was sure that at some moment he too would be hearing the old cracked guitar, same dawn, same thunder, over a world Grandpa and probably Kipling wouldn't have wasted a how-de-do or a glob of spit on.

Instead of getting up as bidden she had sunk farther down on the hard-packed ground, and thought the warm wetness on her cheek must be the tears she was aching to let loose, but it was just the terrier giving her a little tentative, inquiring lick, asking why she wasn't scampering along after the boss for whatever the excitement was. Its three bulging black buttons the same size, off a lady's coat they might have been, stuck in the tan tousle, one for a nose, the upper two half hidden under drooping thatch, did suggest a baby's vast blank voracious wonderment. She wished she knew how to speak to the nose, but being human, returned the wishful gaze of the eye-buttons instead, reading a world of sentience into them to suit her need. As a high-IQ member of her genus, Corky seemed used to this cross-purpose and prepared to play along with it for a minute, though the nose quivered in contradiction.

"I wish you could have known my Grandpa, Corky. There never was a man who understood dogs the way he did. He'd

had a lot of them, hunting dogs, you know, but then when he'd
have to be in a city he couldn't keep them, and it would be very
sad. I'll tell you a story of his, no, not a story exactly. It's a
'receet'"—she spelled it for her bemused audience—"for washing day. That means when you do the laundry. An old frontier
woman wrote it down long ago and her daughter, by then an
old woman herself, had shown it to him. You see, when he read
anything like that that interested him, he'd never forget it, he'd
know it word for word the rest of his life.

"It begins with carrying water and lighting the fire to heat it,
and then dividing the laundry into three bunches, white, colored and 'rags and breeches.' Then there's a lot of 'biling'—in
lye, you wouldn't like that—but the colored you just 'scrub
hard, don't bile'—and 'renshing' and starching. 'Thro rensh
water in flour beds, scrub porch with sopy water.' The rags you
hang on the fence. But it's the end I like best. You're to go
change your dress, 'smooth your hair with combs, go set on the
porch and rest, and rock a while and count blessings.' Now isn't
that nice advice for the end of a hard day? But I see you're not
listening . . . Here's a sort of picture you may like better before
the story."

Of course she had stopped speaking aloud at some point, but
her face and thoughts kept the forms of narration, as to the kind
of friend who would be asking for more, really caring about it;
remembering alone didn't fill the bill just then. "My brother
and I usually saw him in places like this, camping, but one time
I was waiting for a bus with him on Riverside Drive and 116th
Street, that's in New York City and a place that's a regular
funnel for wind when it's blowing up the Hudson River. Three
nuns were just starting across the drive from the other side
when a big gust got them and whipped their long black skirts
straight up over their heads, like this"—she illustrated it for her
diminutive audience. "They turned into three crazy headless
creatures made of funny long whitish underwear from the waist
down to their big black shoes and three witches in a tornado for
the upper part, dancing around like crickets on a hot stove.

Grandpa laughed so I thought he might choke, and later on the bus he let out two or three of those aftermath laughs people get, saying, 'I just can't stop thinking about those damn nuns!'

"But the story I was going to tell you is about an oldtime revival meeting. He knew loads of stories like that, kind of ribald you might say, some of them; he never was one for gup of any kind. Everybody at this meeting was getting up the way they do with a lot of Amens and Praise the Lords, telling all the good things the Almighty had done for them. Then just at the end an old feller stood up in the back row, with a peg leg and a harelip and an ear trumpet, all curled up with rheumatism. The preacher, happy to get another one into the fold, shouted, 'Yes, Brother, now you tell the bretheren and sisteren what the Good Lord did for you!' The old feller shook his ear trumpet, making the most terrible face he could on top of the one he already had, and in his wheezy old voice yelled back, 'He ham near *ruined me!*' You see . . ."

Come to think of it, that grandfather's father had a degree in philosophy from Heidelberg, just to cap his American education, made quite a name for himself around the world as the author of scholarly tomes, and two other sons went more or less the same route. What kind of atavistic throwback was that one, the eldest, to have been what he was, so differently endowed, and so unlucky? Or was he perhaps really the luckiest?

"Yes, I'm coming," she called cheerily. "Let's go, Corky. Into the ice water, up an' at 'em, do or die." She hadn't heard or spoken the second of those exhortations in what Grandpa would have called a coon's age. "*Su! andiamo! avanti!*" would have come more naturally to her lips as late as an hour ago and would have meant the same to Corky, who was now bouncing as high as her waist with a scrape of the claws on her jacket each time, in a wild acrobatism of glee and anticipation, uttering the special, shrill yap-yap that expressed no other mood; it had nothing in common with her equally piercing notes of warning or greed or need to go out, or just undirected joie de vivre, except that all were barks.

As she set off to follow Marilyn down the little trodden path—not toward the canoe where the footing would be bad but to the side facing the floating gardens—the "receet" reminded Dennie of one of her grandmother's harshest criticisms of her former spouse. She said he was dirty, would never think of washing himself or his clothes until he positively smelled. She was herself a fanatical bather, laundress and general cleaner-up, in that respect *maniaque* as the French say, and found his negligence, his ability to sleep between soiled sheets, for instance, atrocious. She had taught her own children to look askance at their father for that, or at least to expect the worst when slyly scrutinizing his collars and cuffs. But how could you keep clean on a camping trip and why should you? Getting grimy was half the fun. It was unfair. Besides, on a good day they often did wash their clothes in the lake, with Ivory Soap so it wouldn't sink, and spread them on bushes to dry. In the city, with hot water and a Chinese laundry handy, although he was certainly not dapper and his suits were never in the latest men's style, they thought he looked about like anybody else, only much handsomer, with his upright carriage, except during the spasms of choking, and grey hair that stayed thick to the end, and the glance, from behind wire-framed glasses, that even in a crowded clubroom would seem to be alert for animal sounds or some far birdflight to be identified. He would have that look at times even in the cocktail lounge of the University Club in New York, where in his last years, eased by a minuscule inheritance, he was a member and played bridge with industrial and Wall Street magnates, some of whom would look puzzled by such dignity and social charm from a man of barely enough financial "worth" to pay his dues.

The number of kinds of birds he knew, and could name just from their wing motions at great distances, was to the twins an absolute marvel. And at night when the three of them huddled for sleep under the same blankets on a mattress of pine branches, in the much-mended canvas tent of what must have been Civil War vintage or thereabouts, they loved his smoky, sweaty smell alongside. Together with the loaded pistol a few inches from his head, it gave them a luxurious feeling, like a massage; talking about it once, she and Rick had agreed that where it affected them most was their scalps and their toes, though it was soothing in the middle too. The sensation was of safety, perfect and permanent, as if no harm, beyond maybe a slight burn or bruise, could ever come to them in their lives.

―――――――

"I followed you down the path, still determined to let you swim by yourself if you wanted to be that crazy, and found you laughing your head off. I must say that huge mass of cooked spaghetti bobbling in the water, just where we would have to step in, was fascinatingly dreadful, worse than a bed of live eels to be walked through barefoot. An insult to nature; the fishes had spurned it, so had the birds; if it had been full of blinking white eyes it wouldn't have been more repulsive, and it really seemed to be making a sound as it bobbled in the wash, voicing some loathsome, sinister defiance. It must have been there quite a while. We figured it couldn't have been dumped by the last campers, so considerate about everything else. But who on earth would cook so *much* extra spaghetti? Or perhaps they were a large group who had left in a hurry for some reason, just as the meal was ready, and emptied their enormous pot there. Anyway, that great belly-laugh of yours was entrancing, and so contagious, it spun me right around. It was a side of you I hadn't seen that trip but remembered well from two years ago, when you had the whole gang at the villa in stitches with your description of an idiot nursemaid your mother once hired to look after you. I wonder if you have any idea how it beautifies you to laugh like that, with your eyes, your whole voice and heart, and body; you were rocking back and forth. You're not, if you'll forgive me, all that goodlooking most of the time and you often seem to do your best to keep it that way, as though you enjoyed offending, in appearance too; it suits your rather brutal sarcasm, your strident act of walking alone, which of course has its admirable side.

"But then, oh and so much more when you'd dropped your

clothes and intrepidly started in, giggling as you avoided the spaghetti as much as possible, you became a goddess. And I let myself be influenced far more even than you know, more than in following you into that icy water, more than in what happened between us right afterwards. I'm deeply mortified and chagrined by the rest now but I'll make myself say it. Your sudden charm spread out like magic over all your attitudes, turned them all good and wise, and so I let your repudiation of family, in one click of an instant—not for long but never mind—free me from mine. I stepped away, as if they'd been a pile of dirty old clothes, not just from the funeral, but from so much that had been weighing on me, most of all in those I loved; from their failures and confusions, and my confused failure to understand what made them do what they did and be what they were; from my very love I walked away, going into that spaghetti-fouled water after you, the chill like knives on my flesh; even from my love for Rick, my darlingest, great-hearted twin. Yes, even from my grandfather.

"But here's a question on another plane, I could say, another planet. Surely when you stripped naked and started in, and afterwards when—no, perhaps some other day I can get the words out—you can't have known or suspected that we were being watched from over there where you'd seen the boat. Or did you think of it, and make it an act of pride to court whatever embarrassment and even danger there might be from our flaunting our nakedness exactly there, in that spot? Something tells me, as I've said before, that you had a good hunch, had known all along that it was Mr. Allen's boat and had to have been stolen, not left there by him, and that it was the thief, soon to be our visitor, that we'd heard over there in the brush. I'll never know, and perhaps would have followed you even knowing. I saw you without patrimony, without antecedents, sublime in your courage and total self-creation, believe me I did, as Venus rising from the sea and as beautiful, only without that twining garland of hair she holds with one hand across her pubic part—you know the Botticelli; and I was one of those honored handmaidens, made lovely too by your presence, holding an imaginary cloth to wrap around you when the fat-faced zephyr would have finished blowing you ashore. The only male figure in the picture, as I think most often in your mind, is that caricature, though the myths have it otherwise. However, those androgynous Greeks are a far cry from the pruderies we grew up on.

"And a farther one, if that's possible, from all the women's lib jabber about the new woman that we hear even here in Italy but not as much as I did in my few days in the U.S. How pathetic, how piddling those programmatic rantings sound, compared to that vision on a cockleshell, of spume and ecstasy and perfect power and grace, with the knowledge of an immortality of happy amours wafting her to shore. So in my sudden blast of freedom, or dementia if you like, I saw you.

"And so I let you lure me into the betrayal. Not of Carter, my husband, particularly. We both know what that would signify, though even that equation like everything else isn't what it was, now that he and I have talked so much and I'm even letting him see this scribble as the pages get filled. I drop them on the floor of my little study, far from our fancy reception rooms, and he comes home from work and reads them, asking first if he may. I don't go so far as to pick them up and hand them to him. I pretend not to hear. We both pretend it's of no importance. But I mean the betrayal of so much else, that I see now as the deepest human necessity. I mean the sin of putting desire before memory. It was your doing that I committed it, and I don't blame you and haven't for a single minute; of course not; how could I? I was itching, longing to break out of the whole prison of responsibility past and present, to step clean away from the funeral and from my son too, and you just turned the key without even intending to—I think. Actually your intentions, at quite a few points in the story, are still a mystery to me; your wanting to hear about the Rocca was straightforward enough, almost ghoulish I'd say, but that's neither here nor there.

"The water was of course much too cold for any serious

swimming. We swam a few strokes and having made our point, or yours, picked our way back across the wriggling abomination. You said Dante was a native of spaghettiland and sure missed a trick, not having it in that form in hell; I said I seemed to remember that Marco Polo brought it back from China so it wasn't really Italian or hadn't been very long. I didn't say that Venus had a much longer western history than that—yes, it was just certain kinds of memory I had exorcised, the inconvenient ones. Corky was a few yards along the shore fishing for salamanders, or rather she seemed to have recognized the futility of the attempt and was just hypnotized by them; she would reach thoughtfully out toward one, with one funny little cocoanut-shell paw, not quite even touching the water, and stare and stare. She was as entranced and befuddled in her way as I in mine. I stumbled on a stone, I suppose because of my rotten eyesight, and you had to grab my waist to keep me from falling. The shock of your touch went flaming all through my cold body. I thought of descriptions of people in the electric chair, in the last split second of life . . ."

It was worse, far worse, than the orgy at night in the Dolomites, with the same lean, small-breasted body for a partner but an invisible, untouchable one, with a massive wall between. She heard herself whimper. With a strand of spaghetti caught between her toes and a secondary, at the moment negligible, shudder of cold, she stepped onto terra firma and pressed herself full length against her shining, wet, half-frozen, mythological friend. "Oh, Marilyn, darling," she blubbered, "hold me! Put your arms around me!" To hell with spaghetti—oops, excuse the pun, her remnant of brain interjected, it being Dante she had then in mind, not in connection with the slimy horror he hadn't thought of for the Inferno, but the power that in his cosmos made the planets hold to their courses: love, love, love it was, divine to be sure but missing no tricks in its effects on living creatures, from which in fact it might be said to emanate. The consoling, intellectual flash, superseding Aphrodite, was for the second of its duration so bright that she came close to addressing the object of her sudden passion as Beatrice, pronounced Italianwise: Bay-ah-tree-chay. "I adore you. I've never felt anything like this in my whole life!"

The adored one smiled thinly, with just a hint of condescension and superior insight playing around the now doubly-empurpled lips, which then smashed full force, tongue out like a lumberman's thumb, on the corresponding piece of the beseecher's anatomy, while her arms were locked in a double nelson around the rest of it. The two tongues thrust and writhed in exquisite battle, as breast hardened against breast and thrashing legs like four birches in a windstorm sought more perfect contact, at some risk to equilibrium. But Dennie had two bruises already, and the bodies parted just before the crash.

"I could go for you too, it looks like."

"If what?" She was still struggling for breath.

"If you'd stop thinking there was something peculiar about it, or shameful, or out of the ordinary. All that stuff you got from your Mummy and her ilk."

Dennie couldn't help giggling, even with her crotch about to explode. "It's the last thing I would ever have discussed with Mummy and I don't know that she had any ilk. But if you think . . . Oh Lord, look at me, I'm streaming. If that isn't answer enough!" It was true, the erotic juice was gushing down between her legs. Still in one corner of her being appalled at herself, reeling with incomprehension, she was nevertheless rocked more by this other *force majeure*, as helpless as a kitten being flushed down a toilet, something she and Rick had seen done by a schoolmate, to their lasting horror, when they were six. To hell with corncobs, dildoes; she was on the verge of orgasm just from propinquity.

But it would not, after all, further that cause or any to freeze to death. With heroic self-suppression and a few curses over it, they hurried to pull on their several bulky layers of clothes, before running hand in hand back to their fire, overtaken by Corky, who wasn't going to be left out even for the pleasure of watching salamanders. The plumey black and tan tail, measuring in length more than half that of her body, waved bannerlike as she waited for them, announcing, as her vocal cords did, that whatever the next move or the glad tidings in the human sphere she was only too ready to be in on them. Dennie was annoyed at being reminded of something a Czech friend had once said, about single old ladies keeping small dogs for sexual excitement, training them to lick their genitals. She put the nasty thought out of her mind, more easily in that still another delay, a new trial of heroism, was now demanded. She was sure that Marilyn was as swollen with lust as she was, but with what seemed superhuman denial, she was insisting that they unpack the dufflebag and put up the tent before going any farther. It would be the utmost folly to lie bare on that cold ground and without protection from the wind; besides, look at the sky down there to the south, the black mass rolling their way, the white-caps splattering the lake. She had heard a clap of thunder too. Of course with mountain weather you couldn't be sure, but it was always shifting and unstable for a couple of days at the Solstice; the signs now were all of a storm on the way. It would be hard to pitch the tent later when they would need it the most.

"Don't fret, honeybunch, it'll only take a few minutes. Yes, I know, I feel the same way." She grinned, looking for the first time unmistakably lascivious, and gave a stout poke at where a breast must be; even Dennie's hefty protuberances couldn't raise a bump through that amount of drygoods. "And don't worry about my having the curse. It's about over anyway."

The red tent, folded in a package no bigger than a small-size Kleenex box, was light years from the beat-up canvas of Dennie's youth. Of some synthetic, waterproof material, it had a floor all of a piece with the rest, a zippered doorflap with a swatch of mosquito netting for that opening in hot weather, ready-made metal pegs and poles telescoped for packaging; marvelous; and three could have slept in it easily, four in a pinch. On the trips she'd been remembering they used to cut their own poles and pegs at each new stop. A few strings were knotted or missing; the bowie knife came into use; the hatchet and narrow but sturdy saw had already served to replenish the reserve of firewood and were lying on one of the two rather unsteady log benches they had found on arrival, along two sides of the fire.

Marilyn had been right as usual. It took only a few minutes, even with stoking the fire so it would hold for a good long time. No pine branches needed. There was a double air mattress to lay over the nylon flooring. Quickly, on hands and knees inside, they spread the double down sleeping bag over that, in what the late sunglow, not yet reached by those angry clouds, turned in Dennie's view into a little red chapel, a place of that profound withdrawal that alone can bring forth the true meaning and experience of beatitude, and having commanded the dog to shut up and go to sleep at the end where their feet would more or less be, were about to zip themselves in with their bliss when they heard the clumsy splashing.

The boat was coming straight toward them, from the floating gardens of course.

"Would you mind tying him up a minute? I'm allergic to dogs."

It was true that in spite of everything they both smiled. After all, it might have been someone not nearly so pleasant in voice and manner.

———

He nudged the boat in beside the canoe, which he had to step through to come ashore, after loosely tying a line to it. That would be all right for a few minutes; the wind wasn't strong enough yet to bash them together.

"Please excuse me for breaking in on you. I hope I'm not interrupting anything. I just wondered if I could borrow a spoon for a little while. We forgot to bring one along. Hey, this is a great spot you found. Ours is pretty nice over there too and we get the view of that big mountain, I forget what it's called, back this way, but you've got more room to move around. Boy, is it cold! My fingers are numb practically, just coming this little way."

He was thinly and very shabbily clothed and did look cold, as well as haggard with fatigue, but his motions were spry and of an electric energy becoming to his powerful six-foot build. He might be thirty, or a few years less or more. It was hard to tell, through the several days' dark growth on his cheeks and chin; his head was curiously close-cropped for a regular camper or drifter in the wilds, and the hands he held out to the fire to warm appeared to have been quite well manicured until recently. His smile, Dennie found herself thinking, was very like Luigi's, a quick wrinkling around eyes of indeterminate color, and a flash of teeth not as white as they might be; still, the impression was all very courteous and disarming, especially in the glint that her Italian friend had had too, of some little extra shared amusement beyond the immediate circumstance. Altogether an attractive young man, or perhaps not so young.

Corky had been barking full tilt the whole time, in Marilyn's arms and before that at the stranger's approach, when she sped to take up her stance in one spot after another of the coastline to be defended. However, it was no more ferocious an exhibition than she had put on over their swimming shortly before.

The visitor had had almost to yell, and did again now. "Mind if I sit down just a minute?" Laughing a trifle, Marilyn tied the tiny monster to a tree and told her to stop the racket, which she rather glumly did, hind legs spread behind her like a duck's in flight and chin down on forepaws, eyes wide and aggrieved on the scene she was excluded from. "You girls all alone here? Aren't you taking kind of a chance? I mean, things could happen, I guess, like I don't know what exactly." He glanced at the knife, saw, hatchet on the log beside him, and the still unopened knapsacks. "But I see you're not novices. You seem pretty well equipped."

They murmured agreement. Would he like a drink to warm him before he left? Marilyn's offer was a surprise, in different ways, to the other two. He said he'd prefer a joint, if they had one, but they didn't so he consented to whiskey. "Just a splash, thanks a lot, then I have to get along." In a tone of casual amiability, almost jollity, she said a splash was about what they could spare, and went rummaging in one of the bags for the flask and a paper cup, as well as a plastic spoon he could take; they had plenty of those. He was staring hard at her face meanwhile, and when he rose politely to accept the cup he burst out, "Whadda you know! I was sure I'd seen you before somewhere, and it just came to me. It was in Iowa, about five years ago. You were reading poems, and I happened to be there." Dennie understood him to say *reading palms*, which she knew Marilyn also did on occasion, but the word had really sounded more like *pomes;* was that on purpose for some reason? In general, his speech was not what she would have called slummy. "I even went up and said hello to you afterwards, but of course there was a crowd around and you wouldn't remember."

Marilyn was duly astonished, and still more flattered. "For heaven's sake. Were you a student there?"

"Hell no. A night watchman. But I used to go to those things, concerts mostly. Were you still around when the Amadeus Quartet came to play? It was about the same time. Boy, that really got to me, especially a Ravel thing they did." As he spoke he was casting rapid glances, not at the face he was addressing but over their setup and baggage, with just a suggestion, a new one, of the furtive and calculating; his fingers, large and of great strength by the look of them, strummed along the sawblade beside him, as if it were a musical instrument, or else testing its sharpness. But his wide smile, when he reverted to the *pomes,* was all open, direct and admiring. "I remember one you read—wait a minute, I'll get it—about a sparrow-hawk, right?" He scowled, chewed his lower lip, knocked at his head: the overgrown schoolboy with the right words just eluding the tip of his tongue.

"Yes, there's one like that," Marilyn said. "I may have read it there."

"I've got it! Your voice just then brought it back. 'Clouddriver, wind-thrasher, steel-beaked and taloned slither of flesh and our great distances . . .' Then something about Icarus and his burned feathers, how does that go?"

"Enough!" Marilyn laughed. "If you did all your lessons that well . . . But I think it goes, 'My womb carried and disgorged you, its single, life-long progeny.'"

"That's it! 'And every nine months I labor again, to send you flashing forth again against the sun, steel-strong, wax-foolish.' Wow! See, I went to the library and read it the next day; looked up Icarus and hawks too. I was a city kid, alley cats and sewer rats were all my natural kingdom. Nothing like this around here, I can tell you." As though arriving that instant at a large decision he sprang to his feet, with a look of sudden hostility, not at the two women but at the woods and the setting sun and the dog that had for a while distracted herself by chewing on a small log. "It could give you the creeps. Thanks for the warm-up, and it certainly is a pleasure meeting you both."

On his way through the canoe he paused to bend down and examine something on the bottom, testing it a second with a jackknife he pulled from his pocket. "You've got a little leak here. If I just had some epoxy, I could fix it."

"Where did you get your boat?" Marilyn called, in a tone of normal curiosity between strangers, nothing controversial.

He flashed the big smile. "I borrowed it. And if you don't mind, I'll borrow this paddle just for the night too. I'm getting tired of this old board. Don't worry, I'll get it back to you in the morning." He tossed their stern paddle into the boat and with some agility stepped in after it.

"Hey, you bum," Marilyn shouted. "Bring that back!"

He was still grinning. "Toodledoo. I really must go, my friend'll be wondering, except she knows you're a couple of dykes, not what I go for exactly. Yeah, we were watching the whole show over there. Some poor suckers would pay money to see that, even with a fucking lake between."

To back away he gave a few clumsy but Herculean strokes with the paddle, sending the boat into a vicious whirlpool spin, then paddled off where he had come from.

"I suppose we both knew, and weren't letting ourselves know, that he would be back. One thing I've puzzled over so often is what made him leave that first time. And why didn't *we* pick up and scram then, when we could have? Or couldn't we, with one paddle? He could have overtaken us at once, if he had any such intention. Is that what you were thinking? But I suspect he had worked on you so with the poem and his fantastic memory of it, and his having bothered to go hear you in the first place, you couldn't think ill of him, in spite of the paddle and that horrid gibe at the end, that disgusting word he threw at us. I could understand that; I suppose one doesn't often have such an audience, one that actually hears, and remembers, and is perhaps changed by the poems. I can imagine that a single listener like that could make all the work of your life seem worthwhile. At any rate, you did look more gratified than miffed after he had left.

"As for what made him go, I can only think of two explanations. He was famished, as we were to find out, and may have thought we wouldn't start cooking with him there, or only under duress; it would be more fun, less of a strain all around, to wait and make a cheerful, sociable occasion of the meal, as we did in a way, and save the knife-point for later. The alternative would be some peculiar impulse of decency, for a minute or two. Hungry as he was, he might have decided to go without food, rather than be brutal or rude about it. Yes, he was desperate, but people have died for stranger reasons, throwbacks of one kind and another to what they might once have been. But then, to go on with the hypothesis, he despised himself for that weakness and acted accordingly, with his plan already figured out. The thunderstorm would make some changes in it, but not basically. Well, I can see some flaws in this picture and don't know why I let it intrigue me anyway, except as it bears on the whole nature of good and evil, love and crime, guilt and redemption. Big words, *n'est-ce pas?* You could find better ways to put it, if you'd forget Professor Drumbledebruch."

―――――――

The spell was broken. No question of going back into the tent just then. The night would take care of itself, at a very different pitch Dennie now hoped, revulsion having set in more quickly than after her one previous, if in a sense solitary, fling in that department. There was nothing to be apprehensive about, Marilyn said. They had a fine bed of coals, just right for the chicken, and she could hear about the fortress while it cooked; there wouldn't be a better time.

"Not like your mother's ski story, begging your pardon. You know, just a few tableaux." She extracted her cassette from a knapsack and with an inflated cushion beneath her and a bench for backrest made herself comfortable, pen and notebook in hand to supplement the tape.

"But what kind of non-concoction or something"—Dennie rather wanly giggled—"was it that you wanted it for? I forget. I must have been sleepy when you explained." She didn't add that the previous day had been a long, tiring one, starting with a funeral of more consequence than her friend could recognize or than she had herself at the time. "I wasn't following very well."

In the firelight she caught a thin purple smile, cordial enough, as unintimate as any of the day before. "I told you, you'd have to read up on a lot of critical theory to understand. I'll give you a reading list tomorrow. You'll be thrilled, it'll change all your thinking from A to Z. One of the top brains in the field, I may have mentioned him last night, says it takes seven years to understand his theorems, that is, the basic signposts to all linguistic constructs, but most intelligent people find they can go a long way on faith in the meantime. Right now I wish you'd just tell me what occurs to you, and I'll take what I can use."

"That won't be much, I'm afraid." She was aware, only when the words were out, of a slight barb in them. Really it was her mother she was being asked to spill out for that little black box. It was all her doing that her children had any such experience to relate, and that Dennie could still treasure her abiding love, like her mother's before her, for that grand plebeian character Assunta, the "not-quite servant woman" as Marilyn had called her, and victim of conjugal tyranny. Some victim! rather like a tornado at grips with a poplar, as were several of the nearly destitute mothers of families lodged in the Rocca at the time, although of course not all the husbands were as weak and wayward as Ottavio; some were hardworking masons or fishermen when work offered. Dennie had even rather loved the little old lady miser, the Signorina, who through mad romance happened to own the vast, incongruous enclave. This would never do. She had also gathered, perhaps from one of the graphs on Marilyn's walls, that the usually theatrical lighting of the scene, by day or night, would not be very welcome either.

She would tell most of it silently to herself, or to Corky if the dog was willing. "I'm glad Carter isn't here for this part, he's had to hear about the Rocca so often. And we've seen the outside of it together a few times, from down along the harbor, or from friends' boats. There are lots of luxurious villas and yachts around the place now, hotels, restaurants, expensive cars; you know how fast such things happen in Italy; it's gotten terribly fashionable. But there was nothing at all like that when we went there. The local landowning aristocrats who came in summer had a telephone, but the only public one in miles was in a café way down at the new end of the village, built up since the war . . ."

She heard her voice as droning and depressed, and wondered if they would hear the swish of the boat coming their way again.

"But Marilyn, just one question. If something nasty happened to us here tonight, you know, the kind everybody talks about nowadays—not that I expect it to but if it did—would that figure as reality?"

The investigative author's expression, as she signaled the start of the tape, was that of someone taking a joke in stride, and in good spirit.

IV

HER FIRST SENSE of the place was of course overlaid by many images and events from later years, and even more by many accounts of it that her mother used to regale listeners with, as she'd had a knack for that kind of talk until it went out of fashion, at least in her social neck of the woods. For instance, what Dennie knew of the Signorina story was all on hearsay, although on that it was probably safe to believe Assunta, who as a poor provincial girl had fallen in with the rich little miser lady ages ago in Rome and so had watched the whole business. The Signorina was always called just that, with no proper name, or in the village "the Signorina of the Rocca." The story was of how such a beady-eyed, shabby spinster, never beautiful and who bled for every coin that left her purse, had happened to acquire that extraordinary, even for Italy, piece of real estate, through her infatuation with her confessor, a Monsignore no less and a scoundrel, or as Grandma Jones would put it, a cad. Anyhow, Dennie was quite sure that her earliest true memory, not of the Rocca alone but of her life, was of trudging up there for the first time at the age of four, with her mother and brother and with Raggedy Ann dangling from one hand.

It was spring 1948, not long after the negative coup de foudre that had parted her parents. It seemed the hundreds of worn and winding stone steps up from what was left of the old village were still not cleared of rubble from the bombings, though local people used them, so somebody had steered the foreign signora up the long way around, by the dusty approximation of road on the sea side. They walked through gently sloping fields first, leaving the harbor with its fishing boats behind and with peaceful views of sea and a tiny island opening here and there beyond the fold of the hill. Then she had clutched her mother and shrieked. They were right under the highest swooping point of the ramparts, the road seemed to have vanished and in its place was the edge of a tremendous cliff dropping nearly sheer to the sea. The little stucco building surmounting the fortress wall above them would turn out to be a lookout built by the Italian navy early in the war, and in later years she and Rick, if they happened to be up there, would hold their breaths when a driver, of car or bike or motorbike, coming up for the first time, would sizzle to a stop at that corner. Their grandmother, who came with her Dodge car for a month one summer, never did learn to slow up for it, any more than she did for donkeys or ox carts on the road below, and was puzzled by some of the looks she got.

The village was one of two, both war-ravaged because the Germans had used their excellent little harbors, on a single-mountain peninsula. The children's father had been working off and on with other American archaeologists on a dig on the mainland. Their mother had noticed the village from there, in what had so abruptly turned into a bygone stage of her life, and since she was getting next to no support from her well-off ex-spouse or his skinflint family, she was looking for the cheapest possible summer lodgings. There would have to be room too for her dance partner and another young man, a pianist. At twenty-seven she couldn't hope to get back to classical ballet, at which she had been less than a star anyway, but she had something more contemporary, more personally expressive in mind, and in her new liberation, was hellbent on resuming her career. Starting it would be more accurate. Of course there was not so much as a chicken coop for rent in the village that year; plenty of *sfollati*, the bombed-out inhabitants, were living in both the Rocca and the companion fortress, gloomy and much more inaccessible, the other side of the harbor, but she might find a room or two in this nearer one if she wasn't too particular.

Particular she wasn't and three weeks later, giving time for a few repairs, they were installed. She had fallen in love with the place, howling squalor and all, as soon as they had crossed over the garbage-heaped dry-moat, by the bridge that was once a drawbridge, and through the massive portone and stone-roofed ogival entryway beyond, into the uppermost of many semi-ruinous courtyards, all festive just then with oleanders in bloom, pink, white and blood-rose. In this the young Mrs. Comstock behaved exactly as her own mother would have, and had on a number of occasions with her own two children in tow, and would again when she came to visit and turned the place more topsy-turvy than any pirate crew or invading army of past centuries, as was her whirlwind way. Grandma's Italophilia, in general of quite a different cast from her elder daughter's, was nevertheless marked by the same romantic voracity for the next-to-impossible, or grandeur on a shoestring.

However, by the time of her assault on the fortress the enormous main room used by her progeny, for everything but sleeping quarters, had been cleaned up and even made marvelously beautiful, though with the cheapest possible furnishings. There had even come to be electricity, enough for one weak bulb with a handsome string eel-trap for a shade of sorts over their central table, while kerosene and candles still served for the far corners and for Assunta to see what she was doing at the charcoal stove. The human racket outside had begun to diminish too, as the village heaved itself back in shape like the rest of the country and the families there could gradually move back down, to their own and the Signorina's vast relief. They were supposed to be paying a tiny amount of rent but rarely did, were really squatters and not at all kind or polite to their harassed landlady. Many were communists or had sympathies that way, had expected the Party to win the elections in the spring of '48, so had

had plans to take over the Rocca and a lot else; that the Demo-Christians stayed in was a bitter pill and made for further recalcitrance about the rent.

"They are rude, uncouth, terrible," the Signorina would moan. "They make everything filthy—they dump their garbage in the moat, they let their children throw old shoes in the cistern and laugh about it. *Maleducati!*" She refrained from adding, out of delicacy and because in this they had no alternative, that they used any spot they chose for a toilet, usually on one of the upper walkways rimming the ramparts. She dreamed of installing electricity and renting rooms to a crowd of elegant foreigners, *gente per bene,* who would pay well and have good manners.

Even so, she was aghast at the stylish young American lady's wanting that particular barracks, or stable, whatever the space had once been, then so dilapidated that even the poorest of the *sfollati* had spurned it. She dreaded looking ignoble, making a *brutta figura.* It was bad enough that she had been caught without warning, in a food-stained cotton dress missing two buttons in front, her thin straggling hair quite unwashed, and shoes . . . Well, they were her only shoes; she had kept delaying the torment of spending money for a new pair. These were canvas, with rope soles half disintegrated from kilometers of walking, walking, walking, at least once a week, all the way around the peninsula to the prefecture in the other village, with a shopping-bag full of documents. Always more *documenti;* a question of war reparations, huge sums being given out by the government in Rome and in all honesty not relevant in this case. Her property, of which she had taken possession in '39, just as hell was ready to break over Europe though it would take a little longer reaching that spot, had been damaged in many conflicts over its four-hundred-year history, only not in that last one, by miracle, when nearly everything had been flattened right up to its walls on the harbor side. However, as that clearly *was* a miracle, attributable to her own prayers and her faith in staying there alone through those terrible nights of bombings when every soul in the village and Assunta with her little boys too had fled to the hills, it was only right that she should be rewarded for her piety and get her fingers in the pot if possible.

As to those shameful shoes, it was difficult to keep them hidden under what was both dining-room and parlor table, during that first colloquy with young Signora Comstock, as the slightly humpbacked proprietress was too short for her feet to reach the floor from a sitting position and she soon got an ache from trying to keep them daintily crossed out of sight. The shoes wouldn't have been in quite that condition if she had been willing to take the local bus on her business trips instead of walking, but she was not comfortable on the bus, even if it had ever left when it was supposed to. It wasn't just the jostling and hard seats or even standing all the way, one gets used to such inconveniences, but the atmosphere, from everybody's knowing she was rich and stingy and dressed like a pauper. She knew it would have been far better for her if she had been a titled aristocrat instead of just landed gentry from way over by the Adriatic, with no roots in Tuscany at all, even if the local aristocrats' little patch of beach, as good as private since they owned all access to it except by boat, was about to be strewn with hundreds of sea-urchin shells and so ruined for that summer, some said by communists; it would take the winter's storms to clean it up. Still, they'd have been better treated than the Signorina on the bus if they'd ever used it.

It was Assunta who cut the gordian knot that day, while the twins, tired of standing around in the dingy second-story apartment, got themselves gruelingly stared at in the narrow court, almost alley, below. That was supposed to be the owner's private terrain but a flock of grimy children had filtered in to scrutinize the strangers and particularly the doll, the only toys they knew being what they invented themselves out of sticks and stones and rubbish. Then when stare-period was up, they and the little Americans were suddenly all playing together with the Signorina's old nanny goat. The goat quickly tired of the sport and bounded up the dark stone stairs and into the

apartment, to be chased back down with cries of outraged pro-
priety. Several little girls begged to hold Raggedy Ann and
giggled, getting their tongues twisted over her funny name.

"If the Signora wants it," Assunta was arguing with her
boss, or benefactress, "why not? It's not as bad as it looks, she
says she will pay a little toward the repairs, the mason can
build a stove in a day, the door only needs to have its track fixed
so it can slide . . ." It was also her persuasion that brought
about the use of the long unhallowed chapel on a lower court-
yard, for a dance studio. The Signorina rarely went to church
any more and had contempt for the local priest and his hussy of
a housekeeper, known as his "old fiancée," but feared opprobrium from on high as much as from faces on the bus. "But
they are *artisti!*" shouted Assunta, not much taller than the
Signorina but a dynamo in both soul and body. "And art is in
itself a holy occupation, *non è vero?* It has always been in the
service of the Church, look at Michelangelo, look at all of them
with their Madonnas. The Vatican wouldn't hesitate, it grows
richer every day with its ill-gotten properties, that bunch of
robbers." "Shut your mouth," said the Signorina, forgetting
decorum but glad just the same to be swayed by the argument.
A still further dispute was over the tunnel rigged up as a toilet
by the German army, whether it was usable, whether anybody
else was now using it, and so forth.

Assunta's basic motive at the time was to pick up a little
cash, at last, as cook and housekeeper for the Americans, her
handsome husband Ottavio being no breadwinner at the best of
times. His excuse most often was having been a prisoner of war
in Albania for five years—oh, the misery of it! nobody who
hasn't been through it can understand such suffering; after
which, having followed his family's exodus of five years before
from the capital, to a godforsaken ruin without plumbing but
where there would at least be no rent to pay, he was generally
busy playing cards in a bar down by the harbor, unless he was
having luck in infidelity.

Handsome Ottavio certainly was, though, except for a period

when the last of his teeth went and he had trouble adjusting to an ill-fitting set of dentures, and he could be charming and affectionate when not in a fit of temper; and although it was plain, except perhaps to himself, that steady work of any kind would never suit him long, he had occasional spells of glory. One was from his being hired for a few weeks one year as driver of "the biggest trailer truck ever made," going the whole perilous length of Italy from heel to Alps, which filled him with love of his family and hair-raising tales of near-death on the road. An earlier boost to his ego, on a lesser scale, involved the newly ensconced Americans. That was when the rented old upright piano was delivered to the upper portone, or to the far side of the ex-drawbridge. Farther the truck couldn't go, so happening to be around for once Ottavio took charge, magnificently. It must have been a school holiday, such as seemed to come along every week or two, in honor of some holy name or proud event in the nation's history. Rushing here and there with mighty cries, Ottavio rounded up every possible male, his young sons, the old hunchback, the mentally defective basketweaver, the tubercular schoolteacher with quarters adjacent to the Signorina's; even the lighthouse keeper, a government functionary! was roused from his daily snooze. Somehow the piano was heaved and hauled down sagging steps, through gates, over every sort of obstruction, with Ottavio shouting commands and injunctions at every inch. He loved playing foreman, a chance he didn't often get, and potential drama brought out his excitable best, especially with a prospect of wine all around at the end. He would insist on Assunta's making love with him immediately afterwards, although it was the middle of the day and she had plenty else to do, what with running the American household now as well as the Signorina's.

So for the first summer or two the piano whanged away all day in the mouldy little chapel, while Assunta took care of everything domestic. They tried to spare her the evening work—she could just leave the meal for them, but they would have missed her company and for her too that was the high

point of the day, however tired she might be. She enjoyed both
the conversation at that hour and the exclamations of praise for
her cooking, also it removed her from the likelihood of grumps
or worse when Ottavio came home. Their two sons, eleven and
thirteen the first year, earned a few soldi helping her carry the
heavy bags of provisions and jugs of drinking water up the
endless steps, or escorting the children much farther down
the other side, past outerworks and fields and a farm, to the
only available patch of public beach. The little stretch of sand,
broken up by gigantic boulders onshore and off, was on the
cove next to the one just treated with thousands of barbed
shafts for upperclass feet, although the well-screened patrician
beach pavilion alongside still resounded with equally barbed
laughter and tinkling ice. At the other end, with the fortress
looming into the heavens above, the beach ended abruptly in a
shoreline of razor-sharp lava rocks, where if left to themselves
Assunta's boys, barefoot all summer and with soles like hooves,
would be running on the lookout for sea urchins and other
edible tidbits. It was they who told Rick and Dennie that still
farther that way, under the fearsome lighthouse point where the
sea was midnight blue instead of the pale green of the shallows,
the remains of an American airman's body had been found only
last year, ten meters down they said. Another American flyer,
forced down, had been literally torn to pieces by the people of
the neighboring mainland town, over beyond the long dyke
between lagoons rich in eels. That was because the aim from
above, like the Almighty's, could be faulty and a number of
people including some twenty children in school had been either killed or left minus a leg or arm or hand, a day or two
before.

The boys made no association between these matters and the
nationality of their little charges, to whom they grew quite
devoted. It was too bad, they would say with a replica of their
mother's mournful shrug; *peccato;* meaning in that connection
not sin but a pity, a terrible pity. War, as summarized by
Assunta, was always terrible.

The younger boy, Giuseppe, was a natural-born comedian

but would tremble and even faint sometimes at a sudden loud noise, his mother said because of the bombings there when he was small. He taught Rick to wear octopuses, and not just baby ones, wrapped around his arm and poke them in people's faces, which usually meant Dennie's face, her screams were so rewarding. To make them let go, you only had to bite them in the eyes. Except for the Signorina's saint's day or some other gala, they were almost the only seafood that ever went into that other family's pot. The catch from the boats was whisked off in trucks to Rome, with some left for the fishermen's families, but that was one of the many occupations that were not for Ottavio, an inland man, terrified of the sea; and the Signorina, who ate with them but out of her own separate larder such as that was, would warm up a little mouldy cooked spaghetti rather than waste good lire for something fresh.

It was Giuseppe too, when the twins were a little older, who initiated them into the scary underground passageways, at the risk of quite a calling-down at home, since there were said to be vipers in those dank corridors, along with bats and rats and a danger, as superstition had it, of dreadful, nameless disease. None of the squatter children would even cast a glance that way. The disobedient trio climbed in through a high hole by the lower portone, where a big chunk of masonry had been shaken out in some bombardment or other, and with a flashlight stumbled along what seemed miles of sinister curving and branching catacomb, its side-chambers long since void of their business as arsenal and storerooms, hearing strange squeaks and wingbeats and drippings of moisture that was probably not blood nor even wine—oh but who could tell?—to glimpse at last the deliverance of daylight and emerge, with superhuman efforts because the opening, at another spot of wreckage, was much too high, several meters aboveground in the inner wall of the moat. Dennie had once jumped from that high on a dare in their grandmother's barn in Connecticut but that was into hay. Thank goodness she had left Raggedy Ann safe in bed, she was thinking as the boys taunted her into letting go.

The two legitimate entrances to those caverns were grilled

and locked. One was in the field above their salone, on the way to the navy lookout. It was swept every three minutes all night by the revolving beam from the lighthouse at the other highest corner, and in that fierce wheeling glare the twins were sure they saw ghosts shaking the rusty iron bars, grey shapes of prisoners and garrisons of ages past and probably also of the wicked Monsignore they had heard whispers of, although their mother and Assunta always dropped such subjects when they came in. He was just an evil spook to them in the early years. Still, they had their listening posts and devices, and when they were eleven or twelve and enthralled by amorous iniquity they would spin out the drama for their contemporaries, much as their mother did for hers, only the twins had each other for support and interruption. "And then you know what that monster did? I guess he was goodlooking, and he made that poor little old maid miser fall in love with him, so she would go to the bank and take out millions and millions of lire for him that he was never going to pay back, and that's how he bought the Rocca. And all the time he kept a swank apartment in Rome and a regular ladyfriend that he was sleeping with, can you imagine? Then when he died all of a sudden the Signorina had no proof of any loans at all, and she still loved him so, she went and bought the place all over again, just to go and live where he had been."

She had been both teaching school and trying to run a boarding house, with the young Assunta's help, while herself living like a churchmouse then, as always. But of course as her confessor the villain knew she had become an heiress, through the deaths in one year of her father and two brothers, in some combination of car crash and epidemic. A bitch, three meters tall, was Assunta's description of the priest's regular mistress, her right arm shooting skyward in illustration while her always voluble face said no, she'd have to stand on a chair to do the measurement justice; she had seen that other lady a few times because the unholy one, that *scellerato* of a priest, would send her to pick up smaller loans when he couldn't be bothered to go himself. Dennie never did grasp why he'd wanted such a white elephant as the Rocca when it came up for sale sometime between the two World Wars; maybe it had to do with his being in bad odor with the Church and not allowed to say mass by that time. Anyhow, he shared the running expense with a group of nuns who had a kindergarten in the crummier parts, where the *sfollati* and the Comstock brood would later be, while he besported himself high up alongside the lighthouse, in what must have been once the governor's or commanding officer's palace and where the Signorina when it was hers would scarcely presume to tread, still less be domiciled. Then bang, *finito;* she had never seen him there though she had visited the place once, walking the many kilometers from and back to the railroad station on the mainland. "But he didn't happen to be here that day," she would say with a gentle, wondering sorrow. Perhaps she hadn't had the nerve to write and tell him she was coming; that would be the kindest interpretation.

The skyscraper bitch didn't even wait for his funeral to rush up from Rome and make off with everything movable, down to the brass door fittings of the governor's quarters, an act to be duplicated, minus the brass, by the Signorina's nephew and sole heir, on the very day of her death. Neither of those predators got the most valuable piece of hardware, because it had fallen from over the drawbridge and lay hidden deep in trash. FILIPPUS II FECIT read the grand escutcheon, with coat of arms and appropriate ornament, for Philip II of Spain who must have spent fortunes on the string of such fortifications, most of them less grandiose, to protect his alien foothold on that coast.

Dennie was still older when she came to know, piecing hindsights together, that her mother, blond and quite a beauty in those years, had turned down some glamorous proposals, personal and professional, to follow what she thought her star. She knew people in the high-flying new movie world in Rome, there were spots for her, and she became friends with the princely neighbors near the Rocca from whom the Signorina for all her adjacent property could barely get a nod. There was at least one attractive young marchese who was wild to marry Mummy, pinko opinions, twins and all. Oh and that heavenly Italian tenor, a teddy-bear man the children called him although he was an honest-to-God opera star from La Scala, who brought them candies and burst into an impromptu concert one night outside the portone as he and other guests from the villa below were leaving. It seemed he just got carried away by the beauty of the scene from that height and he was right, it was marvelous, with the lights of fishing boats way out crisscrossing the moon's path, because except on long trips the fishing was all with dragnets at night. Something from *Tosca* it was, about the stars shining, maybe composed just a mile or so across the bay in what was still called Puccini's Tower. Several years later, in wild excitement, the twins at the opera in Rome would recognize the aria and the words, "E lucevan le stelle." Most of the *sfollati* and the Signorina, agleam with wonder in what she must have thought was a bathrobe, rushed from their beds to listen as the glorious voice belted out over the sea. There was a burst of wild cheers afterwards and then most wonderful of all, first one boat and then all of them out there blinked their lights three times in applause.

Well, he seemed to be crazy about Mummy too and vice versa. But she stuck fiercely to the dance. The show was put on finally, at an invitation affair in Rome first and then on a stage in London; hideous flop in both cities; the London *Times* noted that the would-be danseuse was such an earnest and pretty young lady, it was a pity she didn't stick to the knitting she was obviously born for, and stick to her native USA too instead of inflicting such performances abroad. The twins sneaked out of bed one night and found her alone in the salone, weeping dreadfully. They wanted to bring her a bouquet to comfort her but the oleanders and wildflowers were all burned up by July, the only bloom was rosemary over the moat and Rick came near breaking his neck as the goat would later, reaching full length for it with Dennie holding his heels.

Mummy took humiliating jobs in resort nightclubs, leaving them with Assunta at those times. Except for her tears, they were glad she'd lost her silly partners and wasn't using the chapel any more. Now when she was there she could go to the beach with them and nobody was better company for that; they used to deflate their big beach ball on purpose so she would have to blow it up again, she made such funny faces doing it. And she was something of a chip off the old block in her taste for adventure, though without being accident-prone or needing to be the heroine of whatever it was, as was the old block's way. One time, when Dennie was six and in water-wings, the two of them decided to swim out to a yacht anchored quite far off-shore, while Rick built castles on the beach, under orders to keep watch over Raggedy Ann; nobody there would do the doll any harm on purpose, but sometimes when she was left un-tended the other children would get a little rough playing with her and squabbling over her, so her imitation-patchwork dress and white apron had had to be mended and washed several times. Dennie had total faith in her mother's strength and judg-ment and would never forget the awful growing realization as she began gulping the sea, that this time the infallible one had miscalculated. It was much too far for such a little girl, at least one of no great physical prowess, and in supporting her and trying to propel them both her mother too, although she went on making a lark of it, began to show signs of tiring.

Holding the boat's ladder at last and naturally assuming, since Mummy was always welcome everywhere, that they would be invited on board for at least a short rest, they were dumbfounded to get a negative shake of the head, a rather sad one, from the vessel's hired boatman or perhaps captain. Then even little Dennie, already half slung over the gunnel, could see the trouble, which she would know the name for only years later. The crewman, a perfect movie pirate in physique and garb, was playing Cerberus for eight or ten ladies and gen-tlemen in various degrees of expensive beach-type disarray, who were flopped every which way over the afterdeck, mo-

tionless, speechless, unconscious, with their eyes wide open.
Clearly the sympathetic pirate was under orders such as to
prevent his even lending a life preserver to a mother and child
likely to drown without it but who managed not to somehow.

"Mummy," Dennie asked later, "why were all those people
asleep with their eyes open?" "I don't know, darling. I guess
they were seasick." Such elegant boats were no longer a rarity
off that cove, and just three years ago now Dennie had been a
guest for a day on one of them, in just the condition that had
mystified her then, anchored at almost exactly that spot; if such
a pair had clung to the ladder by her elbow, needing a few
minutes' asylum, she would have known nothing about it.

They missed a few summers at the Rocca, out of the eleven
before the Signorina died and the great place went up for sale
once again. There was one at Grandma's house in Connecticut,
and one mostly at St.-Jean-de-Luz where they caught the
mumps and were miserable. That was occasioned by their
mother's only foray into movie-making, number one mirage of
escape hatch, the adult Dennie had observed, for people with a
yen for the arts and no particular talent; not that she was in
much of a position to comment on that score, she was coming to
acknowledge. She and Rick begged, once the mumps were over,
to be sent to America for a camping trip with Grandpa Jones,
and bank accounts were stripped and jewelry sold and it was
done.

Then the family was reconstructed and her mother's last
name, originally Jones, had changed from Comstock to
Willoughby. At least she'd added a syllable each time, became
her routine wisecrack on the subject, she'd never be able to
leave Stevie for anything less than Beelzebub; to which her new
husband's jovial and in a way prophetic epicrack would be,
"She means till hell freezes over." That she had always been
called Evie of course made for some companionable rhyme-
gags too. There were some weeks one year on Stevie's yacht
Hocus Pocus, precursor of the Honky Tonk, Lou Crease and a
couple of others before the present Moby Dick IV. Rick and

Dennie were able to endure the boredom of the boat because
their grandfather, divorced from Grandma since what they considered the dawn of history, was going to meet them somewhere
in Maine, with the same old tent and guitar, and two weeks of
rapture would begin.

Later the Hocus Pocus was somehow transported to Italy
and moored below the Rocca for a month or two. Stevie, burly,
kind-hearted and usually smiling, was a good sport about the
place, took the Signorina and Assunta and the boys twice for
picnics on outlying islands where there were goats and remains
of Roman imperial villas, and even consented to sleep up in
their much enlarged quarters, instead of on the boat. It was
quiet at least; the *sfollati* were gone, all but the sick schoolteacher's family who were going to be evicted; Assunta and her
family had finally been able to move into an apartment of their
own on the lower court, next to the once more closed-up chapel,
which cut down the screaming quarrels of the old arrangement.
The twins missed the racket and gaiety and playmates they
were used to, there had always been as much song and laughter
as pain and rage in the swarm around them, and on feast days
the braziers outside every door would be enveloped in jokes and
high spirits and delicious smells, everybody would seem to have
forgotten the huffs of the day before. But even Assunta had
always been somewhat standoffish with the villagers, and along
with the rest of the grown-ups was overjoyed by the new, if in
her case relative, peace.

Long before that, during one of their mother's absences after
the great fiasco, or it might have been just when it was occur-
ring and she was getting herself flayed in London, there had
been a visit that caused consternation and surprised Dennie
with a flicker of distress even now. Assunta handled the matter,
as she had handled contingents of first the German and then
the American armies not many years before, only they had
stayed a while and she had to cook for them and keep a pleasant
expression on her face. In this instance she behaved more like a
skilled overseer of one of those imperial villas, trained to duties

as often political as logistical, with the difference that some of
those operators, former slaves it might be, had risen to riches.
She had picked the wrong pew for that, in all ways, for one in
trying to start a career as dressmaker just as her country got
bamboozled into that infernal war that was none of its business,
so she had to flee to where women made their own dresses or
did without. A twelve-year-old's confirmation dress now and
then would be the best she could hope for, plus some mending
for the Signorina. But that lady had no mind for rags and
tatters just then, a year of unpacking having been bewildering
enough without the Italian navy's building a lookout on one of
the two most scenic spots on her property, without so much as a
by your leave, when the stupid government had already taken
the other for its lighthouse. Who did they think they were? was
the unlikely little owner's view, and ten years later she was
saying to the new foreigners, "That Hitler, Shitler, what
was his name?" She had to have picked that up from her American soldier "guests" in the last phase but wasn't aware of it;
too many *documenti,* and other problems; Caesar's wars were
much clearer in her mind than that one. But then, ever since
the cursed, the *maledetto* day when Ottavio stopped being a
P.O.W. the dark narrow rooms she had chosen to live in—out
of all that potential splendor absolutely the dingiest possible,
sheltered however from the winter winds—had been such a
scene of uproar or a dread of it, it was a wonder she could
remember the glorious name of Mussolini. Ah, but not glorious
any more, she would remind herself, swallowing hard.

The visit Dennie was recalling was in no way military or
political, though requiring from Assunta as much finesse as
anything history had thrown at her. The twins had turned
seven. Eventually they would hear that the man in question not
only owned an Alfa Romeo sports car but in the extremity of his
plight that day had perhaps pushed it from a cliff into the sea
somewhere off the mainland, to avoid pursuit, but that was
never confirmed. Anyhow, he was pushing a beat-up old pedal
bike, the only kind of vehicle that would pass without notice at

the time, when he appeared at the upper portone at three in the afternoon, hour sacred to the nap as he must have known. The huge doors being always open in daytime, the stranger strode on in and began shouting for attention, sounding as hectic as he looked. A strong, tall man of probably not much over thirty but with black hair already greying at the sides and an air of being ravaged by nerves or circumstances. Dennie and Rick had only a quick glimpse of him as he stood calling out by the small gate to the lower courtyard, where their bedrooms still were that year. Most often the strange middle-aged basket-weaver would be working on the ground down there, opening and closing his mouth like a stranded fish and often stopping work to rub his stomach, but he was napping at that hour too or else was off around the hills gathering reeds for his beautiful creations. Seeing no sign of life in that section, the visitor brusquely turned and struck off toward the Signorina's alley instead.

"It's *babbo!*" Rick was grabbing her, in fascination and terror. "It's our father! What shall we do?"

Assunta took care of that. Somehow she guessed at once who he was, and had evidently heard enough beforehand to make her fear for the children. She excused herself a moment, under the pretext of conferring with the owner, and sent Giuseppe racing around by a back way to whisk them in silence out the lower entrance; they were not to make a sound until they were far away or come back for two hours. Actually it was only their father's parents, not he, who had had designs on the children, blaming their mother for everything including his more and more insensate business shenanigans. But the elder Comstocks' schemes, whatever they amounted to, had soon faded under the growing threat of scandal attending their summa cum laude son. He himself had made no effort even to see the twins since the separation, already had a new wife and baby, and what he was needing in such a hurry that day was just a refuge. Something, connected with a Greek vase unearthed in fragments not far away across the bay, had gone precipitately wrong, and having no time or choice he had grabbed at that straw, of getting his first wife to help him ward off trouble for a day or two.

Assunta explained, and would have done so with the kind of courtesy that invites no further discussion, that the American family he claimed to know were on a trip to France, that no rooms whatever were available, and that furthermore the whole place was in process of closing up for reconstruction. He left without thanking her and at such a clip, she never could see what had kept him and the bike from going over the edge at the notorious first corner, under the lookout. That evening at supper Rick said to her, "That was our *babbo* who came today, wasn't it?" For answer she gave them both a sorrowful hug, then wiping at her eyes said gruffly, "*Mangia! mangia!* Here I made you your favorite pasta and it's getting cold." Dennie used to imitate that "*Mangia, mangia,*" poking a spoon at Raggedy Ann who had a seat beside her at table on top of a pile of books, and Assunta would sometimes pretend to feed the smiling cotton face herself and they would all have a wonderful time laughing together, but nobody was in any such mood that night.

The only other time they ever saw her cry was at the death of the old nanny goat, the only hoofed creature sharing that inchoate home; it was only beyond the moat that you would often see an old goatherd with his flock and in fields far beyond the stone triangles a team of oxen with the farmer singing or hallooing orders behind them. Assunta had always been the one to milk the goat as long as she had milk to give. After she missed her footing the livestock inside the walls was just chickens and rabbits, to be eaten, and stray cats so nearly starved they looked like skinny kittens and produced kittens the size of mice.

The twins never saw their father again, which gave them a topic of slight kudos among schoolmates at one stage. It was certainly nothing to put beside the loss that Dennie had suffered the year before. That was when she took her first headlong plunge into the knowledge of violence and grief, down it seemed to where the aviator's body was found, and now fresh from her mother's grave she was perplexed by the sudden new freshness of a sorrow almost thirty years past, or perhaps by a contrast that didn't bear spelling out. Some unpleasant characters, of whom there would be many more later, had begun to appear on the beach now and then, usually by boat, small rented outboards and such. Not communists, nor ordinary ruffians; the neo-Fascist movement was on the upswing, and these were generally young blackshirt types with enough money to drift up the coast from Rome for a day or two, just for the hell of it. An extra-rowdy bunch were fooling with guns there one day, shooting across the whole crowded little beach at targets of one sort and another set up in the bushes. It became so disagreeable, if not dangerous, that Giuseppe hustled his small wards away; they grabbed their belongings and ran, discovering only when they were back in the Rocca that Raggedy Ann had been left behind. Tears; desolation; nobody would go all the way back for her then, especially with the shooting still going on. When they went again the next day, a kindly fisherman's wife, often there with her children, ran up almost in tears to give them the doll, its face destroyed by bullet-holes. She had seen it set up for a target, with horrid shouts of laughter—"Ah, those thugs! *quei mascalzoni!*"—and had retrieved the poor ruined thing after the gang left.

Assunta said she could sew on a new face and button eyes so you couldn't tell the difference. But Dennie went on clutching the precious bundle and sobbed no, what her darling had suffered was the truth, it couldn't be wiped out and she didn't want ever to forget it. Then in the evening, long after Rick was asleep, a search party was gotten up. It was Ottavio who finally thought of the moat, and after a bad time racing through the wrong sections of it carried her, with murmurs of comfort, like a father, back into the lamplight. He had found her asleep across the old king's escutcheon, half buried in stinking refuse, with the remains of Raggedy Ann in her arms. She had gone there because the little owl of legend, the *civetta*, had a nest in the wall above, and after dark they would hear the sad, piercing notes of its call. It was speaking of death, she had often heard the Rocca people say; that was why she had needed to be there that night.

Rick, who earlier had been almost as stricken as she, was pretty mean about that part of the episode, saying she'd been playing prima donna the way Grandma Jones always had, as they'd heard their mother remark in unfilial moments. She'd known perfectly well she'd give everybody a scare and be the center of attention, and although she pushed him off the court-yard steps for that so he sprained his ankle, secretly she knew he wasn't being so dumb. But that wasn't the whole truth. She went on sleeping with Raggedy Ann, was quick to tears over nothing all the rest of the summer, and would just peck at the wonderful meals, even cakes, that Assunta made for them. By fall she was so thin and pale under her suntan, her mother took her to a doctor, who prescribed vitamin pills.

Years later she would still wonder now and then when and where in the family's peregrinations the grubby old wreck of a doll had been thrown out, or maybe just left behind because a suitcase was already too full. She remembered a fisherman's widow whose twelve-year-old daughter's death had her half cracked, so she would stop almost anybody to tell about it, saying, "She speaks to me every day. She says, 'Mamma, when are you coming? I'm so lonely for you.'" People would always stop to listen, no matter how often they had heard it before. The strongest habitual voices of the Rocca—and how they would carry!—were of mothers calling live children at a great dis-tance, usually from one of the upper walls, "Bruno-o-o . . . Beppina-a-a . . ." with a swooping lilt down an octave at the end, mournful and all-penetrating and with never a crack in the voice, like the sound of the nature of time if there could be one; they might have been calling a child to come forth from an Etruscan urn, that was how it felt, and it would be many times every day. Then it was night and only the *civetta* was calling, for the Signorina and everybody there before her, all the poor ghosts shaking the iron bars in the hillside and blinking every three minutes as the great light swept past, and all the sailors and marauders shipwrecked off that point long before there was any Rocca, which was why the lighthouse came to be there and why the fishermen could still bring up ancient amphorae, even whole ones, in their nets. Assunta would smile if she spoke to her some day about the crowd, victims and sidekicks of the world-dominators and all the rest, that Raggedy Ann had joined. On the other hand, she might not. Certain subjects tended to make her clam up and look away rather fixedly for a moment, as if her attention had been caught by a bumblebee at the window, or a spot on the floor.

V

THE CHICKEN WAS READY, and so was the storm. The last few minutes Dennie had been so engrossed in her Italian reverie and its bearing on yesterday's funeral, she had hardly noticed that Marilyn was moving about getting things under cover. Dusk turned to night-black, the first near thunder boomed as the sky split with lightning, showing the wall of rain driving toward them up the lake. It hit a minute later, with a wind that threatened to rip the tent from its stakes, or carry it off stakes and all. They had thought Corky was inside it, out of a sense of what was coming or just from boredom, for a snooze; she had been with them by the fire not long before, after the last of several scampers into the woods on the track of some wild creature, they hoped not another porcupine. She was not in the tent, nor anywhere in the vicinity. In raincoats yanked from the dufflebag they ran here and there, calling. In a moment's lull in the wind, they both thought they heard her, not yapping, it was more like a little half-choked howl of distress, far away, off by the beaver pond, it seemed, and that was where Marilyn had her eyes fixed when the next jagged bar of lightning threw out its hideous illumination.

"I see her! She's over there, by the point!" That was beyond the beaver dam, farther than on her escapade of the afternoon, and this time, in the storm, she was evidently terrified of trying to swim back to them or retracing her way through the swamps either. The next thunder was no peal or clap, but a bolt to flatten mountains, synchronized with the nearest and fiercest stroke of lightning yet, an instant's crisscross shredding the sky, and that one struck no farther than the wild iris bed, on the shore opposite where the dog had been seen. Then Dennie was yelling with all her might into the deluge, "Marilyn! Don't! You'll be hit! for God's sake, wait! At least wait till we bail, you'll never make it . . . ."

Even her weak eyes, when the sky lit up again, could make out the water level in the canoe; it couldn't all be from rain, it hadn't been pouring that long; the leak had widened. But Marilyn had already pushed off and disappeared into the black fury, pitting her own will against it, though with only the smaller of the two paddles now left and the canoe riding so low in the water, the wind-slashed surface was bound to fill it fast.

Dennie's document reads at this point: "Had you seen his boat over there and thought he would do Corky some harm if he could? Was that it? Was that why you set out on that lunatic venture, without even stopping to bail? You never said so. And neither of us ever said what we must have known then, that he had fixed the canoe to sink, put his knife through the hairline rupture in the bottom seam when he was leaving the first time. I suppose I can see why we never said any of this—when could we have? What I'll never understand is our putting such a fact, what he had done to the canoe, and the meaning of it, out of mind as long as we did. Simple, I can hear us agreeing: by the same process that gets most people through the regular horrors of life; just deny what you know, enough of the time to keep going. How he must have laughed at us—as God must all the time—in our sweet little bravery and pretense that all was well."

Agreement, on much of anything, wasn't what had figured between them ten minutes earlier. During most of her command performance, Dennie had played the well-trained diplomat's wife, kept her intimate and compulsive memories to herself, fed out what she knew was wanted in the way of geometry and female subjugation, with stress on the piquant and the ludicrous. Only toward the end, in a fit of perversity, outrageously, she had burst out in another vein, to suit herself, not about her own family or childhood, of course, but the surrounding human scene in its "endurance and forgiveness"—a formulation brand new in her mind and that struck her as having some merit though she might revise it later on. Faces, voices, moments, for the cassette and its owner to choke on. Dennie's combativeness at this stage, surprising to herself if not to her audience, had been across the board, and they both knew it, although it was only after the tableau of the mother mourning a dead daughter that Marilyn turned off the tape and uttered the monosyllable "Shit" in a most uncharacteristic tone of sadness, which clearly had nothing to do with pity for the poor widow's plight. More likely it was just the sound of one more little human failure, with Dennie this time, being dropped into whatever list she kept in that respect. They had reached a point of definite hostility. Frigid politeness would have been the best they could hope for if the storm had traveled another way.

Now exposed alone to the spite of the cosmos, abandoned in such dread solitude as she had rarely had any inkling of, Marilyn's forgiveness, as much as her survival, became the main object of Dennie's yearning. She felt her very sanity hanging on that friendship and was appalled by her own priggishness in letting it be threatened by some trivial sense of discord, over sex, art, or the confusion known as human values; as if she had anyone but herself to blame, if blame there should be, for her own passion of an hour before; as if her own pattern of so-called normal life, or the ones she had formed into such an accusation just now, were any argument against what her grandmother would have called aberration. Marilyn might even be right about her stone triangles; they had withstood sieges in war, perhaps they were indeed what was left to count on by way of human expression, under the assault of forces more insidious than armies. Dennie was ashamed of her story-telling, and though dazed beyond any sexual thought or interest, ashamed of her previous shame.

No human or animal sounds reached her through the uproar of the elements. At moments she was riven by the practical question of what she would do if her friend had drowned. Marilyn was a strong swimmer, as Dennie remembered well; even in that dark turbulence would make it to some point of shore, if she hadn't been struck by lightning or injured in some way by the canoe's going down. But what if she had chosen to drown? if her wild act of courage had been a flamboyance beyond what it seemed? She had spoken of having had such an impulse once in her life. There was no background for it now, unless from some disappointment she hadn't mentioned, not from their brief flare-up and Dennie's repudiation of it, a matter of minutes, not months, of attachment. There must have been many such abortive flings in her life; yes, and that could be exactly it. The scene she had counted on for her creative salvation had wound up as a picture in which Ms. Groves would be less than one of those starved stray cats, ineligible for the common sufferings and delusions of women and proud of it, but herself more suffering and deluded than any in her dual incompleteness, as woman and as artist; at least her rather feverish pursuit of theory and material for fiction hardly seemed to signal much self-confidence as a writer. A quite startling glint had come into her eyes at a description of the original 16th Century toilet facility, a stone four-seater cantilevered some two hundred feet over the sea, its front wall and door long since missing, so it remained as a constant public invitation, more to constipation than performance, considering the view through the holes. Marilyn had even murmured something then, in apparent pleasure in the image, the opposite of her little growl of scorn at other points and her four-letter comment at the end.

She just might, in a jiffy's decision, have determined to shove through feces and all, since her alienation wasn't so easily expelled, even if this wasn't the glamorous Mediterranean but just a Vermont pond in a thunderstorm; it was dramatic enough for the purpose just then; it would do; in which case the narrator would have been the murderess and in a hell of a pickle herself besides.

In her terror and compunction Dennie cursed herself. She could at least have played down the ever-present sense of family, all the women with children to call for in their wild, time-splintering voices from the ramparts, with their implications of goings-on in all those marriage beds, the man-woman-child triangle that had no place in the listener's mathematics. But what rubbish. As if Marilyn had given a damn, set on her pins as she was so much better than most people; if she had drowned it was by accident going for her little dog; which coming right down to it wasn't much more comforting than the suicide idea.

The raincoat would have been good for a drizzle. Dennie was drenched and chilled to the bone, also pelted with twigs and other tree-trash whichever way she tried to face, her contact lenses were streaming veils of water and becoming painful, and as she turned to try to flee to the tent if it was still up, a huge branch cracked and cracked again like cannon fire a few yards away. The thunder and lightning had moved off a little toward the highest mountain, the one they had seen from the other shore, but the wind and the deluge were more violent than ever; she had to bend double fighting her way up from the lakeside to where the fire had been, and although the tent that her hands finally found seemed to be only half unmoored and she was able to worm in, it was a thousand times worse inside, with the nylon slapping and clapping as in the hands of fiends, reminding her of a certain French schoolyard of her childhood, and the knowledge of her isolation and blindness sharpened by the constriction, unbearably. At least down by the lake she could keep listening, for something, anything not meteorological.

She crawled back to it and fell or was blown in, off the rock they had first landed by. Her hands were by then too cold to tell rock from vegetable matter; the water was shallow there, only up to her waist, but finding any kind of hold, for hand or foot or knee, was such a chore, she got swept up for a moment by the absurdity of it and was half-persuaded she must be laughing out loud, as she'd heard of Himalayan climbers doing at the last point of hopelessness. How long it took before she was lying face down in the bushes at the edge of the rock, and whether she was in fact out of the water and not just dreaming it in the kind of delirium or numbness known as shock and exposure, she had no idea. Her ears, however, seemed to be still functioning, and in a sudden stoppage of wind, a signal in an unknown language, more alarming than the racket before, she heard nothing. Nothing at all; no boat, no voice, of human or dog, even the lake water seemed to have fallen under the spell of an eerie stillness, and she supposed that the rain must have no less suddenly stopped.

Yesterday's grave, her mother's, for the first time penetrated the several layers of her defenses against it. Rather a cold fish she had been at the time, and on the flight from Rome too, to put in her useless appearance.

It was the Rocca, recalled for how different a purpose! that brought her mother suddenly now into warmth and presence, and the further tableaux of that time that came to brighten this unlikely night were charged with the vividness of her company as also by her telling of them many times, in many settings later. Of course the leading characters were the Signorina and Assunta, but Marilyn's idea of the other female in the trio as the "alien lost soul between" was certainly wide of the mark. In the present vision of the matter, the three were giving life to one another in about equal degree, even if only one of the three would in the on-stage picture be known by her first name, Assunta. Of course the Signorina is a figure of fun, as the miser character has always been, but how many true clinical misers have paid cash for a fortress for nothing but romantic love, for a ghost at that, and the ghost of a scoundrel to boot? It becomes apparent as the scenes unfold that the young Signora Comstock, eventually Willoughby, has found up in that grand and beautiful ruin a sense of human attachment once known, if separately, for her mother and father, and now, outside her own motherhood, long missing in her life. The laughter that sounded now like the great, the happiest denial, like a stepping forth smiling and well-dressed, well-lit too, no darkness about it from the grave, was gentle, wry, far from ridicule.

Perhaps she was just helping Dennie remember, starting with their first sight of the place and that first colloquy upstairs in the dingy apartment where the visitor, always alert in such matters, noticed three small amateur paintings on the wall, framed: of trees, cows by a barn, a bowl of fruit. They were the Signorina's work, of long ago, copied, she said, from those of the famous woman painter named Klein, she couldn't remember the first name, the American lady must surely know it; with canvas and brushes and oil paints so expensive, not to mention frames, she couldn't risk wasting all that money on original ideas that might be failures; in copying "la Klein" she could be sure of good results. Her other handiwork was ecclesiastical. She brought it out with excessive modesty, a certain pained self-effacement, only on the insistence of the Signora Comstock, who had caught a glimmer of it through the glass door of the sideboard. It was a complete set of priestly vestments that she had put hundreds of hours into, but never quite finished embroidering, with a great deal of genuine gold thread among the silken reds and blues. She sighed; such a long work!—she hoped to finish it some day. The theme was all bees and roses, the symbols of Santa Rita, for whose chapel somewhere or other the holy garments were designed: at the request, the newcomers would soon learn, of her dead adorato, the rapscallion Monsignore. The tricky bastard threw that embroidery job at her to keep her out of his hair for the rest of his life and then some. However, the embroidery work on the vestments, along with prayer of course, was presumably what saved the Rocca from being bombed; if she could finish them, perhaps Santa Rita would bring about a second miracle, of war reparations for the damage that was not done.

By way of conclusion to that first meeting that changed all their lives, they strolled up to look at the stunning view from the *vedetta,* the navy lookout, and the pretty American lady and the twins all exclaimed in delight, not just at the sea and the mountains and the small harbor, but at the mass of wildflowers in bloom all over the field up there. "Flowers?" the Signorina asked. "What flowers?" They showed her. "That's not flowers, that's hay, that's worth a lot of soldi. Cash. Assunta, you must tell the farmer tomorrow to come and cut it right away before it's too dry. He said he was too busy? Ah, he just wants me to pay him double, just like the mason, like all of them. But I have the *documenti,* at last, for the electricity, and the electrician is a decent fellow, not a thief like those others. He promised to have at least one wire in by the end of the month."

Whatever the celestial role otherwise, no saint came to help in the matter of the baby chicks, that same summer. There was a dank, dark, windowless cellar at the bottom of the Signorina's apartment building, with a story used as a storeroom between, and down there early in June she imprisoned a hen, under instructions to sit the requisite number of days—Dennie's mother could never remember if it was twenty-one or twenty-three, something like that—on some very expensive eggs the Signorina had gone to a good deal of trouble to buy; and oh! the soldi! But her people were landed gentry from way back, over in the Abruzzi, not ignorant city-dwellers, and she knew it didn't pay to raise inferior stock. The stupid hen didn't appreciate the quality of the eggs, or the location, would try to escape every time the owner opened the door a crack to put in food and water, showed no sign of sitting at all. After the requisite interval, the Signorina broke an egg open and found a putrid mess. She bought another batch of fertilized eggs, equally expensive, and the same thing happened again. The hen was damned if she was going to sit in that dark hole, nearly scratched the old lady's face off trying to get out, so was boiled instead. It was hardly edible.

Except for the *documenti,* there was not much occasion for the Signorina's proper name to be used or known thereabouts. Her

first name turned out to be Anna. There was nobody left alive
to call her by it but for her saint's day, Assunta and the boys
insisted on a real festa, beginning with a picnic on the beach.
The Signorina rummaged in a trunk, brought out a torn and
dreadfully crumpled white sleeveless dress that came to her
ankles, and a pair of cracked purplè sunglasses with a piece
missing. She squinted through and around the hole, radiant
and insecure as a young bride. In the evening Assunta left the
Americans to themselves for once, to put on the grand dinner
over in the apartment which Ottavio mustn't miss either. There
were just the five of them, but the alley rang with laughter,
song, jubilation.

Another evening had a grimmer side. By '51, '52, the village
had been restored enough so most of the *sfollati* had moved back
down, to everybody's relief, including theirs. The tubercular
schoolteacher with his pale, unsmiling wife and little boy were a
year behind in the rent and had been served with a final evic-
tion notice. By mid-afternoon, all their possessions were piled
in the arch-roofed entranceway inside the upper portone, waiting for a camion that never came. They were in full view of the
American salone, its great sliding door being always open for
ventilation, where by ill luck the Signorina had been invited to
dinner that night, as she was once or twice every summer. A
glorious occasion to her; she washed and ironed for it, washed
her hair too, smeared on a jagged swatch of lipstick, a present
from Dennie's mother several years before and used at no other
time. There was wine, and better food even than on her saint's
day; furthermore others were footing the bill. The family by the
portone, still waiting, avoided looking that way, and everybody
at the jolly table pretended not to see them too. There were still
a few other *sfollati* left in odd holes and corners; there began to
be murmurings, a sound of running and hushed confabulations,
audible among the loud echoes in the salone. At last, giving up
any hope of the camion coming that night, the family under the
dark arches unpacked something to lie on and sank down there
for the night.

The Signorina always stuffed for the next week at these galas, and only after a third helping of dessert would say, "*No, grazie, chiuso*, closed," drawing a finger across her throat to show to what point she was full. This time she left half her meat, a choice cut, and took only a spoonful of Assunta's prize rum-cake, before being taken sick. An American friend of the family, in fact the twins' prospective stepfather, Stevie, visiting there for the first time, tried to escort her home. She got a little way out the door and vomited, disgorged wine, beef, bread and all, and then proceeded to stagger on her own, too ashamed to accept any further assistance.

A still worse event, in a way, was the unannounced visit of her nephew and sole heir, a young doctor living in Milan. Later it became known that he was trying to get his aunt committed to an insane asylum so he could have his inheritance right away, but he was all hugs and smiles and love of beauty at the start of his overnight stay, his first and only one ever. The Signorina, who hadn't seen him in some years and had very strong, not to say excessive, family feeling, was both overjoyed and dismayed. There was no wine in her house and absolutely nothing to eat except a stale hunk of bread and the one wretched apple her orchard managed to produce. It was late, the stores below were closed. In desperation Assunta fled for help to the Americans, who gave everything possible but it was not exactly fit fare for an heir. The nephew left with an ugly expression at dawn.

One wartime episode told by Assunta in their sociable dinner hour, not directly involving either the Signorina or the "ter-ribleness" of war, for years had a peculiar hold on the imagina-tion of both Dennie and her mother, as they had sometimes idly remarked together. It was an odd, trivial and uncharacteristic sort of bond, more so because for once Rick was way out of it, couldn't understand their feeling or why they bothered to re-member the account, except that it involved the deepest, darkest blue water under the lighthouse cliff, where the Amer-ican flyer's body was found. The American soldier in this case, billeted up there in the Rocca, must have been an acrobat or

else crazy. Every morning, Assunta said, he would run in undershorts to the worst part of the cliff, worse even than what the
original Spanish outhouse was cantilevered from, and dive
headfirst that terrible distance into the sea. Then instead of
swimming to the beach or at least the gentler approach over
that way beyond the outerworks, he climbed back up "like a
crab."

Of the Signorina's death, in winter when they were in America or maybe France, Assunta wrote that she had died "come
una santa, senza nessun lamento." Dennie's mother was very
smitten by those words and in quoting them, when translation
was required, was always pained by how poorly they came out
in English. "Without any moaning or groaning" didn't sound
saintly or fill the bill at all.

If there had been any warning, so she could have come in
time to play the loving daughter she had once been, speaking
some truths or half-truths or bald lies to make the dying
woman, who was after all only fifty-eight, feel that her life had
had some purpose, however amorphous, of course she would
have done it, if only to settle some inner accounts of her own.

Lookit, Mamma, if you haven't figured it out by now, there's
not much sense trying at this late date. You know we loved you
as well as we knew how, and that's as good as most people can
say, mustn't turn greedy in your final reckoning, you know that
would leave a bad impression. You sure mixed a mean martini
in your last years with Stevie here, that must have given a lot of
pleasure to a lot of people. Speaking of which, about the name
of this boat you two say isn't a yacht, it's just a trawler that
sleeps six and you run it by yourselves, so all right, this little
boat, I know there was a difference of opinion about its name,
you were pulling for Orlando Furioso, and he was for Dry
Martini, and you compromised on Moby Dick IV, you mustn't
go to your grave feeling bad about that; the altercation was
friendly, in fact darling, everybody said so, and the outcome if

not very original isn't a cultural disgrace even if the preceding three got it from the movie and the sad life or the name either of H. Melville was far from the minds you've been associating with; don't let it worry you for a minute, you've kept up your Book of the Month Club subscription for years, you're dying in as much odor of cultural sanctity, at least in my humble opinion, as if you'd finished that Ph.D. dissertation on Leopardi you used to talk about, no kidding, the country is littered with Ph.D.'s who are just intellectual maggots compared to you. As for the dance, the real topnotch ballet it was to be at one time—

Ah, *la danse!* How she had worked and dreamed and schemed and suffered and made her children too suffer for it as long as any shred of hope remained. Of course the entrechat six and even quatre had had to go by the board, the tutu gave way to many yards of gauze in one type of effort and to skin-tight underwear get-ups as for Picasso acrobats in others, while the old piano banged a gamut from Lizst to Schoenberg and John Cage as she worked, and worked and worked, to project the magical—had she dared say mystical?—body-language that would really speak to her time. Dennie remembered the bitter tearful scene she and Rick made one day, begging their mother to stop and go to the beach with them. Yet she had cabled her stepfather please to find that mother's ballet slippers if possible so they could be put in the grave with her ashes, and it had been done. It was a side of her that her second pair of children had never known, and they looked a little disgruntled about it; when they were four and five, she had been getting graduate credits at Columbia or the Sorbonne or wherever their father, Stevie, who didn't really need to work at all, happened to land in his semi-honorary foreign aid counselorships.

A useful citizen, he aspired to be, and so did she. Her latest stab at pedagogy had been a correspondence course in what was suddenly being called Thanatology: the art or science or sociology or something, of death—how to approach it, how people did approach it, different views of it through history and so forth. This was not, as current jargon might put it, self-oriented; she had had no sign of heart trouble, her own life expectancy looked fine. Out of altruism, or goodness of heart, mixed with a healthy need to fill her days and feel valuable, she had started a service of paid solace to the dying, at their homes or in hospitals and nursing homes; there were office expenses and the field workers had to make a living, so it could not be for the very poor, unless a government grant she hoped for came through, but the rates were reasonable, and it turned out that droves of people dying without a friend or relative on tap both welcomed the service and could afford it.

Business had boomed. Stevie gave up most of his own last hazy international affiliations to help with the book-keeping and installed the newest and best radio-telephone on the Moby Dick IV so they could run things when away from the home office in Marathon, Florida. A chronic trouble of course was bills to be paid after a death, and then sometimes there would be complaints about the employees being too perfunctory in their smiles and getting their various clients' biographies mixed up, using the pet name of somebody's cherished cat to an ailurophobe, for instance; when these objections were called in by the customers themselves, it was apt to be in an arduous squeak or wheeze hard to make out even on an ordinary telephone. The training program needed to be expanded and improved, and staff candidates better screened; that was to have been the next push on the agenda.

Or perhaps the enterprise would have been dropped soon. On her last visit to Dennie and Carter in Rome, not many months before, her mother had been reticent and embarrassed about it, and when mother and daughter drove up the coast to spend a day with Assunta, it was of course not mentioned; that would have been the coup de grâce, if a lot else in Italy hadn't been already. She was shaken, obviously, by the plunge back into her own years there; it was just that there was such terrible loneliness in America, she said without much conviction, and no education in death, it had seemed to fill a need; frankly, she wouldn't want a paid consoler herself, perhaps there might be a better way of going about it; but what? how?—unless you could make society over from top to bottom, as in her youth she had so fervently advocated. Yes, what she was doing was shameful and ridiculous, only no more so than the rest of life in our rotten times. You play with the hand you get, her father used to say— an unfortunate reference; what Grandpa would have thought of the Terminal Consolation Service gave Dennie the hiccups. Actually, her mother that time had seemed to be veering toward some form of Buddhism, if she could persuade Stevie to go to the meetings with her; she wouldn't want to pursue any truth that would cause a rift.

The little country cemetery, on its pretty New Hampshire hillside, had seemed yesterday the ultimate in alienation and fraudulence, worse than any quackery on the market. Nothing but Dennie's own vertiginous translation now, out of every known comfort and company and protection, into menace beyond comprehension, into the totality of the incomprehensible, as she lay half-frozen in the blackness, hearing nothing, made her mind at last go down in true companionship into that fresh hole in the ground, to share with the urn the last closing off of light, when the little gathering would have dispersed and the workmen picked up their shovels for the end of the job. The place made sense, she was grateful for it and to her mother for having chosen it, even if no relative closer than great-great-grandparents was named on any stone there, and if those names hadn't been there it wouldn't matter much. That such pieces of earth used to stay sacred for a long time and most of them probably wouldn't any more didn't matter either; that one was quiet and decent for the time being, and a moment's peace, between harum-scarum and oblivion, is luxury enough these days, even for the rich.

Grandpa hadn't had that much, and it wouldn't have bothered him. "Bury me wherever it's the least trouble," he'd told his daughters. "I won't be worrying about it." As he'd had to be on oxygen in a nursing home his last months, and the one Dennie's mother found near enough to their main marina that winter was in Fort Lauderdale, his earthly remains joined the crowd there, where his name was no more a meaningless cipher, within hours, than most of his new neighbors'. But when his own daughters were small, there had been such camping trips as Dennie remembered in his old age, he had taught them the same songs, outside the same tent, by some of the same lakes, over which his then younger voice would ring with a quality that Dennie's mother in later years never quite described to her satisfaction, though she often tried, with such words as "glorious" and "heart-breaking." And they would sometimes sing his songs together, in the Rocca or some foreign city most often, the twins and their mother, only there was nobody to take the bass, none of them had his ear and they had never learned it, so the best they could produce would be a gesture for old times' sake, a mini-tearjerker, minus the guitar too. What old home? where exactly was Kentucky, where the sun shines bright? were there really rivers called the Sewanee and the Red?

The lakes she and Marilyn had had glimpses of yesterday, after she bolted the postmortem social affair—promising her stepfather to come back the next day, she was sorry, couldn't take it just then—had been unrecognizable with their fringes of docks and vacation homes and official campsites stuffed with pop-up tents and sleep-in vehicles. Nevertheless, that was the piece of the whirling planet where their songs had once rung true, and under the prongs of her present distress, sharp enough to give death some verisimilitude even if reason suggested emergency exits, she knew for a certainty that her mother had picked the unfamiliar little graveyard because of that, in full awareness of all that was spurious about it but as a way of saying, among other things, "Daddy, I know you'd forgive me but I never felt right about Fort Lauderdale, and that's what got me into that dumb fakery of a business I've been fooling myself with the last few years. You'd have been ashamed of me for it and I'm ashamed myself. Terminal Consolation! boo hoo. Never mind, this bit of ground has some grace left in it, and the trees and the light are familiar and dear to us. I think we might stretch the point a little and call it home."

She would have named the place surely on the spur of the moment, in some lawyer's office, with a self-deprecating giggle and no sense of reality in the matter, since everything pointed to her having a good long time yet to live. She had kept her hair blond artificially for some years but nothing cheap or flagrant, it was well done, and well suited to the remarkably uncrinkled skin of her face and throat, and she boasted of having the stamina of a horse; she had always beaten Dennie at tennis and gave even Rick a good game as late as a year ago. In terms of vitality spent, in a few minutes and for keeps, the soil of New Hampshire might be said to be much enriched.

Dennie thought it must be moss she smelled; her eyes hurt, the darkness had turned absolute, her mouth was pressed to the wet dirt. Hello! hello! hello! Bad connection, nobody on the line, no sound from the living, no answer from the dead, in whose embrace, not by one pair of arms but all, in the grave-yard of her thoughts and every other anywhere, she felt herself suddenly drawn still farther down into the ground and on under it, as by steel cables from a machine fit to pull tons, making her little weight a joke. "Mother, forgive me! Try to understand!" She might have cried it aloud, she couldn't tell, but did know that the astonishing sound that struck her ears then was from the living world, aboveground, and not far away.

It was the plaintive, inquiring cheep of some rather large bird, apparently looking out on a first survey of the storm's toll. The note, far from song but of a sorrowful sweetness, sounded again three times, ending just as another cloudburst dropped, as though to annihilate any small creature so presumptuous as to have survived the others. This time it was rage turned solid, it felt and sounded like a skyful of lead pellets hurtling down.

Dennie wrenched to her feet, and facing the lake and the onslaught as well, screamed, "Help! Help!"

As if anybody could have heard, through such anger from on

high; she might as well have yelled for help to, or from, the grave. As if there were any human being to hear, if she had been audible, except the one chameleon stranger who had as good as warned them not to put any trust in him and whom she had prayerfully hoped not to see again. But having been torn loose from any sense of time, of how much of it had elapsed since Marilyn left, convinced now that her friend must be drowned or drowning, otherwise Dennie would have heard something besides the plaint of a bereaved bird, she was past any such reservations; anything human would have been a godsend. She cried out the word again, twice, from a head addled with the sense of inane disaster, then stopped to put all her strength into the faculty of listening. She thought for a second that she might be hearing the same bird again, or perhaps its mate, saying he or she had also survived though their young hadn't; she knew she must be imagining it, they would keep still till the new threat was past; and past it suddenly was, with a speed as breathtaking as on its arrival.

Surely it was human voices she was hearing, a man's, possibly Marilyn's too, very low, over toward the beaver section, not raised or aimed to give her reassurance. It might be other campers who had come in late, on foot, though the terrain had sounded nearly impassable; whoever it was seemed not to have heard her shouts, and something stopped her from hailing them, or him or her, now, when her panic looked groundless and ignominious, though in fact something terrible could still have happened; it was just that the air had turned on the instant as fresh and serene as if the half hour before had been a morbid concoction of her own, a melodrama of delayed rapport with the mother who had taken that long to make her death believable. Yet she was still alone, wet through and dreadfully chilled and badly in need of changing her lenses, if she could find the case with the spares. Tentative bird chirps from all sides were beginning to sound forth, a feathered flurry of concourse and discourse on damage done, sleep delayed, domiciles drenched or destroyed. She wondered if stars and a little crescent moon might be showing even though the faint radiance of solstice afterglow had replaced the false night of the storm; she could see that much, and was about to call Marilyn's name, in no more than the natural hallooing of people out of one another's sight in the woods, when the most bizarre event of the evening occurred.

Across the quieted water she heard, and this too half-seemed a figment out of her own inner turmoil, a rendition of "Là ci darem la mano"—Mozart, in such a place!—not sung, and not exactly from a flute though it sounded close to one in the lower register. Why, it must be something as cheap as what used to be called a penny whistle; yes, that it certainly was, but played with a skill that some of her music-loving friends would have called divine. It was at least nearly beyond belief from a tin one-octave instrument, and had her on the verge of singing along with it when the lovely aria was cut short and replaced by a ripple of laughter. A few seconds later there was a clumsy paddle-splash and in a minute they were getting out on the rock beside her, Marilyn with a much subdued Corky tight in her arms. Their dripping clothes were plastered to them and their teeth were chattering.

"Call me Fred," the visitor said as he bustled about, with surprising efficiency digging dry pine needles and twigs out from whatever cover had been furnished by lairs or a rock overhang or deadfall cavities. Luckily Marilyn, as the storm approached, had thought to toss a few logs and some paper into the tent. "Or Isaac, if you like it better. Or how about Denton? Wasn't there some Henry James character with a name like that?" He grinned, looking altogether open and disarming and as attractive as on his first appearance to borrow the spoon, but younger, in his doused condition, perhaps no more than twenty-five.

The fire was started, not easily; he was very good about that, going for more and more handfuls of at least half-dry materials. They would give him the sleeping bag to wrap himself in while his clothes dried; they had a change of clothes for themselves.

The canoe had sunk, not far off the point where Corky was stranded; considering his aversion to dogs, it had been nice of him to take Marilyn over there to rescue the poor little thing, just at the godawful worst of the weather too.

"Now that I think of it"—Marilyn's smile held no trace of any previous cause for huff—"what *were* you doing out in the boat, and over on that side?"

He smiled too. The three of them were sharing what little whiskey there was, while the chicken got warmed up. "Nutty, I call it. My friend thought he'd seen a shelter back up on this side, one of those hikers' places, but he's scared of lightning so I said I'd look for it and come back for him. But I never thought a storm could hit so fast. See, I didn't want to make you girls nervous coming too close, you might have thought I don't know what, so I paddled way around that way." His gesture took in half the length of the lake. "Besides, he thought the shelter was up there. I guess that's why you didn't see me. But boy did it get dark in a hurry. I mean, that was some freak-out."

VI

"It was pleasant having a man around, and such a lively and helpful one. I know you were thinking so too, though of course I didn't get the full drift of your feeling for a good while, and I doubt if you did yourself. He reminded me quite a lot of Carter, who after all isn't above deceit now and then too, like all diplomats; it's part of their professional equipment. There could be perfectly good reasons for Fred—we were calling him Fred, you may prefer not to remember—to have lied about his non-existent friend; a man out alone in the woods like that, and as hungry as he was, is bound to look suspect; I thought right away that he'd changed the friend's gender on purpose, as a kind of comic way of telling us it was a lie. That's a familiar ploy in the diplomatic game too, elementary you could say. I began missing Carter, wishing he were there, thinking how much good it would do him to get a taste of the wild, feeling any failure between us was mostly mine, and what a good time and place that would be for the old mythical fresh start we're always hearing about. What you told me before we were through ought to put a different light on this, and I suppose did for a time; now I don't know. Unless he's fed up by now, he'll see this page tonight and may break down and illuminate me; if he's up to it; if we're up to it.

"Fred's features weren't much like his, but some of his man-

nerisms were, that sudden lift of the head in response to a
change of thought, all the little quick gestures of eagerness to
please, the nervous scratch at the chin when there's no itch,
even the slump of the whole body in some momentary
broodiness. And they're about the same height, six feet. Carter
has plenty of muscle too, he works out with barbells and can lift
terrific weights but he's not a patch on that Fred fellow. Try to
excuse my going on about him, if you ever see this; it can't be
welcome, but my God he was strong! (N.B.: at least I put it in
the past tense, as if he were dead, as he may be.) I couldn't
believe it when he lifted up the root end of that tremendous
fallen pine that must have been lying there for years, to chop off
some dry roots from the underside for the fire. I'm afraid Carter
would have admired that and given himself a hernia by getting
into foolish competition with it. But the music on that funny
little instrument and the general good feeling at that stage,
some of the turns of conversation too—you know my darling
husband can be pretty eccentric himself—would have been
right up his best alley, the one I enjoy most anyway.

"So as I say, my marriage felt more, I guess a therapy word
for it might be 'solid,' than for a long time, laugh as you will.
I'd changed my lenses, could see that wonderful pale luminous
streak of afterglow in a single band over the end of the lake,
while the quarter moon turned bright over the part where I'd
imagined you drowning, and worse, wanting to, just a little
before. *Vaut le voyage,* Michelin says, and it *was* worth the trip, it
was lovely, probably the meal too but he got most of that and
our next morning's breakfast besides; it was lucky neither of us
was very hungry. For the rest, I felt—how wrongly!—that I
had stopped being a beast about my mother and her funeral,
and just as wrongly, that I hadn't been attacking you in telling
about the Rocca, it had been just a fit of hypersensitivity that
had made me think so when I was alone in the storm; I couldn't
have told it differently; if there was any attack it was from you,
against me, and I thought I understood that and how little it
amounted to. You do like to play up your harsh side and then

be a pushover for even the most imaginary kindness or affection
right afterwards.

"Jumping ahead, I keep wondering how much of my ram-
bling account of the Rocca, and what part of it, influenced you
later that night, as it had earlier, when you pushed off in the
canoe. That much you did intimate; the thought I had put
down as crazy had been close to the mark; you had intended to
get to Corky if you possibly could and go down with her in your
arms—again, if you could; as you were both fine swimmers and
she would have struggled, it would seem to have called for
preparation, rocks, rope etc. You were just carried away,
maybe only for the first few seconds, by the impulse. Something
in the story, so you implied—you weren't being too coherent
then, and I don't want to exaggerate—had triggered that resolve, one you must have been nursing for a long time, for
anything so extraneous, a picture of strangers in a country you
hardly know, to touch it off. Perhaps it went back to that same
old love affair that brought you close to it the first time. I don't
think so; it must go much farther back; I think of you now as
having teetered for years on the brink of enormous self-doubt
and doubt of any good reason for living. But no matter, it's
none of my business; except that it could explain the degree of
your blind sympathy for Fred, or Isaac or Denton, after he'd
shown himself to be an artist of—I was going to write 'of the
abyss' but that's no vocabulary for you—anyway, something a
lot bigger and more terrible than the penny whistle. Before
that, aside from enjoying his company, I guess we were both
feeling grateful to him for having more or less saved your life.

"I see there's a contradiction there that Carter will spot at
once; he's so good at that. If you really wanted to drown, why
be grateful to the person who prevented it? But he'd saved you
from longer discomfort too, and that could be, seems to have
been, decisive, as I hear it is with most would-be suicides, even
when the resolve is a good deal firmer than your, as I take it,
passing whim. And to emerge to the strains of *Don Giovanni*!
Enough to make almost anybody glad to be alive; enough to

make us both, as I've said, willfully overlook that two hours earlier he had quite diabolically arranged for us to be at his mercy, with a sinking canoe.

"We dismissed other things, like all the wet bills he pulled from a pants pocket and spread out to dry before we ate, going to some trouble to find enough little stones to weight them down so they wouldn't blow away; there were several hundred dollars' worth, mostly fives and tens but I noticed a couple of fifties and one hundred-dollar one. Beyond some little joke about his being so rich, nothing was said about that, nor about his insistence, that too before he would touch the food we were giving him, on going back to the boat for the extra mooring line and stretching it above the rack we had improvised just back from the fire, to hang everybody's wet clothes. The clothes, we could both see, were drying well enough as they were; it was the rope he wanted to dry, or have handy, and we acted as if that were a natural domestic impulse, rather praiseworthy. And when you remarked, with mild amusement, that the boat belonged to Mr. Allen, you had been out fishing with him a few times and knew it well, and said you were surprised the old man would ever lend it to anybody, he never had even to his best friend that you knew of, Fred just said with that boyish mock-wicked smile, exuding the assumption of confidence by and in all present, 'Well, I guess he won't mind this once, it's only for a night. You might ask him to leave his tackle and bait next time. And motor of course.'

"However, things would have been far worse for us if we had read the signs. In spite of everything, I'm still convinced that that hour of friendliness was important to him in some unfathomable way, though I know it sounds like just the wishful sentimentality, the bourgeois gup, he was about to charge us with. I'm only wondering about our stubborn suspension of disbelief and how far we went in it. Did we think it wasn't really happening, that we were in a theatre?—as actors, that would have to be, not spectators; or no, it could be both together, couldn't it? and we wouldn't have been so good at it without years of hard training in less dramatic scenes; in what passes for our ordinary lives. That's what shakes me, not the way the image of Corky does, but they're related, after all.

"I must say he showed a relic of manners, enough to suggest he'd had some once, in eating most of our food, while contradicting himself several times about the reason for his being so hungry. He was too smart to do that out of carelessness or think we were dumb enough to miss it; it was part of his lonesome, elaborate game. But he did seem halfway apologetic at moments, and as if he'd like to make it up to us somehow, while amends were still conceivable. Hence the charming performance, Brahms that time, on the penny whistle, after he'd eaten everything in sight. Or he may just have felt like playing; he has to have had a passion for music, to have learned and practiced so much."

―――――――

"Oh my sweets, my honeys! What a fiesta! Muchas gracias, I mean it. Shall we dance? shall we fuck? do you believe in immortality?" Grinning, he hopped sleeping bag and all to see how the clothes were doing; his own jeans were still wet but Dennie's, nearly dry, fitted him around the waist so he whipped into those and they all laughed at the length of hairy legs left uncovered. For the top Marilyn gave him her wintry navy-blue parka; close by the fire she assured him she was fine now with windbreaker and two sweaters. "And longjohns—see?" She pulled a bit out from under her belt to prove it. Since the time in the Dolomites Dennie hadn't seen her so ingratiating. He thanked her, "kindly" as he put it, and with meticulous care turned the six shoes for maximum drying effect. There seemed to have come upon them all a sense of being in exactly the company that in all the world they would have chosen if they'd had the choice, and in the most surprisingly right place.

Looking into the fire, Dennie murmured, as in sudden release from strain, "I was at my mother's funeral yesterday. I got thinking about it before you came back, in the storm."

"Natural death?"

"What?"

"Somebody bump her off, or you mean she just got sick and croaked? Boy, that's class for you; lucky lady; you don't hear of many like that any more. But I guess I haven't exactly been moving in polite society."

"My twin brother, Rick, probably doesn't even know about it yet. He's in Cambodia, somewhere near the Thailand border I think."

"I know a guy over there, used to be big in poppies and stuff, you know, drug traffic, but I hear he's pirating refugee food supplies now, making a mint they say. Did you have incest with your brother? I hear that's irresistible."

Dennie got on her disapproving pout; Marilyn took it as a joke, inoffensive. Fred picked up his penny whistle and after a couple of warm-up toots announced, "A touch of *Magic Flute*. For your mother. May we all end as peacefully. Not that we're likely to, of course. Me, I've been trying to volunteer for a one-way trip to outer space; at least get some interesting thoughts on the way to extinction, but it seems there's some law against it. Guinea-pig suicide, they call it. Can you see any logic to a prohibition like that, considering what's known as the quality of life on this dead star?" He didn't expect an answer, didn't wait for one.

It was marvelous what he could produce on his little tin pipe, and he did it as naturally as breathing, more so than talking, like an animal happily lapsing from some learned, alien form of speech into the one its genes provided. For an encore he played what might have been something from Brahms, anyway it was one of the last pieces Rick had struggled with on the fiddle, with Dennie accompanying him or trying to, when they were fifteen and about to give up their instruments for good. Listening now, she regretted that rebellion, wondered if her brother sometimes did, sympathized with their mother's unhappiness over it. After one down-rippling phrase it appeared that a thrush high above them was answering, and hearing it the young man—he did look young then—repeated the phrase; sure enough, it wasn't accident, something in the particular notes had taken the bird's fancy, and it joined in the second time from a much closer branch, although this was past its bedtime, if any bed was left. Perhaps it needed to sing simply in celebration of survival and the end of storm and dread, and its partner in the duet might have been doing the same, his features as he trilled were so cleansed of any harshness or duplicity. There were two ugly scars one on each leg, and they had seen some on his throat and arms earlier, but the only conflict showing as he played was between the intensity of the occupation and the pouring sweetness of sound of so different an order of intensity. The thrush gave up, tired at last, or let down by mystification; the man finished alone, then dropping the whistle with a little smile and shrug of self-deprecation, picked up the hatchet instead, to keep his fingers busy.

They thanked him, spoke of the thrush and the unusual brilliance of the stars, replenished the fire, felt deeply at ease. Dennie sat with a wad of foam padding between the seat of her jeans and the cold ground, leaning back against the large log they had found in place there. Marilyn, on a half-inflated pillow brought from the tent, in a gesture of further, sudden relaxation lay back with her head on her friend's lap, her face turned up to the star-spangled balsam ceiling. There was no air of either invitation or retort in her change of position, she wasn't either resuming romance with another female or telling the male to think what he liked; it was just for comfort, in ordinary friendliness, and very comfortable, inwardly as well, she did look. Glancing down at the rain-freshened face her thigh was pillowing, Dennie was startled by its serenity and a sense of having grossly misjudged the character in question. Such capacity for repose, for one thing, she wouldn't have suspected in her. A moment's image came to her of her son as a little boy of three or four, cuddling against her as she rested on her bed or tried to snatch some reading time on a sofa, wanting to be told stories, saying often, "Tell me what it was like when you were little.

What were your mommy and daddy like?" She had hugged him often enough, and racked her brain for Cinderella and the wild swans and the dog with eyes as big as saucers at the bottom of the well and the frog who was really a prince, but too often, it seemed now, had had to hurry to dress for a party or would be impatient for obscure reasons of her own.

Fred, back to his restless quickness of glance as soon as he stopped playing, didn't seem to mind having nothing to lean against. He was sitting on the flat-topped log at right angles to hers, that one propped up at bench height and also provided by previous campers. Along with the semicircle of rocks for the fireplace, uncemented but carried and arranged by others, these conveniences lent a slight sense of the motel room to the experience of wilderness; still, it was cold going out of the firelight to pee, and there could be a bear or bobcat nearby. Apparently tired of strumming the hatchet blade, Fred had laid it on the bench at his side and was now whittling on a small piece of birchwood with Marilyn's bowie knife.

"Do you write poems too?" he asked Dennie.

"No. Or well, actually, yes. Sort of. I used to." In the diplomatic set she was often introduced as a poet, and played the part, but that was not in Marilyn's company.

"I started to write a novel once," he said, with a half-smile between boyishly embarrassed, on the verge of hopeful, eager, and world-weary, or worse, world-contemptuous. He went on more to Marilyn, who had twisted to look at him with new interest. "It was when I was being a guard on that campus where I heard you. Matter of fact, it could have been you that set me off, gave me the idea." At this he became for a moment altogether boyish. "Yes, by golly, I honestly think it was. Small world as they say. I was reading a lot, don't ask me why, and I could see where practically everything they call novels nowadays was just another kind of hustling, you know, untrue, out of joint. Either tired old hat or trying so hard not to be—you know what I mean, so all you get a load of is the sweat over being different. And all of a sudden I thought I had a hell of a bright idea. Not sci fi, either, that's the worst bore. The real malarkey. Of course kind of autobiographical, like first novels always are, but I could see how to stand back from this me-guy and make him do things way off there like a tightrope artist. Oh well, there you are, another pipedream bit the dust." That was to make Marilyn smile. "I know how you appreciate mixed metaphors."

"And what happened to it, the novel?"

His eyes went still merrier. "My living quarters got changed. The new ones weren't conducive to creative activity." He inspected the point he'd been whittling, squinting to sight it against the flame, then started on the other end of the stick. "This the first time you two been out camping like this? Like I said before, I should think it might be risky—two gals out alone, unprotected. Or is this a crime-free state? What state is it, by the way? I wasn't paying too much attention."

They told him Vermont, smiling, and Marilyn said she'd been camping hundreds of times, he'd already commented on her equipment. Dennie said she and her brother used to do it a lot when they were children with their grandfather.

That nearly knocked their new friend over, or so he made out. "You had a *grand*father? And a mother too, till yesterday, or maybe a couple days before. Boy, is that class."

"Didn't you?"

"Not that I ever heard of. I was a foundling, grew up in one of those institutions. Grew anyway, I don't know about *up;* feels more like down when I think about it, not that I do generally. In Cleveland, Ohio, that was. And I bet I know what you two are thinking I am right now. An escaped convict, right? In for murder and all that. Otherwise, what would I be doing here with that boat your friend doesn't like to have borrowed and with all those greenbacks, and so forth." He sounded mightily amused, not quite pleasantly. Dennie's eyes were averted from him, and she felt her neck muscles tense, but Marilyn said cheerfully that they'd be glad to hear anything he felt like telling: "Otherwise don't." He said, "I'll give you a choice of scenarios, how's that? But hey"—he reached over to pluck Dennie's sleeve, forcing her puppy-fashion to meet his playful gaze again. "I really enjoyed that Italian setup you were telling her about a while back. The rock place or whatever you called it. That really got to me. I mean some of those details, about the toilet and the lighthouse, and the old lady, she's great . . ."

This time neither of the women was smiling, though the guest still was.

"Oh I forgot you didn't know. Yeah, I was in the boat, right over there, where those trees come down over the water." He pointed across the fire with the knife, toward a spot between the spaghetti beach and their landing rock, across high thick underbrush that made the lake seem farther than it was at that point. "See, I'd changed my mind about leaving, I thought I'd come back and make friends, only I could tell you didn't want to be interrupted so I was going to wait till you finished the story. That's all, nothing sinister, so you can unruffle your feathers. But then that hound of yours"—he made an obscene face at Corky, who was unhappily tied to a tree out of his reach—"started raising holy hell at me. Couldn't you hear him, or her or whatever the fucker is? So I figured a different approach might be less disturbing to all concerned. And then wouldntcha know, the little bastard went all the way round over that other side, I could see her keeping her eye on me the whole time while she was whipping through all that muck. And look at her now, just drooling to get those fangs into my leg. She better not!" He calmed down, with a little effort, and got his nice gregarious smile on again. "Of course I couldn't quite hear all you said, and I guess I missed the end." They were both embraced, positively hugged now by his confidence and enthusiasm, as he leaned way toward them from his log. "Boy, I'd love to see Italy. Never been overseas. Oh, I've been out of the USA all right, in kind of a hurry sometimes; Mexico and Canada, but they're over*land;* one time on that little draft question, Vietnam, other times on private business. So I suppose you speak good wop, huh? Not like the kind I get to hear. Gee-zuss, you've had *all* the advantages, looks like. I tell you, it's a real treat sitting around with privileged people for a change. Where I've mostly been lately . . ."

In his clamming up then he looked more bored with the rest of the sentence than secretive; there was even around his mouth a hint of his suddenly being bored by his audience altogether, not wanting to waste his breath on it. He jumped up and began hurriedly changing into his own still-damp clothes. Marilyn, laying her head back again like anybody dreamily with friends by a campfire, said what about the scenarios he'd mentioned.

"Ah, the creative side; so we'll all be poets together." His laugh was for the first time rather shrill, but short, like a whinny. "I've already told you the first one, the most plausible, except I didn't say what kind of murder, did I? As if it mattered, except to make judges fat and lawyers rich. Molière, you should be with us at this hour. Oh, gimme those old ten commandments . . ." That brought still another face, another voice, and in a convulsion of mock gallantry he was yanking Dennie to her feet and into a wild hillbilly dance around the fire as he sang, "Oh gimme those old ten commandments, gimme those old ten commandments, gimme those old ten commandments, they're good enough for me!" Whirl, bend, giggle, whistle, change direction; Marilyn laughed, pulling her feet out of the way. The next lines called for a stomp side by side, hip to hip, arm around partner's waist. "Don't steal, don't squeal, don't screw, except you-know-who"—squeeze and kiss on the girl's forehead there—"honor those schmucks who fucked you forth, don't take what's his name's name in vain. Don't covet, oh no no, don't kill till they tell you to. Ashes, ashes, London Bridge and all that, oh poor people," upon which he more or less hurled the lady onto her seat and with all laughter on the instant blotted from his face, demanded, "Tell me the truth, do you know anybody who's not a thief?"

She was still smiling and breathless from the dance and not over the surprise of it.

"Why, yes, my husband."

"Didn't I hear you say he works for the State Department?"
"Yes, he's . . ."

"A hundred years to life, no parole. Next case."

She couldn't quite get rid of her smile, even felt it widening a little. "Well, my father . . . He died ages ago, I only remember seeing him once. But he *was* a kind of thief. He smuggled ancient vases and things out of Italy to sell to museums."

"So you had one honest person in the family." He seemed about to sit down but thought better of it, and of a rival impulse too, judging from his glance something to do with the boat. "I'll fill you in on number one later, the scenario I mean. The others you'll have to give me a few minutes to think up. It's time for a piss and my TM anyway. Or is the transcendental passé in your set? Maybe you've got some quickie type of meditation . . ."

He swept his damp bills up from the ground, pausing once as though to listen to some untoward sound from quite far away, then vanished into the woods, knife and two-pointed stick in hand.

———

"Wasn't he as good as inviting us then to run for the boat, leave everything, save ourselves, maybe save him from himself?—if that was possible without a motor; if he wasn't hiding just out of sight, for a joke. I guess you were thinking of that last possibility, because it was just with some lip motions and a bit of other sign language that you seemed to be saying he'd probably gone for a fix, if anything had stayed usable in his pockets. Even with just the paddle we'd have made it away, half a minute was all we needed; he'd have had no way of following. But if the suggestion did flick across my mind, it didn't linger. You certainly wouldn't have gone for it, were just looking amused, and in command of the situation as always, saying you might as well do your yoga until he came back. Walk out on all your precious camping equipment, for no good reason?—ridiculous; and I imagine the blow to your pride would have been still more unthinkable; you're not one to be put to flight so easily, by no wild beast but a mere man, a fine musician too and better yet, appreciator of your poetry.

"And I myself was in no mood to dream up trouble. I hadn't had so much fun dancing in years, not since my poor crazy painter friend shot himself; we used to dance in little disco dives he'd found in Rome, where you could be pretty sure not to see anybody from the diplomatic set; that would be when Carter was away on some mission for a few days. But what drew me to our strange friend even more was my having been able to speak of my father the way I had just then, and never had before except alone with Rick, with none of the usual strain, shame, embarrassment, whatever it had always been. I suppose everyone gets the feeling about something in their life, like a bathing cap that's too tight. By what magic had he gotten rid of that horrid pinch on my skull? I'm afraid I know the answer now, but then I was just feeling that no priest or shrink could have brought such relief, and whatever he might be running or hiding from, if he was, he had powers some people I know would pay a lot for in the name of therapy."

She watched the loops and bends and other yoga stances she had already seen that morning, in the house before breakfast. They were certainly agile, if not very becoming; it disturbed her to see the performer's crotch, although so heavily garmented, thrust into front row prominence by the legs, right then left, whipping up for the ankle to catch on the back of the neck, while the torso writhed in frantic insinuation: what would those limbs have been up to in the tent but for the interruption? Worse, the position reminded her of the ugly little secret weapon in the first-aid box and its having been used once, on whom she didn't want to imagine. The lion's face was still more repellent, the tongue that had recently wrangled with her own now protruding full force, like an erect penis in caricature, below eyes wildly depersonalized. Jumping up for the next convolution, a straight-legged bend forward, palms to the ground as good as literally exposing her ass-hole, Marilyn remarked, "I must say he has wonderfully voluble eyes, don't you think? I just can't quite decide what color they are; I suppose something like mine, sort of grey-blue but darker; they looked almost brown or black for a minute there. Oh, poor little Corky. I guess we can't let her loose, he might hurt her, but do go comfort her and give her a dog biscuit—I don't think he ate those." She sprang into the lotus position, her eyes still straining toward infinity, though she had said she didn't go in for the metaphysics of all this, it was just for limbering up, and Dennie found herself newly ashamed of her own fat and flabbiness and not having touched her toes or tried to in ages. She'd rather not get so wild-eyed and shrank from sticking her tongue out even for a doctor to inspect, but perhaps she should learn the rest of it. "Only I'm so big in the hips no matter what I do. I'd never get my feet up in my groin like that."

Corky was whimpering pitifully and was so grateful for attention, she untied her after all and held her on her lap by the fire; she kept a finger under the dog's collar, however, anticipating trouble when the visitor returned, if he was going to; just then, for all they could see or hear, he might have decided to slip off the edge of the world. Surprised once more by the warmth of feeling it brought her to have Corky licking her fingers or meeting her eyes with such happy trust—Alan again?—she addressed another silent soliloquy to her. "I advise you, sweetheart, to stay off drugs. They're bad business. I know."

On that score, she figured she was probably better informed even than her companion, if she was behind on other fads and fashions. To her sorrow, though not much from her own body's history. Both her lovers *manqués*, of the years of marriage to Carter, the Roman prince and the young American "provisional artist" as he bitterly called himself not long before the suicide, had been heavy on heroin, coke, ups, downs, just about anything going at one time and another, in very different ways. In Luigi's native social set, it was common garden pastime, and so it came about one sunny afternoon, anchored off the diminutive beach below the Rocca of her childhood, that instead of being the little girl in water-wings holding a boat's ladder for dear life, with her mother's face twisted in dismay beside her, she was one of the motionless adults on board whom no drowning alongside could have disturbed. The boat belonged to a friend of Luigi's; she had balked, priggishly he said, at other such parties and was sick nearly to death after that one. But he had a basic flippancy about dope, as about so much else, could usually lay off if he wanted to and did when his rival addiction—political—demanded; that had switched, soon after their parting, from the Communist Party to something that called itself Maoism, and more lately, she had heard, to the Red Brigades; so far he hadn't been publicly charged with anything, and in view of her own father's record of buying his way around the law she thought she knew why.

Ray, six years younger than she, in the sty of his scattered paints and clay and soiled underwear back of S. Maria in Trastevere, had been far more dismally hooked, and it was only because he was so much more fun than anybody she knew, and more sensitive to her as a female, when not weeping at her knees, that she let him put the needle in her arm, twice. For days afterwards, both times, the dreams overlay real streets and faces. In most of them she and her mother were being beaten away from a boat by a smiling pirate, while an American aviator's voice from far below cried for rescue, he was being eaten by octopuses.

"What on earth are you staring at in that corner?" Carter would say, or "Madame Hofenstein was trying to say goodnight to you, you know we can't afford to offend them just now, I'm afraid you'll have to write and explain you were sick." Ray swore he would lay off, would go home to one of those damned clinics if necessary, if they could just have a night together first; when she turned up for it he had broken everything in his place, squeezed expensive tubes of paint all over the floor and didn't recognize her; out of her own need, which she called passion, she got naked into his soiled bed anyway; a few hours later he was dead.

"Quiet down, Corky."

More and more she felt the need to be telling, not just remembering, so had to make sure of the audience for her
thoughts. "Yes, I know you're a dog but just go on pretending
for a few minutes, would you please? Then I can pretend I'm
talking and have somebody to talk to.

"You see, what I've been telling you, about Ray and Luigi,
was really nothing compared to Rick long before, those three
awful years in school and college, and now my own little boy,
Alan, that you keep reminding me of. Eight years old, can you
imagine that? when the carabinieri came to the door with him
at three in the morning. He was supposed to be staying overnight with a friend. The fanciest ring we've heard about, one
super-rich American of about twenty, and what your non-
friend here was calling the privileged people of several na-
tionalities, they'd made Alan a runner for them; he's quick as a
cat about ducking into alleys and such, and he hasn't got eyes
like mine, he can tell a police car a mile off. They said he had
several million lire worth of heroin on him when he was caught,
and it cost us about that to get him off, not counting the medi-
cal side. They'd been paying him with tiny packets of powder to
sell and sniff on his own. He'd been lying to us for weeks about
the new wristwatch and camera and gold belt-buckle he had,
said he'd run errands around the FAO, the huge world food
organization down our street, where he was allowed to play
sometimes with personnel children, or he'd been smart trading
old toys at Campo de' Fiori. Of course we were getting worried,
he'd be bleary and vacant and seemed deaf sometimes, and
quite often couldn't get to school, just like all the poor slum kids
we read about—ghetto, I guess we say now—in the same trap.
But then he'd be so open and loving and childish with us, much
more than the year before, and would beg for things he knew
we'd want him to want, like a family picnic at the beach, and
we'd think we were being neurotic. We're both always so
pressed and busy anyway, it was easier to think that. Until that
night.

"Oh . . ."

That last was a real groan, aloud. Corky, half dozing by then but pleased to have the silence broken, reared up to lick her chin with a tentative wave of the tail, and Marilyn, absorbed in her note pad since the finish of the yoga, said, "What's the matter? Have you got a pain or something?"

"Not the kind you mean."

"Forget it then. Or do you want to confide?"

"I am confiding. In Corky." They both smiled. Marilyn put another log on the fire and went back to her notes, after glancing over her shoulder and remarking that Fred must be quite a strenuous meditator. "Heavy, he'd say."

Alan's great resemblance most of the time to his Uncle Rick at the same age was often commented on, but Rick had been twice as old when drug-dealing got him expelled from his top-flight U.S. prep school, in his senior year, a month before exams and diploma. At seventeen-plus, he had been sullen, combative, when not totally withdrawn. Alan's little white face between the towering carabinieri that night was tear-stained and terrified—could they have beaten him?—cringing, pleading, hopeless. The officers, correct as always with the Diplomatic Corps, looked almost as stunned. The child had said that was his address, they were his parents: a high-ranking official of the U.S. Embassy! *Incredibile.* Mario the butler, in pyjamas, who had been roused by the clanging doorbell and opened only after some colloquy through the door-speaker, naturally assuming it had to be terrorists at that hour, now stood sleekly discreet, exchanging certain glances, an odd mix of triumph and sympathy, with the embarrassed arms of the law. Yet it was to him, Mario, not to either of his parents, that the trembling child bolted for comfort, even protection it seemed, and Mario said what needed to be said. "Coraggio. Calmati, piccino."

Dennie half imagined for a second that that specter, of her son, so vivid had she allowed it to become, was what at that moment raised the hackles under her fingers and brought a gurgle of growl, which grew louder, to erupt in a strident bark, of the hostile, warning variety. It was not what the two ladies expected. Marilyn soon saw the eyes, not far back from their circle of light: a bobcat, she murmured first, but it was just another porcupine, which Corky, forgetting last night's ordeal, strained wildly to go for, nearly pulling out of her collar. There was a faint skittering on leaves, and the animal shambled away.

"I guess it's immodest to tell you how beautiful Rick used to be, up to that year when the stuff got to him. I mean because when we were little, if we were in shorts or pants, playing around in the country, people often couldn't tell us apart. That was long before I grew this big bosom I still hate and this big bottom I must say I'm glad to have to sit on right now, though it gives me a lot of style problems with clothes. He's very slim around there and got to be much taller than I. When we were nine, ten, grown-ups would smile nicely enough at me and then swoon over him, in grocery stores, at parties. He never had my eye trouble but his eyes are just like mine to look at, and when a smile broke under his dark tumbly curls I remember people in Italy once or twice actually crossing themselves; they thought they were seeing a genuine angel, or a cherub at least. Of course I knew better. He pulled my hair and did things to make me trip and hurt myself, and we threw dictionaries at each other. But we'd comfort each other too, when the big nobodies were in a mess and took it out on us. That's a play on language you wouldn't understand, my little hairy friend; from *les grandes personnes; personne* means a person and also 'nobody' in French, get it?

"It was three years before he stopped drugs, and I guess it didn't help Mummy's marriage to Stevie sometimes. And then Rick had other troubles; kept dropping out of colleges and taking stupid jobs and quitting them, and trying different encounter groups and gurus, like nearly everybody else he knew. It used to embarrass my husband Carter to have him around, though he's basically sweet-natured, really, and would try not to show it. It made sibling trouble; we'd stopped feeling or looking like twins; we were like not very friendly cousins.

"But he pulled out of all that confusion, thank God, maybe better than I have. Got his degree finally, at a crummy little experimental college that went bankrupt right after; that was just to qualify to be useful, he said, no sense to it otherwise, it wasn't what he chose to consider education. And he found his direction. He's on what Carter calls a Third World kick. He wants to help people who need it most. I don't know about that part of it, sometimes it seems as if prosperity made worse kinds of suffering. Anyhow, that's what he feels, and he does help, he tries, he's risking his life for it right now."

She felt her thought go into a most unaccountable tailspin there, as from some brand new uncertainty, out of keeping with any previous view of the matter. But she and Marilyn were snapped from their disparate concentrations by a squawk on the penny whistle, down the little path they had taken for their swim, followed by loud hoots of masculine laughter. Rocking with hilarity, Fred sprang between them, the borrowed parka serving as a container for a huge mass of cold cooked spaghetti. "My contribution to the feast! Here, you have some," and he dumped the wriggling load onto the dog and Dennie's lap. "Oh, I'm so sorry. It slipped. Let me help you." He gave Corky a kick straight toward the fire, from which Marilyn managed to snatch her back, and busied himself picking the gluier strands off Dennie's clothes and the bench, laughing all the while. Funniest thing he'd ever seen, apparently. He then quite docilely acted on the ladies' suggestion that he dig a hole a little way off and bury the whole mess, as should have been done by whatever campers discarded the stuff in the first place. "Yes, people certainly are inconsiderate," he said as he raked over the ground with both hands. "I don't know what this country's coming to. Daniel Boone would never do a thing like that. Mmmm. Spaghetti with pine-needle sauce." He stuffed some in his mouth, chewed reflectively, swallowed it. "Not bad. We should try it warm some time."

"Were you really meditating all that time?" Marilyn asked when he'd settled onto the log bench once more.

"Hell no, my mantra's a poor little thing; got it secondhand in a flea market. I was just enjoying the scenery. And thinking up the scenarios." It was true that his eyes were on the grey side, more than blue, darkening with certain glints of private humor or speculation. Somehow he had gotten his hair wet going after the spaghetti, and as he rubbed it upward with a towel left on a bush to dry, his forehead, in spite of a further scar over the left eye, appeared unusually lofty; brain-crammed, some would consider it, even noble, and his large, straight nose and chin in front view the shape of a steel spade, went well with it. A more impressive figure of a man, in body too, than Dennie had let herself think before, and she had a hunch that Marilyn was indulging the same reappraisal, for all her generic toughness on males. But then, of the two of them, she had been the more kindly disposed toward the present specimen from the start, and she had spoken last night of having some straight male friends.

This one, straight or not, friend or not, but in some such role for the time being, had turned censorious all of a sudden. "I should have put the fire out with that spaghetti. Don't you care about the earth's resources *at all?* Don't you know wood's too valuable to burn and pollutes the air worse than any industrial fuel? It's people like you who're gonna run this planet into"— he signaled for a gag on the way—"the ground. Harr, harr. And couldn't you tie that beast up again, a little farther off? I don't like the way it's looking at me.

"Tell me something. Doesn't anybody live *any*where around here? You mean it's all miles and miles just like this? Aren't there any watchmen, or rangers or whatever they call it, who come around? I thought I heard a jeep, or like a truck or something, way over there a little while ago, but then it stopped. My voices couldn't get through all that quiet. They're tuned to compete with the sounds of civilization, you know, TV and traffic and people off their nuts yelling about it.

"And one more question before the program starts. What do you consider the most valuable human attribute? I mean *per se,* rock bottom, no qualifying circumstances like war or running for office. Me, I'd say *tenderness*. How does that grab you? Or some days I think *mercy*, whatever the hell that means when you come right down to it. I mean, I know how Shakespeare says, the quality of, no sweat, falls like gentle dew from heaven— isn't that sweet? I think I have a kind of an idea, though, what it might be supposed to mean, like blesséd are the merciful and all that. What do you think? I'd honestly love to hear from people with your shall we say background."

VII

As FEAR GREW, so did peace. It was like a bewitchment, or what she used to imagine as that, in childhood; ordinary rules and references seemed to lose their grip and pale away. The quarter-moon, when he spoke of it, became an alternative code of behavior, to be ignored at one's peril. When Marilyn interrupted to ask about the voices he'd mentioned, he said the most reliable was a friend of his named Jumper who'd been murdered in prison a few years ago and he didn't know why he was holding out on him tonight, unless he was busy turning into Dionysius, as he'd proposed to do once or twice lately

The "program" clearly hadn't occupied him much during his recess, and didn't now. He ground out a few scenario outlines, all very desultory and uninspired, and not even funny. The leading character in all of them was either a criminal or a truth-seeker of one sort or another. "I bet I know the big topic of conversation in your set these days. Crime, nez pah? Everything's amok. Scared to go out in the street, get mugged, get raped, get pushed under a subway train or into a sewer hole minus legs and arms; bank robbers and arsonists on every block, teenage gangs bothering old ladies, little kids selling dope. Worse every day. So here's this terrible guy everybody's been trying to save because he plays the flute and has a heart of gold, even if he did chop up a nice old lady schoolteacher when he was fourteen, see, she gave him free music lessons and lent him books and had what's called great hopes for him so of course he knew which mattress she kept everything in . . ."

Marilyn said that was the third time he'd invoked Dostoievski and how about something more original, adding with a smile that it was lucky he'd never finished that novel he'd spoken of earlier, since he didn't seem to know what a story was still less how to tell one. He said he guessed that was right and it could be because he'd never been around people who told stories; in what he called "my crowd" nobody would think of it; their minds just didn't work that way. "But are you saying I couldn't even make it in Hollywood? That's too cruel. I've seen people get stabbed for a putdown like that. Well, one more try . . ."

That was the longest and dullest of the lot, and he was scarcely even pretending to keep his mind on it; he must be either listening again for Jumper and Co. or trying to arrive at some plan of action without them, or else the moon was distracting him. Several times he broke off a sentence to play some little Mozart or pop phrase on his instrument, like someone coming up for air, then went glumly back to the drudgery he had after all brought on himself; there was nobody to hold him to all that fancified autobiography even if they'd cared to.

The long scenario featured a case of arrested development, a so-called underground activist from the 60's, who'd been visiting an old girlfriend at her by now longtime hideout in Vermont. She has been going under a phony name of course, has been on the lam for years, since the last bombing they were in on together. He is one of several caught and tried, did time, has just been released. She's naturally had a bunch of guys since, hundreds maybe; that's all right. Both are still believers in the Movement but can't agree on whether there still is such a thing nor on meaning, tactics, direction etc., besides she drinks like a fish. It's a commune she's in, with a sick lady novelist-poet and some others and two or three literally sick cats, meaning the animal by that name, not the commune members. So sick they shit and throw up all over the place and one had set the group's previous quarters on fire knocking over a candle; it burned to the ground; it was considered wrong to discipline them.

"This one's getting too long."

"No, go on, if you feel like it. I'm recognizing some of my neighbors. And where the story came from too." She named a bestselling novel of a few months before. Fred went dully on, ignoring the accusation of plagiarism.

A renegade ex-cohort turned religious-reactionary had squealed on her and by coincidence the feds turned up just as our leading man, known as Denton in those circles, was visiting. Big hoopla scene, cats and all. He got out through a back shed, wandered two days in the woods, happened on boat, better than sticking to roads just then. Oh, the money. Well, on the way to that visit he'd held up a small-town bank, naturally, or store or disco or motel office, good revolutionary practice, cf. Nechayev—"ever read him?"—on to Lenin, Baader-Meinhof et al. Where they'd all disagreed, that night in the commune that was supposed to be such a happy reunion, was who/what the enemy was exactly. Capitalism of course but on what level?—multinationals, or right on down to the corner liquor store? And if it was just as bad in China, Cuba and the USSR as some there had come around to thinking, while also having long since found grave fault and signs of corruption in Black Nationalism, where should bombings be concentrated? Actually his one-time bed-pal herself, pretty soused by late evening, even got critical of bombs. Said their main effect had been demoralization of the perpetrators; she'd dreamed up a new tactic called Revolutionary Laziness, a form of Passive Resistance—of course nobody there remembered the name of Mahatma Gandhi but the phrase still carried some little echo; everybody is to do twenty minutes' work per hour, develop skill in excuses etc.; in five years private business and public budgets would be a shambles, worse than if the buildings had been blown up.

A big advantage she pointed out was that all you had to sell

people was a rationale for what most of them were doing anyway, but of course as a revolutionary tactic her idea incited
some boozy boos in the room and the argument got so hot, fists
and dishes and cats and diapers were soon flying, even if it was
just a factional dispute. To some in the group, daily violence
was daily bread and several years on pottery-making and
health foods instead had gotten their tempers ready to snap.
"So that's when the feds pour in and you already got the rest."

Audience reaction being nil, that is somewhat worse than
negative, the performer churned out another suggestion or two,
even less enthralling. One featured a neo-saint type planning to
spend the requisite forty days fasting alone in the wilderness,
"like all the great religious leaders," only his character isn't
quite up to it and weakens at the smell of food. Or make the
protagonist a disillusioned dermatologist who's had the brilliant idea of reverting to fur on the human face, and finding zoo
specimens unconvincing, has set out to observe some relevant
species in their proper habitats. "If you like, you can have rural
police get suspicious and carry it on from there."

Marilyn said she'd be glad to help him work out one or two of
the versions if he'd be interested, and he said, "Gee, thanks, I'd
really appreciate that."

Dennie said, "I think that last one is rather far-fetched."

To her surprise the narrator, far from taking umbrage at
that, moved over to sit on the low log beside her and put a
brotherly arm around her shoulders. He spoke with the tenderness he had praised earlier. "You've been in some kind of
trouble, haven't you, sweetheart? Not just your mother being
dead. Something else. Would you like to tell me about it? Sometimes it's easier to talk to a person you don't know at all."

She wondered if he might have borrowed the cake of soap
without their noticing and spent that meditation time washing
himself in the icy water. There'd been a strong odor of body-
dirt about him before, definite if not too unpleasant; now at
such close quarters, in the shelter of his strong arm, she found
his smell wonderfully *simpatico*, rather like Rick's when she

needed consoling long ago. Or like her grandfather's still longer ago, when they used to sleep snuggled up close in the old tent. A smell of loving safety, where no harm might impinge. She bent her head a little against the stranger's chest, not wanting Marilyn to see the tears that were welling up—what for: her mother? just death itself, the shortness of life and prospect of one's own showing up at the end with an F for Failure: useless, wasted, no good to anybody? But there had been no death in view, none she had to see her way close to, when she talked to the unknown, faceless priest in the confessional a few months ago.

———

It was St. Peter's she went to, she who had never been in the Pope's fold and attended no church except out of ceremonial obligation once in a while, when diplomatic corps spouses were expected. A weekday morning, no fanfare in progress, the usual groups of tourists with guides or guidebooks, some solitary suppliants in side-chapel pews, out of pious habit or specific anguish or gratitude. The majesty of the interior smote her as for the first time, sweeping tombs, gilt, marble angels, bric-a-brac and her own spirit, which for once she nearly dared call soul, upward in the grand flight of human centuries to where the most beautiful of domes might in its great eye annihilate all ugliness, of behavior by God's creatures here below or their less worthy art. Here Bramante and Michelangelo by sheer might of absorption spoke Byzantine, Baroque, snitches of late 20th Century in paint or steel, all the lingos going in wrought objects, a little span each, since the saint expired upside down on a cross, hateful joke on his Lord's agony, he who was to have built on a rock and seemed to have ended up doing so, through the bequest of his name.

But the homogenizing swoop that seized her, and for the first time, although she had known the space and its accoutrements since earliest childhood, left a literal language problem she hadn't thought of, which the Babel chatter of guides in their various tongues, not all familiar to her, intensified. The confession stalls with their language signs outside bewildered her. Whatever it was she had come to relieve herself of, she had to decide whether to make the attempt in English, or Italian, or possibly French; her German was fine in a parlor but not to be trusted there, and didn't seem adapted to the case anyway.

The quandary, if it really was one—any of the three possibilities would be all right, she wouldn't be needing the names of birds or fish—gave her a shiver of doubt as to her intention, her degree of honesty in it. If she had told her husband where she was going and why, he would probably have brought up the name of Hawthorne, even called her Hilda, with a perfectly friendly touch of irony in his smile. They had often observed together that literate Americans living in Rome were often to this day touchy about *The Marble Faun,* pro or con, and about no scene more than that one, of the pure Protestant girl, she of the tower and the doves (Oh Nate, Dennie used to address the author, belovéd old friend, old master, how could you?) so burdened by no guilt of her own but just the sight of evil by another, she has to go sweat it out in the papish sauna, in precisely that same temple of untruth and chicanery when not worse, with some clumsy consequences for the resolution of the plot if not her turmoil. Ah well, Dennie wasn't the dove type, had not seen anybody pushed from the Tarpeian Rock, and Carter needn't know; or if it happened to come up, she could be "amusing" about it.

She decided, after some hesitation, on English, and having awaited her turn, found herself shut in with a most exquisitely lilting Irish voice, fresh from County Cork was her guess and toward middle age, perhaps on the young side of it. She had been to convent school long enough to get through the preliminaries without disgrace. And what did she wish to confess? She suppressed the tired old gag phrase "Mamma mia!" that absurdly came to her mind, and the giggle it induced, also a couple of French ribaldries. No, I haven't committed adultery, I meant to, twice, but not this year. I'm just living so many lies,

Father. What kind? Deep ones; I lie to myself, about who and what I am. My son knows. He's only eight years old and I can tell, the way he looks at me. I'm sure he's overheard something about my father being a fancy kind of thief, a smuggler of antiquities, and he thinks I'm no better. And oh Father, he's right! And now he's in bad trouble, we had to send him away from Rome for a few months, to an old friend of mine up the coast, a very poor woman named Assunta.

This last stupid detail might have frayed the priest's patience; other sinners were waiting; a slight clearing of throat and ripple of cloth were audible from beyond the grille but she smelled no whiskey; the upper-echelon Irish clerics she met socially around Rome were apt to be strong on wit, charm and alcohol intake. This one might be new to the job. Yes? he inquired, not impatiently; and then? The drive up the coast with her sniveling, bewildered child, the welcome by Assunta and Ottavio in their tiny upstairs quarters on a narrow cobbled street, engulfed her, along with a wild need to extract some truth from that picture to tell, almost anything, just so it was true. For a few seconds she had lost control and sobbed. How can I say it? With all their troubles and mistakes in life, and there have been plenty, they were so simply good to us. Assunta is short and sturdy and still terribly energetic but she's begun to have cataracts and some heart trouble too; of course the Hensleys would pay them well, still it was hardly convenient, the child would have to sleep on the couch in their diminutive salone and get used to the local public school and so forth, but they didn't hesitate or ask any questions either. Assunta just looked deep into my face and all the years of both our lives were in that look, as I think, I hope, I have heard them now in your voice, Father, you who have to listen to so much wrong-doing and suffering.

She spared him most of the scene, though her trouble seemed to lie embedded there somewhere and her heart was full of it. *Lo zio!* the aging couple both exclaimed, not having seen Alan for over a year; why, he's the image of his uncle Ree-kee; and

Assunta with a loving push immediately put him to work, said
the water from their one faucet was hardly running at all, and
gave him a pail to go fetch some from the one in the street; see
what a help he would be to them! and when the boy reappeared
with the heavy bucket, without even having spilled much on the
rickety stairs, he was showing his own true happy and affectionate smile, of pride partly, for the first time in weeks. "Bravo!"
Ottavio cried, bringing out glasses and a bottle of strega for
celebration, not that this took much excuse for him; this
giovanotto—he graciously didn't say *bambino*—is what I've been
wanting, another grandson.

So from Christmas to Easter the boy was as good as hidden
there. At first he was laughed at in the local school for his
stylish manners and combination of Roman gutter speech and
elegant palazzo diction, but that got smoothed out and when
the three-month probation was over he left more tearfully than
he had come. He was another real son to them, Ottavio said,
just like Filippo and Giuseppe, quite forgetting certain stormy
scenes of the past with those sons. Assunta's still more remark-
able comment was what a pity the Signorina couldn't have
known and enjoyed Dennie's *figlio* too, it would have made her
happy. A shrug, a sigh, a slight skyward lift of the eyes were the
only comment Dennie had ever observed from Assunta on her
having been left not a stick or stone or a single lira by the
Signorina, after being her sole help and companion for some
thirty years; lock stock and barrel, the nephew got all.

Of his main inheritance, the Rocca, sold at once and which
Assunta's older son Filippo was having to help transform at
least on the inside, and all its swank new surroundings, all she
ever said was, it was better when we were there. It was not an
offhand judgment; as she made it there raced across her face,
more voluble now than at a less wrinkled age, the memory of
every postwar squalor, poverty, sickness, screaming rage, along
with the festive times, and the frights of war and faces of three
separate armies before that. It was better, she said; perhaps she
only meant she had been young or younger then; or she might

mean that the kind of wealth pouring in now was more divisive, people had to try to be more human to one another then in spite of everything, in spite of the schoolteacher's family waiting all night with their evicted possessions by the portone.

Somehow abashed by the authenticity, not of the unseen priest's faith which she couldn't gauge but of his English pronunciation, her own striking her for the first time as artificial in comparison, Dennie stammered something about the ride back to Rome and how she pointed out the Rocca to Alan, at the one point on the coast road from which it was visible, far off across the bay. She had chosen that road rather than the inland expressway on purpose, in order to see it and tell him how she and his Uncle Rick had spent some of the loveliest periods of their childhood there. He said he knew all about it, had been up there several times with Filippo and his son, except for the outside walls it was going to be just like any hotel anywhere, he and some other boys had fun one night pretending to be ghosts in the moat and scaring the new owner's wife to death. He didn't care what kind of a child I had been or where, not any more; Assunta had become more the mother he could trust. I suppose I'd wanted to feed him some kind of family feeling, and maybe some sense of obligation in the whole human flow, and the Rocca used to mean that to me, the way this basilica can for a minute if you come in the right mood. We drove then around the inland side of a hill with a grove and a bit of ancient wall showing on top, and just out of sight was the archaeological dig where my father learned some of his tricks, and it seemed my son knew a lot about that too and was thrilled by it; not the scholarship; the fraud. You should have seen his eyes. When he was smaller he used to love to hear about *my* grandfather, a lovely honest man who never made a dime or couldn't hang on to it if he did; now it was *his* grandfather, the rich crook, who filled him with excitement and admiration.

Yes, but have you yourself stolen anything? is that what you have come here to ask absolution for? because otherwise . . . She was sure she could sense a smile, not an unsympathetic

one, from the other half of the booth, as feet shuffled in a new
way and the big organ went into a whine beyond the curtain.
Please, I need help! don't send me out of here the same as I
came in! Of course I'm not to blame for my father, I'm just glad
he's dead and wish him in hell. But I've stolen my son's life,
and perhaps my husband's, and certainly my own, and haven't
even a fortune to show for it. I pretend all day long, to myself
too, there is no truth in me. I had a fit of sexual passion once,
two years ago, for another woman, on the other side of a thick
wall. I hear that's not so uncommon, and it can't be a sin not to
tell a husband about it, but it's like everything else, I don't look
at it straight myself. I've gained eleven kili, I mean about
twenty-five pounds, in a few months, from deceit and despair; I
lie about the calories. By far the best thing would be if we were
to let Assunta and Ottavio keep our son and raise him as their
own, he's a stranger to us anyway, and if I were never to see
him again. Not that his father would agree to it, but that's the
confusion and wickedness in my heart, that I came here to tell
you. It offends me to the core, and if I have a core that's where
the rot's worst, to be a mother, or wife; I'm not fit to be either; I
should never have let it happen.

She was to pray for forgiveness and divine guidance, also, the
Irishman slyly murmured, keep her fingers crossed. It wouldn't
hurt either to lose those twenty-five pounds. His stint was over
for the day, the waiting line was moved to the next English-
language booth, and she found herself exchanging a glance of
keen curiosity with her confessor before he flapped away. Not a
bad-looking fellow, of medium height, about the age she had
guessed, lower to middle forties, now for a few seconds frankly
appraising her not as a soul in need but as a woman ditto—in
need of what exactly? he seemed to think that wouldn't have
been hard to answer but not in his line of duty, unfortunately.
She noted his brawny country-born hands, thinning but still
curly gold-blond hair and also somewhat curling thin upper lip
common among Celts, while like brookwater in sunlight his
glance sped twinkling from the expensive headscarf she had

thought appropriate for the occasion, the not so appropriate soulfulness of her dark eyes and full petulant mouth, the expanse of bosom in a waste of well-tailored spring coat, down to the still more expensive kid shoes that Corky had just destroyed now before the start of this ambiguous camping trip. For one instant then her eyes and the priest's had met, before both pairs in pious decorum were lowered; his seemed definitely merry, perhaps just congenitally so but she could have sworn that from one of them she was getting a regular old-fashioned Irish wink. Among other things, the batting eyelid said clearly enough that he hadn't been bored, had actually enjoyed her absurd effort at confession, and when she cast a quick look around her after his departure, as though to make sure it was really in St. Peter's that all this was happening, it seemed to her that the eye of Michelangelo's dome was winking at her too, with just as little opprobrium.

She surprised Alan by picking him up at school, the French lycée, that afternoon; they went to a tearoom off Piazza di Spagna, ate pastries ten centimeters high slathered in the local version of whipped cream, shopped together for his father's birthday present, laughed, chattered about all sorts of things including grandfathers and the unpleasantness of drug rings, and had the time of their lives.

———————

She looked up into the eyes of her present comforter, whose arm still lightly sheltered her; she had felt no weight or pressure from it. "But we were talking about *you*. Tell me"—she met his eyes with the kind of smile often mistaken for candid by slight acquaintances—"have you spent much time in prison?" In just such a tone she was accustomed to ask a visiting scholar or functionary about his stays in China or Peru.

Of Fred's previous boredom and grouchiness there was no trace. He got up, and with a smile as fit as hers for a whiff of salon flirtation, said, "You're cute."

He gave a careful turn to the long slender log he had whittled a point on and stuck in the fire earlier, looked at the little moon as in an inquiry of which the upshot was still under advisement, bummed a last cigarette, his fourth or fifth, from Marilyn; she wasn't a heavy smoker and hadn't brought many. Probably referring back to his scenarios, she was saying she didn't think either crime or ultimate meaning was particularly interesting, "Keats knew better," and at Fred's murmur of "Negative capability" she rewarded him with a rare glint of approval, sending him to the top of the class. "But that was a hundred and fifty years ago for God's sake . . ."

"Please don't refer flippantly to the deity. It offends me. As I said a while back, First Principles, whatever you name them, and The Meaning of It All have got to be subjects of reverence."

She ignored that. "Now everything's in smithereens, we have to think differently, learn to see the pieces and take that for our meaning and universe." Not all the mosquitoes had been blown away; she had to slap one on her forehead, which led to a "Damn!" and a scratch and brought Corky upright, ears pointed, eyes agleam. It had been an injustice, Dennie thought, to call them buttons; now they were like the finest china, or better, live coals.

"So you think *reduction* is what we should practice, huh? Break it all down to the fractions so nothing means anything. I know a lot of people who do that without any theory to tell 'em to. But I can see your friend here doesn't agree with you. She's for guilt, and remorse, and retribution, aren't you, honey? You want the phases of that little moon up there to be telling you something every single time around, right? And you wanna know something, they do, we just haven't learned the language. We don't even think we need to any more, just because we've had a man walking around up there. As if that changed it *all*. I tell you, you see that orb in her new quarter like now—look at her up there, listen to the music of that light! you see that from behind bars, if the hell-light from the tower doesn't get in the way, it can break your heart. Or say you're alone in the hole for a month or two with no windows, just imagining it. Hey you up there! look where I am now! It's me, yeah, your old friend. Right on!"

Dennie had it on the tip of her tongue to tell him he was just a big bully trying to scare them with lurid fantasies about his life and character, although she was noticing, as she felt Marilyn was too, that somehow every sharp tool they had, knife, hatchet, pointed spade, saw, had collected within his reach and out of theirs. However, what he'd been jangling in his pocket was just a new-looking set of jacks, which he brought out with a little rubber ball and began playing with very deftly on a more or less level bit of bench. "Ever play? Dumb kids' game, I dunno why it intrigues me, I can play by the hour." Obviously, no matter what the conversation, he couldn't stand not having his fingers busy. Before the jacks, even as he was gloating over the moon, he'd been turning his beech spear once more in the embers; the protruding cold end was of a diameter to fit well in his fist and he seemed to like the feel of it.

"Oh my, how peaceful," Dennie murmured. Her head rested back against the log, face up to the stars, her lungs filled deep with mixed chill and fragrance of the woods. She was wondering what peaceful moments her mother might have known in her adult life; perhaps there had been a few, attained by what self-deceptions? "It's such ages since I've been away from it all like this."

"Does your soul good," Fred mimicked her but took back the sneer at once, looking quite contrite. "Excuse it. I know how you mean, except whatever *it all* is, I'd just as soon not be quite so far away from it, myself. I mean like enough's enough, like I told you before I'm no country boy and jeez-*zuss*, you dolls didn't even bring a radio out here on the veldt, or did you? You want me to look in those sacks and see if your maid packed one for you?"

Cross-legged, with the dog emprisoned between her shins, Marilyn had been bent toward the fire, squinting into a tiny compact mirror as she redid the magenta on her lips. It was a job she performed about once every hour, always in the same order of procedure, left to right, top then bottom, with the same quick grimaces for inspection and lip puckerings to get rid of any excess. Dennie had thought well before the start of the camping trip that she had never seen so much attention paid to a pair of lips by their possessor, to a degree that might be called for by disease or malformation, neither of which showed any sign of prevailing in this case. The habit was just an idio-syncracy, evidently a way of re-establishing identity every hour, as in station identification on the airwaves, only this wasn't so much for the public as just a private matter between the self and itself.

The tie being re-affirmed, she flashed a smile, or more likely a quick rehearsal of one since the expression it led to was less showy, held in by some passing question or reservation. She might be wondering, as Dennie was beginning to, what the guest would propose to do about sleeping arrangements, in case of rain again; they certainly couldn't have both him and Corky in the tent with them. Or the question, if there was one, might be more serious, unnameable.

Something was brewing, some kind of shift if only perhaps of tone seemed to be imminent, but whatever they might be sepa-rately bracing for was nothing like what then did occur, snap-ping two heads around and sending one body, the man's, flying halfway to the boat. It was a high, penetrating, twice-repeated howl across the water, from the vicinity of the floating hum-mocks that Fred had come from. It sounded again, a little farther along the intervening cove and with a short glissando at the end, before anyone spoke. Trembling and looking half para-lyzed by indecision, Fred stumbled a few steps back as though thinking that whatever it was might be approaching by water. "What the hell are you laughing at? Was that a *wolf?*"

"It could be partly. There are different versions of it. They call them coy-dogs here but that's only the second one I've heard and I've never seen one. Other people do and they're said to be increasing." She got off a soothing bit of pedagogy

about certain coyotes moving east across Canada and sometimes mating with wolves or it might be just wild dogs on the
way; a number had migrated down across the border but as
there weren't many sheep or poultry farms left in Vermont she
hadn't heard of much damage from them. They were said to be
even shyer than most wildlife thereabouts and very smart about
hiding in hunting season.

This display of environmental chic, whether to be credited or
not, brought the color back to Fred's face and thoughts of
human menace to the forefront. That might not exclude the
chief potential menace himself, some of whose glances out from
their circle seemed less keyed to presences from another world
than to possible sounds of pursuit in this one. However, he
resumed his little game of jacks, with no more signs of tension
than he'd shown right along, and grew positively jolly in probing for more details about the Italian fortress, as if his having
skulked around eavesdropping on Dennie's account earlier
were a joke shared by all present, except of course the dog.
Once more, as in connection with her mother's funeral, there
was a question about the manner of a death. Had the little old
miser lady, rich enough to own such a palace, just up and
kicked the bucket? all that money and all those poor people
around and nobody thought of doing her in? Dennie said well,
they weren't that kind of people even if they didn't like her
much, even the ones who were communists wouldn't have
dreamed of it and anyway she probably kept her money in a
bank and not in a mattress. Then he wanted to know about the
ghosts in the underground passageways shaking the iron grille
in the hillside at night, who they might be, who else saw them,
how come they couldn't slip on out, was there some unnatural
power in that lighthouse beam sweeping by every three minutes
that kept them locked up? And how did they get to rate being
around anyway?

"I really wonder about that. I can understand about those
old kings and knights who died in dungeons because they got
captured in war or something, you can see how they'd get to

stick around and haunt the place. But I mean just ordinary guys. Like me." His smile, after a successful grab and catch, was not unlike that lighthouse beam, strong, compelling, transitory. "Some little blob of sperm that never should have been let out, how does it qualify to clank around for a thousand years? Yeah I know in geology that's no time at all, but in *ghost*ology I hear it's about the limit.

"What do you think? Maybe in Italy they understand these things better. Did you ever hear anybody there make sense about all that?"

Dennie had it in mind to say he was barking up the wrong tree, the British Isles were much richer than any Mediterranean country in that kind of phenomenon. Anyway they were both joking, weren't they? It was really just the grand feeling of history in the place that she'd been talking about, from long, long before the fortress was built. After all, the 16th Century was just yesterday; Odysseus sailed right past that promontory more than two thousand years before.

For a moment she thought she smelled incense, and that it must be from having let her recent visit to St. Peter's take over so powerfully, but it was not that. When Fred sprang close to her, to retrieve his little rubber ball after a bad throw, instead of the smell so reassuring a short while ago, the whiff she got reminded her of the sulphur baths she had been to once or twice outside Rome. So I've met the Devil at last, she thought with some amusement, along with a shiver of chill in the spine. Representations of that personage, from various books and paintings, raced to her mind, with a cumulative effect of nothing but self-belittlement: a fool deserves whatever he or she gets. He had asked a civil question and asked it quite engagingly; the foolishness was in her nostrils and a keyed-up imagination, which however, before she could speak, had led her in a further and worse dance. She was staring into the steam from the sulphur pool, the Irish priest's voice in her ears telling her to draw back, and instead she bent over the edge and was seeing a bottomless black chasm, mile on mile of nothing, into infinity, and some force whether of priest or devil was drawing her over the brim. For a second a face very like her own but a man's whirled in the deeps, somebody said "I hear that's irresistible," and she was moaning, "I've been lying about everything." She screamed as she plunged, knowing it was her own volition that had caused the fall.

Fred smiled up at her. "I'm sorry. I didn't mean to bump you. I was just getting the ball. This is hardly the terrain for it; I'll stop. Excuse it, I interrupted you." Evidently she had spoken some of her earlier thought, about time and history, since he added, playfully, "Yesterday and tomorrow's all the same to me." Marilyn meanwhile had had to break off another lipstick job to control the dog in her lap. Corky too seemed to be responding to some peculiar new odor in their midst, perhaps from the pointed log that Fred was once more turning in the fire. Her nostrils quivered, she was straining to be let free and her gaze kept switching from the outer dark to her mistress's face, in an urgent appeal to go after whatever it was.

Dennie wouldn't have known if the moon was in its first or last quarter if their guest hadn't mentioned it. He had made her ultra-conscious of that light and its play on the scarcely rippling black water which seemed to stretch a great deal farther than at sunset, also of the eyes and breathing in the hushed vegetation everywhere, over their heads or at ground level. But her own eyes were also taking in the same moonlight on the Mediterranean, below the Rocca, where lights of fishing boats danced attendance on the goddess and porpoises played; some large imminent decision was being held in abeyance by the thrall of so much beauty and the will, beyond all hope, to comprehend it, there or wherever they were here—Vermont, was it? She felt herself quite literally, body and mind, in both places; might the damned as well as the super-righteous have the gift of being in two places at once? Wryly, she recalled a silly English woman friend of her mother's years ago, who went overboard for the monk Padre Pio and used to prattle about his miraculous cures, the gloves he wore to cover his stigmata and incontrovertible proof of his ability to be simultaneously where he belonged in the Abruzzi and hundreds of miles away; calling it the gift of ubiquity had puzzled Dennie in that case, since the alternative locations of the selfsame gentleman, or saint, at least the ones she heard of, were always in Europe.

She was doing better; was now on two continents at once. No, three. Another landscape had come to surround her, more compelling than either of the others, only land it was not, nor with any moon above, nor any human company. She had never before stopped to consider how sociable, like all of Italy, the Rocca had been, even in the last years when the voices of mothers calling their children were no longer from the ramparts but were nearly as loud, reaching there from below, with the harbor and the encircling sea and hills for the acoustical shell. Even if you happened to stand or walk alone, a rarity at that, you were always in company.

In the third of her present locations she was the only living thing animal or vegetable. Yet there was motion of a sort and a dull far-off pervasive sound off and on, as of many giant planes in formation except that there was no more sky than earth. The enormous shapes she faced, and felt obliged to move toward, were of a glinting black though apparently white in basic substance, jagged and menacing like icebergs, and the sound she heard seemed to be from their slight grinding and collisions below whatever medium it was that held them, if anything did. No Dante, no plaintive sinners with tales to tell; the human story obliterated, and from the unsteady mountains of what couldn't really be ice, an icy chill reached out and struck her to the bone, as by an action willed and purposeful. Mind of some kind there clearly was at work in those towering shapes, which soon had appeared also behind her, blocking any exit there might have been. She would not scream, now or ever again; such noises had probably never occurred except as some higher being's mad grab at illusion, quick as an Irishman's wink, and matter and non-matter would go on fighting it out on their own terms to suit themselves.

However, illusion or not, with space as its subordinate in tow, time did resume or seem to, and in the nick of it, bypassing gregarious if not always sunny Italy, she was back at the Vermont campsite, which more than once for a few millennia at a whack had lain beneath miles of honest-to-God ice, the real thing. She was still shivering; the temperature must have gone still lower in its unseasonable caprice; Marilyn's teeth were chattering and she was rubbing her bony hands, trying not to lose hold of the leash in the process.

"We mustn't be greedy to understand," Fred was saying, probably going on with something Dennie had missed. "Any one spirit, or soul as they used to say, can take in just so much and no more." As though developing the same theme he went on, "See, about your fortress and all that, I don't get the chronology. I never knew anything happened in Italy before the Red Brigades, except Julius Caesar and I've only got him situated somewhere before business suits and neckties. Oh yes and Romeo and Juliet, they're in there; I acted in that once. I was Mercutio. Ouch!" With a gargled shriek he performed a burlesque of the death scene, without quite pitching off his bench. "A plague on both your houses!

"Come to think of it I don't know whatever happened on this side of the globe either and I don't give a fuck. I used to read like crazy, yeah, but not history, that always bored the crap out of me. I saw a picture of Washington crossing the Delaware once. The old lady schoolteacher I told you about, she showed it to me and wanted to tell me all about it, but I got her mouth shut. I still can't see why he bothered. It's been nothing but trouble since. Oh by the way, I just heard about a new kids' game on the market, you know, like Monopoly and all. It's called Shoot a President." He slapped his thigh, guffawed, and was suddenly on his feet. "Somebody's gonna make a pile with that, I wish I'd thought of it.

"Gee, I'd give anything to see Italy. Hey, let's us three go on a trip there together, whadda you say? I mean just buddies, me and you two dames who know your way around. Then we'd have time to work out the A-1 scenario and sell it to the movies and get rich, all three of us."

Marilyn seemed to have warmed up and was veering back to friendly humor again. "And get to understand the point of life at the same time, of course."

"Of course." He grinned back at her, then pulled his spear from the fire and after a second's hesitation chose to hold his own knife instead of Marilyn's in his right hand. "And join up with my ideological pals. You and your history! Twirpville—that's your fortress. Continuity you want, ha ha"—that was two belligerent syllables—"you think it's like coupons you can clip. The last bourgeois luxury. Well, my honeys, you're about to see the plan of action that's winning the world, here there and everywhere and it's no little class struggle or any of that old halfway shit. It's been nice knowing you so I'll let you in on the word for it." His eyes glowed brighter than the pointed ember he had them covered by. "Erase! Get it? Wipe out; eliminate!" With the edge of one of his shoes he made a mark in the dirt and as quickly ground it away. "Like that. Every living thing. Yeah, you too over there!" That was in sudden rage, toward where the coy-dog had been. "We've got chemicals for your kind.

"But people first, they're the worst." An instant's lisp and grimace gave a fleeting caricature of some standard public performances. "That's become a slogan in my gang. I made it up. My contribution to the poetry of social protest.

"Okay. I always like a fuck before I go to work, the jacks just didn't tell me which one o' yuz—yeah, they're my I Ching, I ask 'em everything, couldn't you tell? So I'll be a regular gent and leave the choice to you. But it better be quick."

VIII

"AGAIN, THAT FORCED COARSENESS of his speech," Dennie's letter goes on. "When he was sounding more or less natural, his way of talking, picked up God knows where or how, seemed to me rather Ivy League—am I wrong?—slangy but what my grandmother called 'cultivated,' almost professorial, without any particular geographical trace. The 'yuz' and 'wanna' stuff he seemed to throw in, like so much else, on purpose to keep us in doubt, off balance, in case we should spoil the fun by falling too easily for his charm. Or perhaps it wasn't forced at all and was just a true expression of the winning side in his split psyche—the side of the Devil, of the abyss. I don't know if you saw him poke me in one eye, hard, after he'd demanded my lenses and dropped them into the bushes; probably not, it was all so fast and he'd lashed your arms first with the other end of the rope—that rope he'd been so bent on bringing up from the boat to dry—and I think he had you facing the other way. Along with my burned wrist from the shove he gave me across the fire, and the rope hurting both wrists so much, and I suppose being dazed altogether, I didn't take in for a while how you had perhaps risked worse violence to rush around the fireplace and kiss me full on the mouth, and knelt to kiss Corky on her sweet little forehead too, at the next tree. Then it seems to me you looked strangely back at us both, in longing? in farewell? before he ordered you to drop your jeans and long-johns and underpants on the ground outside the tent. He said threesies would be more fun but it was too fucking cold; I'd have to wait for my turn, 'if time and juice hold out.'

"I despised myself, couldn't understand how I could have let you volunteer and not said anything; it might have amused him to let us draw lots for the honor. My comfort on that score was just that we'd both probably get it, and worse, unless your secret weapon worked. I felt sure that was why you'd been so brave, not that you aren't by nature but it had been without hesitation, reeling though we both were. I'd seen you take your little tin box to the woods a while before and stupidly hadn't thought anything of it; only when I was tied, waiting there, did it strike me that you must have suspected for some time what was coming and had prepared for it, with the trick learned from the Argentine nun, that you had used once in your life before. It consoled me to think you wouldn't have gone with him so peaceably if you hadn't had your secret weapon in place. Corky was wild at first, was used to being at your feet in that red chamber no matter what was going on, and of course had known the man's animosity toward her all along. She let out all kinds of yelps and whimpers, clawing and biting at the leash, then spread on her stomach on the ground as near me as she could reach, her eyes probably fixed on my face, listening, as though every pore of her body were an ear, as I was.

"The listening was unbearable. I had to stop it somehow; not easy; when vision goes as dim as mine was then it tends to heighten hearing, and what I could expect to hear was too much. I thought if I could concentrate on a single scene or subject it would help keep my ears closed, so tried to recapture my two visions of the past hour, of death and damnation—believe me, they're not staples of mine, I've never before that night indulged any such fantasy, or perspicacity if it should be that—but they failed me then. I would happily have settled for either one, the pit or the icebergs, and even wished for them to be final, the true postmortem knowledge of the nothing we are.

They were gone, fled, utterly evanesced, and more surprisingly, so was Italy and all my life there past and present: husband, son, Rocca, friends, a thousand excursions, parties, intentions and renunciations, even the interior of St. Peter's. I could recapture nothing clearly enough for it to make me deaf or make me stop straining painfully at the rope, if only to touch the dog. There were just a few inches separating us; it would have helped.

"Instead I found myself once more at my mother's fresh grave. I was lying face down on it, alone in the dark, and was listening more keenly than ever but not to anything in our current drama; you and the man in the tent were successfully blotted out, I have no idea for how long, maybe only a minute, or the flash they say is the duration of long dreams.

"This time it was a faint weeping I seemed to hear from underground. She was blaming herself bitterly for not being able to help me, for not being there to snatch me out of danger as she used to when Rick and I were little, and even for having herself caused my plight by getting me over from Europe for her funeral. Except for that, she hadn't minded her own death, but that I should most likely be following her, and in far more gruesome fashion, within a few days was more grief than she had ever imagined; if she could be allowed a wish it would be that neither of us had been born. Then somehow we were noting the odd fact of her mother, my grandmother, having died only two years before, at the age of eighty-six, and she was letting her sorrow lift enough to remark, with a little whimsical irony, 'You know, hypochondriacs always outlive everybody.'

"At this, though it was still night, the scene changed. We were running and stumbling, she was dragging me by the hand as if I were still a little girl, across the field in back of my grandmother's house in Connecticut, the home of her own childhood whenever they weren't pinching pennies somewhere in Europe. She was telling me we must hurry, hurry, because it was going to vanish and it was desperately important for me, in whatever time I had left, to understand my 'heritage,' my 'peo-

ple,' my 'blood.' These old-fashioned terms were of course from
her mother's vocabulary, not her own. Really what seemed to
be tormenting her was that unless you could count a fortress on
a foreign sea-coast where we had no true claim, of ownership or
shared history or genealogy or anything but our pleasure in it,
she had never managed to give Rick and me a fixed point in our
lives as that one had been for them. Taxes were low then, when
she and her sister, my aunt Dottie, were growing up; the house
didn't cost much to maintain and would go too long without a
new coat of paint when necessary; it was always what they went
back to, always the pivot of their hearts' world when they were
away.

"It's true I had often envied her the rapture of those home-
comings over the years—the thrill of turning the key in the
garage lock, rushing to bounce on the huge sofa and armchair
never changed in their lives though the slipcovers had been
once, banging out a few bars of jazz or Chopin on the oldtime
Chickoring square piano that of course would need tuning,
dashing to haul out old toys, recognize the nick in the upstairs
wash basin, pat the trunks of the two great Norway spruces that
had stood guard front and back from long before their time,
make sure the view over the immense roll and swell of uncount-
able valleys out back was as grand as they remembered. Those
two trees and the view had clinched the purchase of the place to
begin with, and beautiful it all was, inside and out; nobody ever
accused Grandma of a lack of taste, in architecture, landscape
and domestic furnishings; in the styles and periods she cared
about, American colonial and Italian Renaissance, she was a
whizz.

"But what a sad little manless family, a mother and two girl
children; not even an uncle to drop by, Grandma having been
an only child and soon at swords' points with most of her
departed husband's relatives. I said, 'Cheer up, Mummy. At
least you gave us a stepfather and a pretty decent one, and a
couple of boy half-siblings I've never liked much but still, an all
female ménage wouldn't be my idea of bliss. And look how it
ended up.'

"We had stopped out between the grape arbor and the clump of quince trees, in dread of seeing just that. The reel had gone racing ahead. She had meant to show me a place of welcoming graciousness and wit and fun, firelight, vases of white peonies on the mantel, gleam of silver, happy faces of visitors, a crowd of 'young people'—one of Grandma's favorite phrases, along with 'art and music' and 'settling down in the evening.' Instead we stared at a semi-ruin, empty and threatening in the wan moonlight. A pillar of the two-story veranda across the back had come unmoored and was aslant; through a cracked upstairs window we saw pale scudding clouds beyond a gaping hole where the roof around the original central chimney had burned; there was no furniture and the lawn had gone to weeds.

"I hadn't thought to wonder before why we hadn't approached toward the front door, facing the road, or the usual family entrance through the garage, kitchen and fancy pantry wing that was one of Grandma's many late and extravagant additions; after her own mother's death, she had a stroke of financial luck, thanks to an old gentleman roué of the neighborhood who persuaded her to invest some of her small inheritance in a certain insurance company on the prospects of which he had inside tips. Most of the bonanza went into the house, and by the time she was through and it could at last rival the statelier colonial specimens a mile away on the village green, it was three-quarters fake, correct however and only an expert would know the difference. When acquired, while genuine enough as to period except for a horribly incorrect porch tacked across the front in the rural turn of the century mode, it was just an unpretentious little farmhouse where some poor hardworking family who didn't have time to give a hoot about architecture had just come to grief and died out. Grandma didn't wait for money to get rid of their abomination of a front porch; somehow she contrived to have that fall off at once and a fine replica of the best colonial doorway pop into place outside the front door; a year or two later the splendid double veranda also sprang into being at the back. But most of her reconstruction would wait years. Her daughters were grown and gone before the house contained six complete bathrooms—for one old woman more and more alone—and Rick and I had been ten years old the summer of the big garage-kitchen operation, when we stayed with her. We adored the head carpenter, one of the last of Jordan's real oldtimers, who kept a raw onion in his pocket to chew at now and then and whistled beautifully most of the day; concerning the details of the job, he was probably as mystified as we were by Grandma's routine references to the 'butler's pantry' and 'the Chinaman's room' above it. What butler? what Chinaman?

"On the ghostly visit my mother and I were now making, as though in a momentary respite from our own separate dooms, one accomplished, one imminent, we had for some reason entered the property through the old farm-era gate several hundred yards from the house, and sneaked along behind the stone wall, to be hidden from the road, the way the thief had, also at night. That was a year or two before the furnishings were moved out, when the house was closed up as usual most of the winter, and what we had been stumbling over was odds and ends of heirlooms, a huge broken Canton bowl, a piece from my great-grandmother's silver tea set and so forth, that he had dropped in his haste to get back to his truck. Or perhaps he was tired from carrying the two halves of the ancestral highboy on his back all that way. That was the one valuable Grandma retrieved after the arrest, with the kind of melodrama that was ideal grist to her narrative mill, and Aunt Dottie had it now in Alaska.

"Did we think we were in the position of housebreakers too, for trying to look at such a crucial piece of our own past? In any case, Grandma wasn't aware of our presence. Time had slipped a little, the roof hadn't yet burned or the wistaria pulled the white wooden column askew, and she was lying on her chaise longue on the porch, presumably communing with her beloved view, a marmalade cat and a shut book on her lap. My mother murmured in distress, 'Oh dear, she thinks it's afternoon. I don't know if we should tell her or not.' Grandpa, even long after they were separated, used to say that the only way to keep her sitting down was to sit on top of her, but when at home alone she did cling to the ritual of afternoon repose for a little while, to be achieved only in that one chair, a relic from her days in a TB sanitarium, with her soul nourished by that one view; she loved the Bay of Naples too but it didn't serve that particular purpose. Nor did Connecticut on this occasion. We became conscious of strange breathings and scuffling somewhere in the background, as the cat arched from its drowse, froze for a second's monitory appraisal and then dashed for safety out by the always locked woodshed.

"It needn't have been alarmed. The presences were just pickup hired help and stray latchers-on from neighboring towns, who had come back to pilfer a little. One of them my mother recognized as an unemployed hairdresser who had ingratiated himself with the old lady by driving her to bars and liquor stores, after she had lost her license because of an accident while driving under the influence. He was one of a number of such characters who knew a good thing when they saw it, and a very good thing it was for a year or so, with Grandma not knowing if she was writing a check for ten dollars or a thousand. So mother and Aunt Dottie, to be referred to by her thereafter as Goneril and Regan, with help from old reliable Stevie, had to move at last for a state committal, and the hullabaloo we were now suddenly witnessing, worse than the fire or any architectural reconstruction, was one of the results.

"As her last act as a free woman, maybe ten minutes before state custody went into effect, she ordered a moving and storage company to strip the house of every single possession of every sort from attic to cellar—books and bookcases, light fixtures, antiques, junk, china, old clothes—with special reference to radiators, refrigerator and kitchen stove. The two last were quite antiquated and not worth a fraction of the moving and storage costs, but served to express her feelings at the time toward the wicked daughters she had had the misfortune to spawn. So we were getting a shot of the movers in frantic haste, like so many ants or automatons with buzz-saws, hurling the accumulation of some fifty years, with all the dreamings and schemings, decisions and parsimonies attached to almost every item, into an anonymity that they seemed to look on as a highly significant masterwork on their part. As each enormous crate was filled pell-mell regardless of categories, hammered shut and hoisted to the waiting vans, while we two hiding by the quince trees held our breath in dread of something being broken or even just insufficiently appreciated, the faces of all that crew glowed with complacency. No longer ants or robots at all, they were revealed as so many philosophers putting a last proposition in place, for incontrovertible proof of the worthlessness of human affairs.

"The next scene we had to watch, a reversion to the one with the cat and the chaise longue, was quiet but just as distressing. Grandma had apparently realized that it was not afternoon but the middle of the night, and laboriously getting her poor arthritic joints in motion, she began prowling around the kitchen and pantry, opening the paneled cupboards and even hauling herself upstairs to rummage in long unused closets and bureaux. The stairs were so hard for her, she had moved into the downstairs guest room years back, in fact the very summer when her most awesome overhauling scheme, complete with wall-moving and enormities of plumbing challenges, was realized. That costly undertaking had given her a dressing-room and her very own bath—as if anybody else were competing for any bathroom most of the time—adjacent to her much enlarged old bedroom, the one she had always had when her children were little and way back in the short time when she had a husband in residence and the girl toddlers would ask embarrassing questions about the blue bichloride she used as a contraceptive. Now in that upstairs elegance, no sooner achieved than vacated, she was crawling painfully around, bent over, mumbling more and more angrily as she looked for the whiskey bottle that some transient companion had been hired by her daughters to keep from her. Barring that, almost any sort of mouthwash would do, or more of the pills for which she got prescriptions filled in half a dozen drugstores around the county, with the help of her insidious, fly-by-night retainers.

"But the cupboards up there were as bare as Old Mother Hubbard's—not the only resemblance between the two solitary old ladies, although Grandma had cats instead of a dog at that stage. Silhouetted at the dressing-room window we saw her profile, always a source of grief to her because of the overlong, Dantesque nose, which she had managed however to make merry about, telling her daughters they must thank God for having inherited her character and their father's nose. Now against the wasted cheeks and the never large eyes narrowed by fury and frustration, it was that of a Hallowe'en hag, just as Rick as a little boy had once drawn it for fun, complete with hood, cat and broomstick. Happening to see the drawing, she had taken on an expression not exactly hurt or vexed, just somewhat musing, and said, 'Oh Lord, is it that bad? Well cheer up, Sonny; that's why we're all so virtuous in the family. If I had a beautiful pug nose there's no telling where we'd be.'

"My mother whispered, 'Now she's going to call for the ambulance. You'll see.' That was becoming close to a habit at the time, under pretext of arthritis, diverticulitis and other irrelevancies, and from her manner on entering the vehicle you'd have thought it was her private barouche. Rising to an occasion was one gift she never lost.

"I cried out to my mother please to come away, it was too grim, too sad, what was the use of our looking at all that? Besides, I was terribly cold. Two hundred acres of farmland gone to scrub and brush, desolate, no good to anybody; and that heritage pitch was ridiculous. Neither of her parents had come from Jordan, Connecticut. She and Grandpa bought the place, with money borrowed from both families, after his heart trouble, when his wife wanted to make a gentleman farmer of him, and he was only there a couple of years before the marriage blew up, Grandma never stopped calling herself a Californian and would demand to be buried there beside her parents, refusing to see that the land of her birth hadn't existed for decades. So at the end she was washing her hands of Jordan and of New York City too where she was raised and educated, I gathered because her duty-ridden lawyer father, my great-grandfather Ratcliffe, sacrificed his own and his wife's abiding devotion to California to what he thought a chance of a better career; through love of culture and fanatical frugality, he sent wife and daughter traveling around Europe in style more than once for months at a time, hence Grandma's romantic passion for Italy that was now affecting us for better and worse down to the third generation; she had then spent half her short married life as the wife of an American mining engineer in Mexico. This ruined house and landscape were just the half-century's obsession of one woman—an achievement of sorts, all right, and I realized what it used to mean to her, my mother, but it was nothing to me and had finally been betrayed by the perpetrator of the long fantasy herself.

"I said furthermore how many people in the world nowadays had any kind of forebears' home to think about, or one of their own for that matter; it was indecent to thrust such a bygone luxury on me, I wanted no part of it. The Freds, or Isaacs or Dentons—whatever our present companion's name really was—all over the USA would laugh their heads off at what she was showing me. Think of the tribes and whole nations dispersed if not destroyed in our century, think of the homeless, fleeing people Rick was with right now. I thought I heard her answer, very sadly, that she used to talk that way too when she was young and it was true but not the whole truth. And what might the rest be? What anybody in the graveyard knows: that cruelty multiplies and societies die from loss of memory. Expand the faculty as far as you're fit to, Roman Empire, Stonehenge, whatever, it won't be a reliable instrument and it may be the most dangerous one if it hasn't started at home. That could be the most poverty-blighted street, or a concentration camp with a grandmother on her way to the gas chamber, indeed ultimate horror is everyone's birthright now and God help those who don't see it, but if you let that fact shame you into ignoring your own nearer, less noteworthy legacy, you will be contributing in your small way to future criminality, national and individual; to what happens when people no longer remember us, their immediate antecedents, however erring and ordinary, and so have forgotten how to remember anything.

"Quite a little speech, not like her at all and I told her so; evidently in that week since her death she had been thinking how much wiser she might have been in her recent business, the Terminal Consolation Service. But then suddenly, as house, trees and everything around us began growing dim and tremulous, and she too was on the verge of fading, she looked away, shaking her head a little as if in awful disappointment in me, almost disgust, saying quite tartly, 'Are you in such a hurry to get back to your present reality? have you forgotten what that is? Are you falling in love with that killer who's raping your friend a few yards away? At least I can see you're a tiny bit jealous, or piqued in your pride that he didn't pick you first.'

"I screamed, 'No! No! don't go away! I'll stay, I'll listen! Show me how it used to be, tell me about the cream separator, and the phlox and sweet peas blooming right over here and how the Concord grapes used to smell on the vine—there were such bushels of them—and about the dances in that room, with music from the old wind-up victrola, wasn't it? and the awful cheap pensions in Paris and Florence. And jumping in the hay . . .'"

———

Straining with all her strength against the rope, Dennie managed to stick a foot out just enough so the dog could rest her chin on it. The wind was rising. There were some light noises, nothing terrible yet, from the tent.

The reel was lurching both ways, backwards and forwards, faster and faster, out of control. They were walking in a mediaeval town that might be Lucca, seeing a hearse drawn by two black horses, followed by a large crowd of mourners on foot, heads and shoulders swathed in black hoods, without even slits for the eyes, guided only by the somber single-note rumble of three bass drums draped in black up ahead; along the sidewalks business stopped, men took off hats, people made the sign of the cross. Then it was a sunny little French harbor café on a small Mediterranean island; they were sipping pernod and watching pleasure boats maneuver in and out, while domestic chores were in process on boats at anchor and something funny was being narrated at the café table, making everybody laugh, so that even strangers at nearby tables paused in their own talk to look that way in hope of catching the fun. It must be a story being told either by or about Grandma Jones, not yet Mrs. Ratcliffe-Jones as would come to be her legal signature, out of detestation of her husband's name and love of her father's, which aside from other factors sounded, she thought, more aristocratic. The dashing young lady swinging into a Mexican saddle and galloping off, on a horse generally considered uncontrollable, at least so the tale would run in later years, looked pleased enough to be plain Mrs. or Señora Jones, but then she was not yet a mother and not long a bride.

It was with that same bravado, one summer month in her fifties, as if her Dodge car brought from America were also uncontrollable, that she was seen charging the fearsome lookout corner under the fortress wall, the coast of Italy dropping some two hundred feet from the edge of one front tire and twin grandchildren screaming on the back seat. Halfway in time between those two gallopades, of Mexican stallion and Dodge convertible, was a very different flash, in Geneva. There too she was hurrying—taking her time, about anything, was not in her nature—but on foot, after her day's work at an English-language school, to where her precious older daughter Evie, eight years old, was recovering from a nearly fatal bout with double mastoiditis—penicillin as yet unknown; the operation would leave deep lifelong scar trenches back of both ears.

For some reason the mother in that picture, for all her scunners against her husband's tribe and a tendency to scunners in general, had never quarreled with her distinguished parents-in-law. The elder Joneses happened to be in Geneva too part of that winter, for something to do with the League of Nations, and when their little granddaughter could leave the hospital they took her in with them, in her huge turban of bandages, until she was well enough to go back to school. It was at a window of their rented ground-floor apartment, furnished in what came to be known in the family as Swiss-ugly, that little Evie waited and waited for the adored mother, the Grandma-Jones-to-be for Dennie's and Rick's childhoods, who would come swooping down the street, long skirt flapping, hat askew, at the first possible moment. A few years later, when the girls were up in their teens, there would come to be terrible screaming rows in the female threesome, but until then Evie, far more than her sister, did dote on their mother—as she would eventually on her children.

It seemed as important to Dennie as it was absurd now to grasp the moment that was being waited for, the heavenly daily reunion of mother and child, so long before her own birth, but the image blurred, there was no time, the black-wrapped drums of Lucca were pounding in her ears. "But obviously, we're a *race* of assassins," a high-pitched British journalist was saying with stylish glee at a party in Rome. "After all, we're carnivores, who have had the misfortune to develop some contrary characteristics, called inhibitions, but they're falling away rather rapidly." Carter, home from the embassy, was mixing a stronger martini than usual; as a rule he was almost absurdly discreet about bringing home office secrets, but sometimes the trouble would have broken in the Italian press and by morning would be all over the world. Generally U.S. citizens caught in nefarious trafficking, in drugs and arms for terrorists most often lately; or it might be their own government exposed in some duplicity, and from her husband's drooping mouth and eyelids and shoulders, and his failure to have a romp with their white poodle, Dennie would know there were ramifications that probably neither he nor his superiors there were getting the straight of. He had aged fast in the last year or two, at thirty-seven was being taken for well over forty, from career stress she had been choosing to think but that might take some rethinking if there were time.

A disparate huddle of European friends, those most victimized by wars and tyrannies, filtered into view, not trying to shame her with their private tragedies but having that effect anyway, and one, grieving for her, seemed to say gently, "Ah, *ma pauvre Dennie,* what I would give to help you now! You have helped us so many times . . ." That was Michèle, as generous as devout, of the ready laugh and long Gothic features, Dennie's oldest friend, from school days in Paris. Only once, very briefly, she had spoken of her young father's being tortured into idiocy before he was killed, by the Gestapo in Paris, three months before her birth; it had further been the pleasure of someone in authority to have her mother, without news of him in the weeks since the arrest, brought to see him, at a certain hotel in Montparnasse, in the penultimate stage, when he knew neither her nor his own name nor anything any more at all. The pictures of him, the handsome smiling student, law student, bridegroom and equestrian, were on the family's walls and the features were much more deeply imprinted on Dennie's mind than those of her own vanished father, which as far as she knew were not on loving display anywhere. From envy, might that be, of martyrdom versus ignominy? Carter, who had come to share Dennie's attachment to the "saintly" Michèle as he called her, remarked once in that connection that "from lack of singularity" perhaps there could be no such thing as tragedy any more. Dennie had refrained from adding, "Or comedy either," meaning that the extinction of a certain illegal provider of museums ought to be funnier than it somehow was. But that was a subject better left dormant between them.

Other voices were growing nastier. "Americans! . . . you Americans! . . ." One was of a clerk in the Rome Post Office; one sounded very like their own butler, Mario, after hours. Poor Carter, no wonder his face was so lined; of course any

American scandal is a joy to the world. "But it's gimme gimme just the same," Grandpa Jones used to say about international relations, but then he was an old reactionary, for all his repertoire of songs and sweetness of nature, and the last two decades added up to what he might have called a helluva long coon's age. At least she'd be giving a lot of pleasure to a lot of people by getting herself raped and stabbed, not on any foreign soil but beside a darling little lake in Vermont, USA, by one of her compatriots.

Shut up, all of you! Go away! Can't you see I'm busy? Right now, if there was still time, she had to concentrate on something human and true and that really happened. Her mother was right, she must use whatever seconds there might be trying to see what she and her brother came from and the sense or senselessness of their lives.

Second only to that wandering brother, Rick, off among dangers just as unimaginable as her own present plight, it was Assunta she most yearned to conjure up. Instead she got the League of Nations, just in passing though, as explanation for the apartment in Geneva. Dennie's great-grandfather Jones, the mighty if self-effacing old scholar whose portrait she had been taken to see at Columbia University, had been a friend of Woodrow Wilson's and for the rest of his life would spend his valuable spare time monkeying around with that era's mirage of world peace. The sick child is on pins and needles at the window, for hours it seems, but at last—oh, at last!—the beloved presence swishes into view down the street, with some little package, of cookies or a mechanical mouse or a volume by Jules Verne or from the English-language bookstore it might be Sir Walter Scott or Robert Louis Stevenson. Of lower fare than that in children's reading she would not hear, although she would herself in her later years be seen mainly with the Reader's Digest.

It is an apparition in brown that signals the end of the vigil; brown and old rose were that mother's colors, never black, and because of a somewhat olive complexion that she would bequeath to at least one of her grandchildren, she detested blue. Apparently no other woman in Geneva wore brown so she was easy to spot, and as Evie would some day tell her own daughter, when their eyes could finally meet through the windowpane and the hugs and kisses and the million things to ask and tell were only a minute away, she was fit to bust with joy. There was such a pickup of life that came rushing in the door under the brown cloth coat and little feathered hat, better and faster-acting, she said, than any shot or drink or pills ever made. She would swear she was well, would want to rip the horrid bandages off her head or be seen with them in the street if necessary, anything just so the awful separation was ended.

The thing was, money or no, nothing could ever be ordinary around Grandma, or ever had been, as far as her grand-daughter could make out. Every situation had to be *extra*ordinary, a gala, unless it was a wake. Dennie herself had often heard her excoriate "people whose souls are dead" and in the same lofty tone "people who eat potatoes"; a beautiful view, not only her private one in Jordan but any, must be exclaimed over; a meal must be a party. In Connecticut a ten-mile trip for groceries must entail a drugstore counter stop for a chocolate soda and woe to the participant who wears a glum face or prefers strawberry or still worse, a sundae, or absolutely beyond the pale, a banana split, one of her dicta, not altogether a joke, being "We don't like bananas." Until the serious stuff set in, she had a craving for chocolate, though between meals in Europe, where drugstores hadn't yet diversified to that point, she would settle for a nip of port at a café instead. Obviously no husband, even if willing to forego potatoes and bananas, along with her pet bugbear, tobacco, could have survived long; daily humdrum home fare, in conversation either, was simply not in her capacity to tolerate from another or dish out herself. Anything smacking of the back seat, or second place, in any respect, was just as inconceivable; the school jobs she took for a few years, in order to give her daughters the kind of education she had had herself, were many because short-lived; after a year or less she always quarreled with somebody among the female higher-ups and would move on, until scholarships and a little family help freed her from the indignity of regular hours and subordination to anybody on earth.

"A premature women's libber," Aunt Dottie had called her a while ago, not unsympathetically, in spite of having been cast as Goneril or Regan not long before. But except in the first few weeks of the incarceration, that was just Grandma up to her old antics; she might still be trying to connive with lawyers against her cruel offspring but she bloomed under their visits just the same. "But in the interest of what exactly?" a militant lady, hearing Dottie's remark, wanted to know. Business? art? scholarship? liberated sex? had she even done volunteer work for the bloodbank or a hospital? organized political campaigns? Well, it was hard to answer; a saying around Jordan, roughly from Presidents Coolidge through Eisenhower, had been "God help any cause that Frances Jones decides to support"; and you could certainly leave out the sex angle. There had been a doomed romance or two along the way, doomed being the kind she was made for, and she seemed to have welcomed certain snuggles and smooches in those contexts, but given her period and social rung, plus a bad case of father fixation and a holy terror of any suggestion of the less than ladylike under that roof, under that skin, anything involving undress would have called for a license and ring. But look, she created a house, and an image; no party she was at could ever be boring; people were apt to be more daring about their own lives, and funnier too for a little while, after they had been with her. Evie and Dottie, when themselves in their fifties and no longer having to pick up the pieces, and with their own youthful promises long since fallen sick by the wayside, came around to thinking that was a pretty good contribution to human welfare.

They weren't alone in that view. The eligible young Carter Hensley for one, who came from a family moderately prosperous and immoderately dull, was entranced. So it came about that he and the granddaughter of the house made love for the first time on the floor of the attic, which within a year of their marriage would go up in flames.

"Magnificent! Terrific!" he said after Grandma's star performance at the dinner table, where what was left of the best crystal glasses and Meissen plates and Irish table linen, rather rarely brought out from their elegant cupboards for several years past, were of course in use; the thief had left enough for that small party and the silver, as always in her absence, had been at the bank when he did the job. Carter, laughing with an abandon seldom seen from him before or since, had already been softened up, as people generally were, at first sight of the be-chintzed and sunny living room, with its books, Persian rugs and antiques carefully short of ostentation, placed to be almost if not quite unnoticed in a sense of comfort and well-being. "Lovely," was the word there. Dennie's mother and stepfather had also come for the weekend, and for dinner a decorous old widower and suitor, now just a faithful friend, on the order of an old dog, but once under the misconception that he and the untameable Lady Frances, the Duchess as he called her, were engaged to be married.

It was the right-sized gathering and Grandma, in an old-rose velvet hostess gown, brown-dyed hair fashionably set, was in fine fettle. Of course nobody else got a word in edgewise, and the extra manhattan before dinner, if not other extras sneaked in the pantry beforehand, made her repeat some parts of her stories, but that could be put down to age and it was hoped that the nice young man from the Foreign Service wouldn't notice. There was the recent drama of the robbery, and her exciting trip in a police car to recover the highboy, to be narrated, for one burst of high comedy; then came Kaiser Wilhelm bowing to her from his carriage on Unter den Linden, when she was a young lady, and how years later she dragged her little girls at six in the morning to see Mussolini ride horseback in the Villa Borghese. "I don't suppose you'd remember this, Evie." "Oh wouldn't I!" said Evie. Stevie guffawed and the old dog chuckled. Whether as *grande dame* or poor abused little woman or in any of her other personae, Grandma was all for democracy on home ground but never thought to conceal her fondness for autocrats anywhere else. Next came a heroic sequence, with herself as heroine to be sure, surviving sandstorm and stampeding cattle on her latest drive back from California.

Oddly, to Dennie's mind, she had never gone back to Europe after her flamboyant stay at the Rocca, as if all the years of that other obsession—the languages she had once mastered quite well, the museums and cathedrals and oh, the views—were a book shut for good, like all the actual volumes she took such pains to keep dusted. Had she become afraid of Europe? had it hurt her feelings some way, by not caring if she was there or not, or by offering, when she was on her own, only public accommodations and not very grand ones at that? Yet way up into her seventies, until the booze finished getting the upper hand, she would drive alone across the American continent nearly every winter, to play daughter to still older and much richer family friends who might leave her a little bric-a-brac in their wills, and reminisce about covered wagons, gold rushes, virgin sequoias and ruined millionaires jumping on white horses from cliffs into the Pacific. Hence a new stock of adventures with which to regale the New England stay-at-homes every spring.

"My freedom!" she intones merrily, an invisible sword flashing heavenwards. This is after the after-dinner coffee and liqueur in the living room; somebody has just mentioned an ill-fated marriage; she is standing, on her way to nowhere in particular, and it is with layer upon layer of canny play on her own half-suspected inconsistencies, and for an easier target, the world's, especially in its conjugal configurations, that she rises to her evening's dénouement. "I want my freedom!" she proclaims again, like someone crying only half in parody, "My kingdom for a horse!" and the little audience having duly cracked up, she proceeds on a subtly lowered pitch, though still holding the stage with prima donna stance and glance, "Give me liberty or give me death." That had become her most frequent actual quotation and she would profess utmost pity for anyone who didn't know the source of it. "*What?* never heard of Patrick Henry? Merciful heavens, what is the country coming to?"

"She's so complicated!" was Carter's glowing comment afterwards, and from him there was no higher compliment. That was because his Pittsburgh-bred mother, notable for neither humor nor IQ, had spent years in Jungian analysis and made an instrument of domestic oppression out of the term "simplicity."

As late as last year Dennie's mother had told her, almost as in a confession of weakness, that she had never stopped having dreams now and then, real ones in sleep, about the house. They were not peaceful or happy dreams. They would be of the thief in the night, who in one period appeared as Adolf Hitler, approaching along an upstairs hall as mother and daughters cuddled in almost sexual affection before the Franklin stove in the old so-called master bedroom; or of the fire setting roof and exits ablaze all of a sudden without cause or warning. Actually the fire had been started by a careless stopgap tenant, drunk on a New Year's Eve, to whom the daughters had given a dirt-cheap rental after the grand exodus, until they could decide what to do. So a stranger, in their words a blithering idiot, decided for them; somebody else would have to pay for the reconstruction. No member of the family would ever cross that threshold again, even to assess the damage.

In their stealthy lurking among the quince trees, Dennie's mother had perhaps been granted one wish after all. She must have wished for them to be collaborators in her final dream.

IX

SHE COULDN'T UNDERSTAND why it was taking so long for the
needles to make contact, he had seemed in such a rush to get to
business. Perhaps he was impotent; or Marilyn might be skilled
in wiles, delaying tactics, that her unhappy friend tied to the
tree outside preferred not to imagine. Or perhaps it hadn't been
very long. In her racing pursuit of memory and the secrets of
the grave she had lost track, time might have stopped, the
woods become enchanted, the man in the tent revealed as a
knight or necromancer able to divulge the holiest of secrets if
only one were pure enough in heart to understand. From the
sounds she could no longer blot out it didn't exactly seem so.
One giggle had penetrated her inner soundproofing—a peculiar, rather strained one but still of that general category, and it
was followed later by another, more breathless, and then by
some low grunts and moans both male and female and certain
dull thrashing noises, as of the most ordinary, unopposed copu-
lation.

Dennie, in her humiliating immobility, exclusion and plain
pain—not just at the wrists, her previous injuries to foot and
forehead were acting up too and the strained position against
the tree trunk made her back ache dreadfully—went into quite
a maelstrom of what she had imagined her mother calling jeal-
ousy, not altogether inaccurately; the word was just a touch on

the mild side for what came over her and the image of Fred, however fleeting, that went with it. Captivating, he was; if Marilyn did seriously wound him with that gruesome weapon of hers Dennie would find it hard to forgive her, assuming they didn't both get their throats slit at once; even then, she fancied it would be more the hurt to that particular male that would be the unpardonable offense. Whatever the duration of this fit of longing, one instant or quite a few, it totally cleansed her sense of their chameleon visitor, for the time being, of anything that was not strength, charm, comfort, poetry, generosity of understanding and near-genius on the penny whistle.

Wasted on that belligerent freak of a non-woman and oh yes let's come clean for once, that phony poet with her skinny purple lips and neo-critical gibberish designed to squelch all literature past and forever more. Enchanted wood and lake indeed these must be to have forestalled the earlier erotic madness, midsummer night's horrid practical joke, through the arrival of such a presence.

One contradictory item did reassert itself for a moment; it was not nice of him to take her lenses and poke her in the eye, or push her across the fire either, making for two more areas of discomfort. But he'd been acting in haste, and probably in irritation at his jacks and rubber ball for sticking him with the less desirable woman. She would scold him for that and for the I Ching business in general if there was a chance, tell him it was childish, with his qualities he should be above that sort of thing. She'd had to give Rick a pretty angry lecture of that sort once when they were thirteen and he made a big joke of running off with her first contact lenses; of course he was sorry afterwards and they kissed and made up and he gave her the very finest seashell in his collection, a big one from the Indian Ocean, by way of begging forgiveness. All truly superior men keep a touch of the adolescent if not the child in their natures, she'd heard or read somewhere; women of course couldn't afford that luxury; a female, to grow up strong, had better have a touch of the grand-mother from adolescence on; of which wisdom, Dennie reflected, her own actual grandmother, the only one she had known, had possessed not an iota but her mother, it was surprising to see only after her funeral, had had a fair amount, enough at least to achieve—and bequeath?—some personal stability, though at quite a price in other departments. The thought made the image of Marilyn over there in the chilly red enclosure, naked from the waist down, still less appealing, whatever was going on or about to ensue; porcupine quills, those were her achievement, in her repudiation of all female principle. Their poor knight, needles or no, wasn't in for much joy from that quarter.

Carter's last pleading embrace at the airport struck her now with dislike and disgust, far beyond the vague scorn she had felt at the time. All that was over and done with, had been a sham from the start, she would not fret her mind with it, any more than she had on chucking marital unreality number one twelve years ago. True, the shining alternative, the heroic figure risen by its own bootstraps, which were of some angelic endowment, out of an absolute of poverty and anonymity, everything she and all her friends had been spared, hadn't precisely offered itself, and she was hardly in a position to beckon and contrive. But never underestimate the power of a woman's will, Grandpa Jones used to say only half in joke, having had a rather crippling experience of it. Dennie felt her own will ripening toward irresistible contagion, a better weapon than any hatchet or pointed ember; the man would forgive her life of privilege, would whisper his true name to her; overcome with desire for her alone, would dump his sorrows and struggles in her arms, then kill her if need be, but five minutes of that union would be worth an eternity of what she had been playing at for so long in the name of life.

A hindrance might be that she would freeze first, unable to move and so far from the fire if there was any left. She wiggled her outstretched foot and was glad to get a little whimper of response from Corky. A new kind of clatter in the leaves, some change of temper in the wind from across the lake suggested another storm brewing; the moon, *his* moon she fondly made it be, must be clouded over, unless it had already set. This really must not go on much longer; if only her will could penetrate the tent; from which a scream then issued, short, high, hideous, and not of the wounded male. Marilyn's death cry it had to be, as the dog must be thinking too, such a thrashing and straining and gurgling had erupted in the little body, for once too distraught to growl or emit any of her usual vocal repertoire. Silence a while; leaf music; water slapped hard on rocks; from somewhere down the lake a similar screech but in four notes and more rhythmical and this time Dennie was not dreaming and knew it for an owl. With all her soul she wished and tried to believe that the first scream had been that too but both she and the dog knew too well from what throat that one had come, the same that was now, for the two listeners' further consternation, as Corky was not liking this much better, giving voice to what must be some little conversational pleasantries, in which the man's voice also took part, preparatory either to the couple's reappearance or the next round.

It was to be the latter, with another cry of orgasm from that unlikely or rather absolutely unthinkable vehicle, while dog and woman outside congealed in all ways. But there was a short interlude first, with entertainment for all, if all had been fit to take it so. It was a little concert on the penny whistle, not classical this time but on the order of rock, very funny and energetic, with elegant detail and a beat to get bodies going in the aisles. It might have lasted a minute or two, followed by the two voices joined in some murmurous merriment, then the works again.

"So it was plain, and I had been every kind of a fool, more than you know, since I didn't tell you there were a few minutes there when I would gladly have scratched your eyes out over that man. You hadn't sacrificed yourself at all; or yes, you had, but not for my sake. You *wanted* him, starting I think from his first appearance when he came out with those poems of yours. Excuse me, of course I realize it was no immediate pleasure but just the purpose he could serve that you had in mind and that seemed worth a minute's physical subjugation and nastiness, as I suppose you consider it. And come to think of it, the baby idea, that you and your pal Agnes had had such schemes for and failed to bring off, probably seized you a little later, in the storm, along with the contradictory impulse to drown. This you'll hate me for saying—and that's all right, there's nothing between us to be lost—but wasn't it in some way my feeble attempt to give you the Italian picture you demanded, and its turning out to be a story that accused you to your depths, made *you* the grotesque one, so much more than the old lady in her infatuation—wasn't it that in part that drove you to both those extremities, one very quickly after the other? As a rather equivocal example of motherhood I think I may understand the first, the suicide bit, better than the other, in fact I can see now that what I took for overpowering sexual attraction that night was mostly an urge to join my mother underground.

"But of course your second plan of action, to produce a child, gets more general sanction, as indicating some sort of basic human responsibility, no matter how unconventional the method, wrong-headed the motive and ill-suited the prospective parent to that role. How much of your reawakened desire was visceral, how much imposed by some marvelous combination of theory and ignorance, I have no idea. Anyway, fate had brought you a perhaps dangerous but otherwise ideal accomplice for your purpose; the genes would be excellent, anything worrisome there being obviously just the work of social forces on an innately superior being, and assuming there were no serious violence afterwards and he would choose to depart in peace, you would scarcely expect ever to see him again. True, he knew your name from the poems but he'd have no claim on you or the baby, or on anything else by the smell of it; whatever he was or had done, the signs were all of his being in bad trouble and headed for a dependable, permanent disappearance in one fashion or another.

"But the best-laid plans, of women too . . . There were a

couple of things you hadn't figured on, and horrible they were, to both of us though with some distinctions. You had meant to submit, and instead were made to enjoy, to a point of ecstatic abandon such as I rather doubt you had ever reached or even dreamed of before. It was a coup d'état, by a force well organized and aided too by the element of surprise; it dethroned your pride, blew the whole structure of your self-esteem to smithereens, threw your fancy palace guards out the window. Apparently he'd allowed you to wriggle back into your pants before coming out. I heard you thank him for holding the tent-flap back for you to pass; you sounded weak, bewildered, almost craven; you turned the flashlight on Corky who was straining to jump on you, and then me, showing no great haste to relieve our distress, and when the beam arched back across your two bodies, as though from utter, delectable weariness in your limbs, I could make out his arm lightly around your shoulder and your left hand cupping his stubbly chin. There was another storm coming, you said softly, as if it didn't matter much.

"I suppose you were in what's called the mystical moment of post-coital bliss or something of the sort. I wouldn't have known, not having at that time experienced much of it myself. For him, it was evidently a high point in his farce but not one he cared to protract. The very next instant, if you càn bear to remember, he was once more the human beast we had seen before, as crazed now with hostility as if you had after all installed your secret weapon and he had just come in contact with it.

"The prospect of another storm probably had nothing to do with that change of mood, just with his course of action. I'm convinced that until you mentioned that, his idea was to have a go at me too, I suppose leaving you as I had been during your exploit and still was, tied and gagged. He'd have had to be ugly enough about that, and would I then have welcomed him with the all-consuming adoration I had worked myself up to a little while before? I can neither confirm nor deny it, I would have to say if this were testimony in a court. I wish I knew. I don't know why it seems to matter so much at this late date but it does, I feel the most important decisions about life and my life hinge on it. I'd give anything to know that, and which of the three of us that night was most the . . . oh silly me, I was about to write *sinner* . . . An obsolete word, isn't it? This is a poor listening post for linguistics, but from some talk on the Moby Dick IV before Mummy's funeral, I gather we just speak now of crime and criminals, and they're society's fault, our fault, so there's only the common blame, right? That could be what drove me to St. Peter's that day last spring. I was craving to hear the word sin—*péché, peccato*—and face my own nature head-on. But our night in the woods seems to have been more effective that way than the confessional."

———

"You dumb bourgeois broads, with your fancy foreign accents and your L.L. Bean whatsits and your fucking mommas and grampas and college degrees and your shitty little poems as you call them—yeah, po-ems like in po-insettia—and your still shittier little ideas about how to clean up society . . . We didn't get around to much of that, did we? but I know your type, give us another meal to sit through and you'd have the schmeer all over it. Wanted a peek into the lower depths, didn't you? just an itty bitty peek to see what it's like down there and why all those terrible people do all those terrible things, woof woof, welfare schmelfare, nothing like that where *you* come from, oh no, everybody's clean as a whistle and honest as the day is long up there, nez pah?"

During all this he was racing around collecting what he wanted of their possessions, hatchet, saw, flashlight, sleeping bag, some soft drinks, raw bacon and the last of the bread, and hurling them down the bank into the boat. At the start he had pinioned Marilyn's arms to her back with a deft knot of the parka sleeves, thrown her to the ground and driven his pointed stake through the cloth with one blow to hold her there.

"Well, thanks for the screw. Not bad for a dyke, except you're more the brick wall type, aren't you?—not like Lady

Dumpling here; I suppose I could have had the pleasure way back then in Iowa if I'd played my cards right, huh?" That time his laugh was like a fox barking. "That pig slop you read out there! you didn't honestly think I'd *admired* it, did you? I mean could anybody outside a Mongolian be *that* benighted? 'And every nine months my womb . . .'" he mimicked her public intonations and barked again, more shrilly. "You did give me a good laugh, though, so thanks for that. Never heard such shit in my life. Couldn't believe you were being *paid* for it." He checked the jacks and whistle and still damp bills in his pockets, then sprang toward Dennie, knife raised. With his face almost touching hers he broke into an amiable smile and in a tone gone suddenly ingratiating, almost cavalier, went on, "I honestly hate to do it in a way, and miss out on that nice trip to Italy we were going to have. But you understand. You wouldn't want to see a superior guy like me betray his principles, would you? We all gotta remember that motto I told you, 'People first . . .' And I gotta keep the respect of my pals up there."

He cut a quick slit in the parka over her left breast, pulled the gag out of her mouth. "Don't worry, I'm an expert, you'll hardly feel anything. If you've got any last words, okay, but say them quietly please. I can't stand melodrama. It makes me mess up the job. Like the last one; I gotta tell you about that. Most of my victims as the media call it have been gentlemen, but this one was a girl, a Porto Rican kid, fourteen or so; family ran the grocery I needed a few things from, like the cash register that had about six bits in it for all my trouble. Come on, my little guinea hen, laugh, can't you? Doesn't *any*thing strike you as funny?" With his index finger a trifle lifted from the knife handle and the blade grazing her hairline he yanked the corner of her mouth to the side. "I said laugh!" She made her mouth spread on the other side. "Louder! I couldn't hear that!" She forced out some kind of sound. "That's better. See, she was yelling her head off, just couldn't stop, it drove me nuts so I shot her in the neck instead of the way I meant to. You're such an understanding type, not like your bony friend here, you can get the picture."

To her surprise, as she gasped for a last breath, he backed away a few inches, letting the knife down by his side, his eyes turned on some upper distance, as though seized by inner debate, even true reluctance possibly. Could that transforming power of will she had imagined in herself a few minutes before be operating after all, just as she felt most emptied of anything of the sort? But it was nothing like that. He was just having a little colloquy with his buddies, or bosses it might be, in the beyond, and this time was so forcefully in their company that he even spoke a few words aloud. "Okay, Joe . . . what's that? Uranus? Yeah, I know. I'll be through in a minute."

He turned back to Dennie. "He says you're so cute, you can come last. We'll start with this one."

He crouched, grabbed Corky by the scruff of the neck and in the same instant plunged the knife in her throat; one swift further motion took it down the length of her belly. "See what a nice quick job I do? Now wasn't that neat? Boy, what a sweet sight!"

It was better than sweet, to judge by its effect on him. On the instant, his voice had gone mellow, his eyes pitch black, a beatific glow seemed to emanate from his very skin. He was a born-again Christian just touched by divine light, a poor downtrodden nobody winning a million-dollar lottery. He gurgled, crowed, beamed, smeared his face and scalp with the blood, in his ecstasy lost all verbal coherence, vehemently patted his sexual organs, laughing all the while. But for having put forth twice in the last hour, it seemed that he would have ejaculated over the little corpse.

But duty called, or something else reminded him that there was better yet to come. Gathering his scattered senses he straddled the prostrate and soundless figure of Marilyn, as good as dead already by the look of it, and had the knife poised for another expert strike, when his arm froze and he underwent still another, no less extreme transformation, this time into a bundle of craven terror, and not at any message from on high. It was just a sound from the wild that undid him, and chilling enough it was, because no longer from a single coy-dog but several, and much closer than before. The howls, not quite in unison, seemed to come from no farther than the spaghetti beach; the animals must have crossed over the narrow inlet up that way, drawn either by the smell of blood or the penetrating pitch of the tin toy flute just a little before. Dennie's grandfather used to tell about coyotes being attracted by certain musical vibrations, even from a voice or guitar but the response was more commonly to a high wind instrument.

The howls sounded again, just a little closer, not much, down the path; the last thin straggle of smoke blowing that way from the fireplace might be a deterrent. The man, in his innocence of any but human life and a rather special sampling of that, was looking paralyzed by conflicting impulses, with one side still driving him to finish the interrupted job no matter what, when a first low grumble of thunder shook the mountains, followed immediately by a great thrashing of underbrush at his back, while his eyes were still fixed in the direction of the coy-dogs. He whipped around as though himself stabbed in the back, by some hitherto hidden assailant, and found himself facing, at hardly more than arm's length, the most improbable apparition of the night.

In flight from the savage hybrids, a doe, with her fawn close behind, had sprung into that clearing, probably aiming to cross it and swim to safety. The human scene smacked them to a stop, in mid-bound it seemed; no bullet or concrete wall would have halted them more abruptly. The two tawny bodies, the newborn's pressed to the mother's flank, went as rigid as carvings of their like on walls of prehistoric caves; the four eyes were as though blown that second to excruciating hugeness; only some faintest quivering at the nostrils, if there had been an observer for it, must be betraying the shock and turmoil within the elegant heads. Behind the doe's terrible responsibility in that sudden encounter, with an enemy worse than the one they fled from, nobody could know what histories lay engraved, on brain and sinew and heart. It could not be certain even that she took in the meaning of the tiny corpse her front hooves had nearly touched. A vision of Artemis, patroness of that species, prickled at the edge of Dennie's reawakening mind, like a prayer. The goddess had whisked Iphigenia from the altar at Aulis in the nick of time; her precious herbivores, as guiltless of bloodshed and cruelty as any in their kingdom, were not in the danger they thought in the immediate scene and really didn't need saving this time; perhaps once more the Olympian one might deign to snatch a mortal lady, or even two of them, from their new-style sacrificial altar instead.

Oh but Artemis-Diana was herself mainly the huntress, portrayed with bow and arrows; it must have been just having her dear ones killed by mortals that she minded, and she was the moon too and their killer-priest had the private line to that deity, so he implied. Dennie herself had happily conceded the claim just a few minutes ago. Obviously, classical civilization was going to be no help under present conditions. This made the second time in a single evening's adventure, with the Aphrodite episode for the first, that it had led her astray.

Now there was nobody to call on but her good, tender and attentive husband, Carter, not for help, even if they'd had any such power of telepathy, just for forgiveness. My dear, my almost darling, I've loved you as well as I could, at least I've really not loved anyone else more, except in a little fit of craziness now and then, and oh, I've done us so much wrong. I know you'll be good to Alan. Try to remember me not too unkindly.

———

They were in the attic, the morning after the family dinner party. Her mother and Stevie had just had to leave in a hurry, because one of the boys was in more trouble than usual in prep school, and Dennie had undertaken to find an old diary her mother wanted for some reason. Carter was eager to go with her, saying he loved attics and it would be fun to get a glimpse of the village from up there. The upstairs guest room where he had slept alone, with one of the late splurges of plumbing to himself, had been Evie's and Dottie's nursery once upon a time, and Evie, with something of her mother's narrative flair, had told him about the stuffed tarpon that used to hang across one whole wall, with an equally enormous reproduction of Rosa Bonheur's "The Horse Fair" across from it. The gigantic fish, said to have been caught off Florida by Grandma herself, dated from the short era when Grandpa could still get her to go fishing with him. Its one exposed glass eye, big as a tea cup, along with the central rearing horse of a dimension no less alarming on the opposite wall, as Evie gaily described it to her daughter's guest, had made the little girls' environment less soothing than energizing. "But then," she added, getting a good-natured laugh for this from her mother too, "not much else about the place was any more soothing."

Grandma knew how to be *touchée* without loss of face, or merriment either, in fact could often turn it to her advantage. "Well now Evie, you know we did settle down in the evenings." "Yes, with the sextet from *Lucia di Lammermoor* on the victrola— Galli-Curci, wasn't it? I wouldn't call that very soporific." Grandma admired music on principle, and went to great lengths to take her children to the opera whenever they were in that kind of metropolis, but made no bones about being herself tone-deaf. "I can't tell 'Yankee Doodle' from a hymn," was her regular way of putting it. Probably she thought the evenings had been quieting because culture was supposed to have that effect and she wasn't listening anyway.

She said she had given the tarpon to a natural history museum long ago but "The Horse Fair" might still be in the attic. It was, adorned with a wasp's nest to scale around an upper corner, way back behind a stack of superseded reproductions of Raphael madonnas, poor original oils of California cliffs and missions, the worst-stained of the Piranesi and a terrible pastel portrait of Grandma as a little girl. Apparently the would-be artist in that case hadn't quite dared to shorten the Ratcliffe ploughshare nose, destined to be a tribulation and source of wit throughout the model's life, so had settled instead for a prematurely doleful glance, as though in some fleeting interval between one distraction and another the narrow grey-green eyes had been caught and skewered like two moulting moths to the canvas.

A few wasps awoke and changed location, confusedly; big drowsy flies batted at the small casement windows; it was a sunny June day and hot up there under the roof; one side of the old central chimney was still warm from their little dining-room fire the evening before, when it had been just chilly enough for that. On cast-off kitchen plates here and there were small squares of bread neatly spread with rat poison, really intended more for squirrels that came in in winter and ate things they shouldn't. It was on the whole an unusually tidy attic; Grandma who was beginning to lose her grip downstairs, when sober still fussed a good deal over this peculiar aspect of housekeeping, but it did give her a pain in the fingertips to throw things away so the large space, sloping down from roof-ridge to eaves over the whole central, or original, part of the house, was crammed in the traditional rural way with ancient leather trunks missing a strap or two, dismantled spool beds of which the slats and springs had probably been taken for some other purpose, mahogany side-chairs missing a rung or seat, bales and basketsful of old letters and canceled checks, shelves crowded with dusty canning jars and tin jar-tops from the period when the kitchen, nothing like the fancy new one of the last twenty years, used to steam summer and fall with that occupation and the wire-screened cage in the cool cellar got replenished with jellies and fruits and vegetables for the year ahead. There were even, to Dennie's surprise, a rusty rifle, fishing rods and golf clubs, pertaining of course to her grandfather, a character rarely mentioned with anything but opprobrium in that house for the last forty-odd years.

Carter's pleasure in it all made her laugh, and made her realize what a chestnut tinge there was to his thick crinkly hair; he was having to stoop except under the actual ridgepole while she stayed upright halfway to the sides. She said, "Anybody'd think you'd just come on the last royal Egyptian tomb, never opened before." He grinned and blew her a kiss, her first from that quarter. She really hadn't had any idea he could be that attractive.

They weren't very well acquainted; the weekend had been planned mainly as a work trip. Dennie, two years out of college and two months out of her glum little mess of a marriage, with an underling job at the State Department and Carter for a boss, had had to accompany him to New York for some foreign-language interviews and now there were translations to be put in shape; she was the better linguist by far, so indispensable. He was said to be more or less engaged to a girlfriend in Washington and that was fine; he was too placid and somehow hesitant to set off any spark in her and she suspected he was rather prone to worry, something she took for granted in women friends but hated in men. For the head over heels business—the "Real Thing" of her grandmother's parlance, reduced by both subsequent generations to a ribald when not sardonic "R.T."—she thought she was on the lookout for somebody more decisive, more dangerous maybe; which vague notions had been only slightly jarred by her present companion's having had a good firm old-fashioned grip on her arm when crossing a street in New York, and by the real enjoyment and naturalness of his laughter at dinner the night before. He was bright, all right, anybody could tell that, and nice; she was lucky to have such a boss.

She just hadn't figured on the power of an attic on a person raised in merely figurative upward mobility, without that last terribly steep and narrow flight of stairs or in fact any stairs worthy of the name at all. The homes of all his growing years had been one split-level after another, according to executive needs of an expanding corporation, with standards of space, carpeting and neighborhood high at the start and rising each time, but also to the tune of much hauling to dumps and the Salvation Army. Not that there wasn't plenty of fine old American past in his family too, D.A.R., westward treks and all. There just hadn't in his lifetime been any place to store it, and neither of his parents' heads was much of a storeroom either; the upper crust in their case had thinned to exactly that—"over

a miasma," he would say once some years later, "of self-absorp-
tion and petty acquisitiveness." It was just impatience at his
younger sister's horrid church-cum-countryclub wedding and
their having felt obliged to travel from Rome to Indianapolis for
it, that wrested this cruel disparagement from him. With that
one exception, although recognized as a sport in his family, and
a disappointment too until he showed signs of heading for an
ambassadorship, he played the dutiful son pretty well and kept
any such thoughts to himself. It was good training for a diplomat. Luckily, there was no question of entertaining his parents
abroad, as they couldn't abide the thought of travel except on
the best-planned tours, with every minute mortgaged and the
menu for every meal provided in writing beforehand.

It was very much the lonely poet, set free all of a sudden
among voices and vibrations after his own heart, who stood at
the attic windows that sunny day, looking first to the south,
over the garden and grape arbor and the clump of quince trees,
then at the other end, to where two white church steeples,
Congregational and Episcopalian, showed quite far away
across a dip in the long wooded descent between. *"Bello! magni-
fico!"* With a pretend schoolmarm frown she murmured the
correct pronunciation and they both laughed. They had gone
through the same little act the day before, driving by "the
center," and he was right, it was one of the prettiest village
greens left in Connecticut, rather mysteriously as the road
twisting through it, the same the house fronted on, had long
since become a hardtop major highway; Grandma's thinning
lilac hedge seemed overcome by the falsity of its role as shield
from the passing world, as much as by the fouling of its air and
loss of root-space. Dennie's mother, too young when the family's working farm vanished to remember much of it besides
whirling the handle of the cream separator in the old pantry,
did retain a dim image of the road as a dirt one, traveled by
more horse-drawn buggies and wagons than early Fords. Some
of this she had most likely picked up from her mother's talk of
it; the forty cows and four thousand chickens and several work-

horses with all their housings and accoutrements were gone by the time she was four. Anyway she said she and Dottie and everybody used to wander back and forth across the road all day long, because the barns and most of the family's land were on the other side.

One sprawling structure, the grand old multilevel red hay-barn, still remained over there, and Dennie and Carter would go musing through it hand in hand later in the day. That last vestige of farming days was to be carried off only after Grandma herself was and for the same reason: it had become dangerous. As to the personal side of that dual development, Dennie knew that a lot of fingers were crossed and her mother and aunt were close to their wits' ends already; Grandma had been hauled into court and lost her driver's license only a month ago, something she had neglected to be funny about last night; there had had to be two thirty-day commitments, over her indignant protests, in the preceding year; her show at dinner, and the dinner itself, had been a miracle, and if the weekend finished without some humiliating scene it would be another. Dennie had warned her decorous guest, when the last-minute idea of his coming arose, that her grandmother was subject to certain spells or attacks; at the worst, somebody might even have to take her to a hospital. But so far so good, and looking over the idyllic landscape from the attic, she didn't see any reason to be more specific. She and Carter had no friends in common, she wasn't likely to see him again outside the office before he left for Venezuela; let sleeping dogs lie; don't spit in the stew.

She told him there used to be a Methodist church too until the congregation got down to one and the building was dis-mantled; imagine, four churches for a population of less than a thousand, because of course there was a little rattletrap R.C. one too, with hardly any steeple, for Polish and Irish immigrant farmers according to Grandma, who of course had never been inside, though she liked "jollying along" with some of the parishioners when it was a question of getting one of her fields mowed. "When in Rome" was a different matter; here *they* all voted Democratic. Actually, in the disappearing farm contest she hadn't beaten *them,* or her fellow Yankees either, by many years; somebody else must be filling those pews now; the only herd of cattle within miles were an absentee's tax dodge and looked as if they knew it.

She'd have taken the blue ribbon for drama about it anyway, whatever the dates, because every wagonload of disconsolate Holsteins and caged Leghorn hens moving off down the dusty road was also taking a more crucial piece of her heart, of her girlhood dreams of wedded bliss, of her beloved parents' hopes. Ahimè! cluck cluck, moo moo and nevermore, oh nevermore; there were supposed to have been plenty of hired help and conjugal readings of Dante in the evenings. The still fairly young Mrs. Jones, generally more given to breaking her bones or to a kind of cough also useful as pathos, emoted herself that time into a TB sanitarium and the little girls spent the winter shuttling between their two sets of grandparents in New York.

It was a good bit of pumping and prodding from Carter that brought all this out. His real, almost childish curiosity, the last trait she would have suspected in him, was eye-opening; she noticed a small cleft, with a look of vulnerability about it, in his otherwise square and hefty chin, and that his strong cheek-bones were so well-shaped, the funny little upward bump at the end of his nose really didn't detract from his looks at all. There was an air of newness, still more surprising, in his interest, as if it had sprung into being in him just then for the very first time, like mushrooms after the end of drought. Good Lord, had he really been that deprived all his life? She had never before gabbled so about the place to any friend, or given it such pro-tracted thought herself, and he still hadn't had enough. "Do we dare peek in those old trunks? Do let's, I bet they're a gold mine . . ." The trunks were at the other end of the attic and on the way he paused to stroke a beam, a floorboard, the chimney bricks. "Gosh, look at the grain, and the width! Do you suppose they're chestnut too? Why, they're absolutely beautiful, and up here where nobody sees them, that's what I love. I know people who'd give their eyeteeth, I guess they'd say big money, to rip this floor out and put it where it would show. Show and sell— like a house afire. But look, you ought to tell your grandmother the plaster's come loose between some of these bricks; you know, these old chimneys can be dangerous, they didn't have firebrick then. Does she know the date?" Well, it wasn't really colonial; even Grandma who would have loved to claim that had to admit that as nearly as could be reckoned, the house must have been built between 1800 and 1810. Still, that made quite an old chimney, and would make for some rollicking risks and curses on the sub-zero New Year's Eve a year and a half later, when the town volunteer firemen teetered on the burning roof, most of them as drunk as the stupid tenant, and what they managed to spray from their hose turned to instant sheets of ice all over them and the cinders of that priceless floor.

Foreign travel labels, pale and curling, still stuck in frag- ments even to the most disintegrating of the trunks, and albums of browning photos in one of them fleshed out the itineraries. Now the real show began, and the two spectators, necessarily pressed shoulder to shoulder, gave themselves to following the plot, which one of them thought she knew already but found she hadn't taken in very well. The central character didn't even go on being that quite to the end; there was some trickery in the synopsis. That of course was Grandma, as *jeune fille*, younger than either of these viewers, with her mother, sometimes with another female companion or two—in Baden Baden, the Ro- man Forum, a gondola, on the Pont du Gard, and with Carter murmuring "Oh, there it is!" posed, as correctly as in all the rest, in front of the Temple of Paestum. He had been tickled to find the famous etching of it, the most valuable of her Piranesi, on the only non-utility wallspace in the kitchen; in fact she had designed the space for just that. "In the kitchen!" "Well, I have to spend most of my waking hours here, like any good New England housekeeper, and I might as well have something up- lifting to look at." The little glitter of the flirtatious that the old lady projected in this exchange, far from grotesque, made her seem quite ageless and still more untouchable in her refinement. The fib about her kitchen proclivities was meant to be understood as a joke; she had mastered a couple of good company dinner menus, but although a fiend for cleanliness had always resented any minutes spent at the stove for everyday purposes; for the rest, her sparkle was just a compliment, a way of telling the young man that he was attractive enough for any woman to put herself out for, and he had responded in kind.

On the back of the Maison Carrée was written, in her bold, hasty calligraphy unchanged in all those years, "Thos. Jefferson's favorite building!"

The ladies wore osprey-nest hats, tight-waisted two-piece traveling suits with skirts to their shoes, often gloves, and one or another was always clutching a volume that must be a Baedeker. Eyes were all straight to the camera, no sidewise glances permitted; what was being documented was respect for the history of civilization and for the expensive privilege of being exposed to it; no laughing matter.

Oh but there were other moments, other facets to those rigid courtesans of culture. Look, here is the same future Mrs. Jones, probably by now a college graduate, once more on a well-chaperoned voyage; it must be a year or two before World War I; the voyage may have been prompted by parental doubts about what would turn into a six-year engagement. Yes, the fiancé is handsome and witty and of impeccable lineage, but he has been in some scrapes, delayed choosing a career; will he stay the course, hold up through thick and thin, provide the proper financial security? The big No for an answer to all that would be known too late, but then the questions had been red herrings, the danger signals were not all where they were looked for. The laughing young lady, perhaps in a stance picked up from the pre-tragic years of her beloved alter ego, the actress Eleonora Duse, is in some kind of gala Italian peasant costume, tambourine overhead, chin up and toe forward in emulation of the joy of the dance. On the next page the fiancé, who in his long life would have no use for either Europe or theatricals of any kind public or private, appears in careless hunting garb, holding a rifle and a string of dead ducks. You can tell at once it is not going to work out.

The worse fiasco of the kind, in a different album, seems on the contrary to have everything going for it, and here Dennie let out a little muffled "Oh!" as though seeing her own equivalent of chickens, cows, hopes, dreams, lumbering out of sight over the crest of the hill. She had never before seen a wedding picture of her parents; if she had ever seen any photograph of her father at all she couldn't remember it. The audience of two has just climbed from that same living room, scene of the ceremony, and porch where the gaudy cake and champagne appear along with the whole wedding party. It is all as smiling and unclouded as can be, except that the groom is in uniform and presumably about to be whisked off to join the army's approach to Rome; he must be attached to some kind of arts commission, with particular reference to works of antiquity stolen or hidden by the retreating Germans. The bride and her equally beaming mother are both, after twenty-four years, altogether recognizable; so, it appears, are the twin babies fondly held by their still uniformed father, one on each arm, on the front stoop right here below, where a minute ago, in the replay scale, the subject was little Evie and Dottie some twenty years earlier in their yellow basket pony-cart. There could be no question of deceiving Mr. Carter Hensley as to any principal identity, in fact bypassing the main question, such as, "Where's your Daddy now?" he was saying, "So you have a twin, have you? a boy, is it, or another girl? My, you were a luscious little thing. It makes me want to kiss you right here on this cheek. Do you mind?"

A long time afterwards, she would discover that Carter had known her father's story all along; it had figured in her security clearance for the job. The next act sped by; anybody would think the fire had broken out already and the director was hellbent on showing the end anyway. Yet this is where the homegrown Duse gets pushed toward the wings, somehow enfeebled in her identity, through the arrival in a dilapidated suitcase, itself probably at least a century old, of earlier forebears of both sexes, mostly unframed and unidentified. All were most likely looking out from and on old San Francisco, although the precious highboy of recent melodrama, until rather forcibly inherited by Grandma, had been in the Ratcliffe home in Hadley, Mass. They couldn't have taken that to the Pacific in their covered wagon; last winter's thief had had a hard enough time lugging it across a single back field; somebody must have stayed put back there and kept the brass polished and ownership unequivocal.

The westward ho bunch, in this particular job of casting, aren't very well suited to the part. These aren't the grabbers and swashbucklers of the bigtime stories; from all the lore Dennie had heard of them they were, as their pictures indicated, rock-ribbed, high-minded, impecunious, with not a scoundrel in the lot; they were all respectful of learning and not strong on organized religion. One published the slim volume of verses that of course is downstairs in honor and not up there in a trunk; one was a born loser so that one's wife had to be extra-noble teaching school; the only one of the lot who ever came near money renounced it on principle, disapproving of some shenanigans by his partners in the Union Pacific railroad. A cut above poverty, a much bigger cut below wealth, they were on record in tales and letters as considering their status the finest achievement of American society, and that pride—in moderation, in not being showy—shows here in the pinch of cheek and mouth throughout, while flights of spirit and a not too uncommon glint or crinkle of genuine, if far from light-hearted perhaps, wit, might alleviate matters from the cheekbones up.

It was so in the features of Great-grandfather Ratcliffe, he of the "my father wouldn't approve" by which Grandma had avoided pretty much anything she didn't really want to do. A replica of the photo, young, black-bearded, perhaps of the period when everybody was doing without everything in order to send him east to Harvard Law School, hung in her bedroom in full power of admonishment now as throughout most of her grown life, perhaps excluding the short marital period; it was hard to imagine Grandpa Jones sharing his nuptial quarters with any rival authority or symbol of reprimand. But Dennie's mother and aunt had remembered no such crushing force of prohibition in his character, except as he might gradually have crushed a good part of himself; they had tender memories of his squiring them to the Bronx Zoo when they were little, to the tune of whimsy and jokes and ice cream cones and a fair degree of zoological knowledge attributable to a lifetime voracity in reading; and Evie, more than Dottie, retained another image of him as a lockbox of fierce disappointments in old age. He was the one-time poet, author of that thin volume, of which no mention was allowed. She said if a summation could have been torn from him it would have been, "It wasn't worth it," and the three wishes of the fairytales would by then all three have been for prompt and inconspicuous death.

So where is all that happy laughter coming from? You might suppose from the golden motes of June sunlight turning attic dust to such merriment through the little casement windows to the south, above the red ramblers in bloom and sweet peas and the garden's walkway border of grape arbor on three sides. It comes also from Mr. Carter Hensley who has just been told that except for the beard and the Dantesque nose he is almost a spit-'n'-image of Great-grandpa Ratcliffe at about the same age; who with a handkerchief has removed a sleepy wasp from his companion's short dark hair, and in a trickier job for fingers unaccustomed to any such, has helped to connect a huge number of almost invisible hooks to eyes and tiny white pearl buttons to buttonholes. This chore he brought on himself, wanting to see the young lady in what must be a garden-party dress of her grandmother's trousseau period, white, of some delicate muslin, massively hand-embroidered, utterly crumpled but untorn, which emerged from a bundle of rags and scraps and discarded dimity curtains and a small fortune in Irish lace collars and cuffs either never attached to a garment or else snipped off for a further use that never came to pass. "She's taller than I am, it'll drag on the floor," Dennie objected, while however turning her back for a touch of decorum in dropping shirt and blue jeans. "The wrinkles! Like the sands of time. Like her face now, poor darling Grandma. Can you imagine the ironing they used to do in those days? I suppose she must wish she could iron her skin. But look, she had exactly my waist!"

So she did, and his two outspread hands could almost meet around it.

Great-grandpa Ratcliffe had whisked back into his picture, his own youth, was very far from censure, and the death that sprang upon the current protagonists and brought another little strangled "Oh!" from the model in the show was not from any experience or wish of his. In this corner of the attic domestic determination had begun to outrun method, rags and broken necklaces and old school reports joined in a jumble almost to be heard as a moan of protest against the incoherence of human possessiveness, until that literal exclamation over a rag of another kind, another history. The object fell from a bushel basket, demoted long ago from proper orchard function to being a receptacle for old toys. The rag was a little more than that; thanks to Grandma's unflagging war against mice, there was some stuffing left, along with the tiny gingham dress, white apron, yarn hair, one black button eye, the black cloth bits for shoes and the face all bullet-holes. "Raggedy Ann! What on earth . . . Did a dog get at her?"

Sorrow, sorrow; her heart felt ready to burst with it all over again, telling of that terrible summer in Italy when she was six and the doll was murdered by a gang of ruffians on the beach, and how they set her darling up against the bushes for a target, and how the kindly fisherman's wife almost crying herself rescued what was left, what had been hidden all those years now in the attic. Carter had disposed of the wasp and now used the handkerchief to dab at her two large tears, making her smile. It was more relief than she could possibly have imagined, unless she'd been hellbent on feeling like a fool, to be speaking of this childhood episode. "Now they'd be terrorists, left right or whatever, and not wasting their bullets on dolls. They were just warming up then." Carter said, "Yes, on an American doll," and then somehow in his arms sorrow and animosities alike seemed to pale almost to vanishing.

They had left a pile of the old curtains on the floor, those beautiful floorboards so soon to come to grief. She was still in her grandmother's wrinkled garden-party dress, with poor resuscitated Raggedy Ann in her arms, as the lives before and before and before slid back into their trunks, the past gave up its voices and Dennie and Carter in a shaft of magical illumination sailed forth into their own golden promises, unlike any ever before. In fact it was pretty much the R.T. after all.

———

"Marilyn! not *now!* Can you hear me? You stop that moaning this instant and do what I tell you. Hurry!"

Here a few lines of Dennie's *soi-disant letter,* as she called it in one self-disparaging passage, are lost or inked out, and a number of the preceding pages are also scrawled over with deletions and exclamations of disgust. She seems to have been close at that stage to destroying the whole missive, mainly if not entirely, as her scribbles indicate, from the thought of Marilyn's scorn of such stuff. Imagine what Professor Drumblink would make of those grandmother scenes, or of the young Carter Hensley for that matter. Worse than Vermont it all was; ridiculous. Little as she'd thought she admired or needed the negastruct or logophiliac whatever it was of her friend's new creed—or call it addiction as some of its stick-in-the-mud opponents did—with its high priests and arcane equations, at some point she seems to have let herself get, well, just a teeny bit tyrannized by it all; you had to admit there was something to be said for chucking out all that old A-plus-B type of character and event that used to figure as literary material, just as the old modes and tonalities did in earlier centuries in music. Or something. In her reversals of mood and general embarrassment she is not making too much sense. Anyway, remembering Marilyn's dismissal of family as a topic in either life or letters, she is trying to skin down the account as near to bare bones as possible, in accord with what might no longer be the intellectual *dernier cri* in Paris but evidently had been at the time of Marilyn's visit there a season before.

However, in her confusion and haste the letter-writer has left some of the more offending pages of period rubbish, about her mother's childhood illness and adoration of her own mother, in the scene in Geneva for instance, and carelessly blotted out instead some sentences that must have been there, on the immediate scene and drama by the lake.

And just at its most thrilling! how could she have made such a mistake?

Oh but that's perhaps the whole point. Narrative is supposed to pall, otherwise language would be threatened in its splendid, if outside the circle of the elect not very illuminating, primacy. One of the mathemes on Marilyn's wall was to that effect, and Dennie had more recently come across a quote bearing it out in a French journal she had happened on. Thrills and grandmothers are equally in disrepute, was the general gist. True, the magazine represented a hostile school, with rival rules and jargon. "Come to think of it," she would scribble on a margin later on, "Fred and the intellectual fashion arbiters of Paris have a lot in common, haven't they? System all, human reference nil. Forms of terrorism? suicide?"

We left them all stunned and motionless with the doe and her fawn equally so in their midst, the knife raised above Marilyn's throat, the dog's body warm in its blood in the dirt, the coming new storm as though suddenly removed from the script. Where had the coy-dogs gone? Never mind, they seem not to figure in the action except in causing the unnatural appearance of the deer and readiness to panic in the so highly principled but city-bred murderer. A wry little question later on, whether the goddess Artemis might after all have taken a hand in the matter, suggests that it was the wheeling of the doe, ending the scene's paralysis, and her marvelous lift up and away through the night, with the little fawn like a mechanical toy in perfect replica at her flank, all quick as a human wink, that finished off the man's resolve and sent him bolting for the boat. For the moment he might have been feeling himself in the grip of some mysterious, unmanning imperative, not astronomical but of this earth and hitherto unknown, perhaps related to what he had earlier had some fun over in the name of mercy. Even as he fled he was babbling, though not without a note of terror, okay, he'd let them off, wrong day, wrong stars. But then from offshore, in a less uncertain voice, as the new wall of rain smashed in, he was yelling threats if they ever told of having seen him. "Like that little hairy devil of yours there, that's what you'll get!"

The violence of Marilyn's emotion had at least served to bend the stake so she could roll over to the little body and press her face into its entrails, and her motions made the nylon knot at her back give a little. She was in condition for taking orders, nothing else. The knot in Dennie's wet rope was impervious to their fingers, but luckily he had missed the razor blade that was in the first-aid box, along with a secret weapon. Dennie grabbed her spare lenses but didn't wait to insert them; he would be back, and quickly; there was nothing to hold him to his wayward impulse in its mix of fear and—and what? could his own word *mercy* have fanned his brow a moment? "It must be this way. Is there any path at all?" They left everything but the corpse; Marilyn wouldn't go without that; they emptied a knapsack for it and she took it on her back but then slipped to the ground in sudden lassitude, almost coma, as though unable to make any further move whatever. Dennie yanked her to her feet and for the first few minutes in the now pelting rain had to half drag her through brush and deadfall, toward the long curve around to the beaver pond. It was the route, if they managed to follow it, that Corky had whisked over just before the other storm.

X

THE SUN ROSE over their left shoulders, not quite at their backs, from behind the low mountain, as they sprawled for rest on a bed of ferns, at the top of a little knoll overlooking the lake. Such a godsend it was, to have happened on that slight clearing just as both felt their strength finally gone and would have dropped to the ground anywhere, even another swamp if it had been that. Instead there was unimaginable sweetness to cushion their oblivion and only a still sweeter wonder, of sound and light together, to rouse at least one of them from it after a while. They had collapsed, it appeared, in a sanctum of hermit thrushes, and before the red disc showed at the mountain's crest, all were wide awake and greeting it at the top of their lungs, although their rest could not have been tranquil that night; or perhaps they sang more beautifully for that, having once again a tale of loss and damage and personal survival, that too, that at least, to communicate.

It was years, she couldn't have said how many, since Dennie had seen a sunrise except through a plane window. When she was seven or eight and the family still crossed the Atlantic sometimes by ship, she and Rick once set an alarm clock so they could go out in their pyjamas and watch dawn break over the ocean; she was too sleepy to care much but she couldn't let her twin down and there was nothing on shipboard, except winning

a silver cup in the junior deck tennis tournament, that trans-
figured him as that spectacle did. You'd have thought it was ice
cream and he was eating the whole skyful of it, and he got very
cross at her eyes' showing a bit less radiance than he thought
must be shining in his own, which were after all an exact duplicate of hers as far as anybody outside could tell, so a failure of
rapture in them was as bad as a defect in his own responses or
else in that particular sunrise. She had to shush him, not to
wake people in nearby upper-deck cabins, since they were traveling first class by that time, not down below as they used to
and as their mother had always in her own childhood. "Lookit,
lookit there!" he was shouting, and in still further excitement
falling into Italian, which he spoke better at that age, "Ma
guarda, Dennie, stupida, guarda lì! Hai mai visto . . ." He was
very thoughtful and bent in on himself afterwards, the way he
was sometimes after hearing his favorite Beethoven sympho-
nies, with that deep, somehow scary glow about his handsome
features as of some far-away knowledge not available to common clay, that could make credulous types and other ninnies
babble about celestial provenance.

Dear Rick, how I wish you could be here, seeing and hearing
this; it's been so long, I don't even know what you look like
now. "And the dawn comes up like thunder, Out of China cross
the bay . . ." Her mind sang a few bars of it, not her voice; not
for anything were the birds to be disconcerted just then. Besides, nothing was the same now as when the song, and the
guitar of long ago, had filled her heart and soul the last time,
just the evening before; Rangoon was not as remote as that
hour. Marilyn lay in a restless doze a few feet away, twitching
now and then in one part or another of her body, one arm lying
across the blood-soaked knapsack she had carried all night.
Sky-shout and birdsong were telling Dennie the stages of innocence. Could that be the same flamingo red the child twins had
exclaimed over? had she walked out of childhood only at the
age of thirty-five, in a single night?—and if so, what name was
to be given to the years of blind error, impulse and somnolence
between?

Lately in Rome, she realized, she had been sleeping half through the morning, often after a second dose of sedative toward dawn, leaving an order for her maid to wake her in time for whatever appointment she had—lunch, hairdresser, dressmaker. Or it might be the dapper itinerant purveyor of fine fabrics, Italian, Egyptian, near-Eastern for both clothes and upholstery, who catered only to the aristocracy, the diplomatic corps and the richest foreign residents. She had been seeing him around noon the day the cable came from Bar Harbor, therefore probably just as her mother's heart unpredictably—and willfully?—chose to stop. The merchant spread his gorgeous cloths across gilt chair-backs, grand piano, Empire settees, all over the airy reception room, and the colors and designs made her sick with temptation, as if they alone were the answer to lethargy and fat. She had had a small baroque sofa in mind, which had become not at all threadbare, only obscurely distasteful to her, but before the shining array a dozen other objects, of household and wardrobe, set up a clamor as of necessity. The Hensleys couldn't afford any of it, Carter's private income was negligible, things were extra tight that year, with prices skyrocketing and the entertainment allowance cut by Washington. She told the man to come back the next day when she'd have made up her mind; she would definitely take something. He would have bowed lower if she had bought at once and would not then have commented as he did, by fingering a corner of his long moustache; he might have been knowing perfectly well that she would be far off above the clouds by that time the next day.

If only the silly recollection were paper, to be burned; but then of how many others, not all so trivial, would the same not be wished? The morning breeze had lost the bitter chill of the day before. It was not cold that convulsed her. True, the temperature hadn't risen much and both parties in the night's fearsome exodus were wet through, but it seemed to be something more in the nature of a hymn that shook her suddenly, as she herself used to shake a misbehaving doll. But this was no sight for a little girl. Golden chariots, huge winged presences—

anthropomorphic to be sure, so deceitful—bearing not harps but immense swords and words of both castigation and mercy from on high, entered her field of vision and were quickly kicked out; she had been to too many half-seen art galleries, probably too many half-heard concerts and operas too, since she was aware of imposing certain expectations of sound on a music they couldn't possibly fit. She must listen better. The thrush wasn't all thrilling upper-register purity, though properly famed for that it got off a lot of casual chatter too, and the famous outpouring went with a number of phrases, not just one; also there was a chorus of cheeps, squawks, twitters and one quite different sustained vibrato, from other species a little farther away. The ancient prophets, the true ones, not the yesmen, knew what they were talking about, in some respects; no matter what anguish might endure or other alarms follow, some sort of covenant or promise was owing in recognition of such grace, after the time of dread.

Pray she could not; she had no wherewithal for it though often envying those who did. But she did rejoice, to the verge of song, of quite other than the Kipling kind—yes, it must be the hymn that had shaken her while keeping itself unrevealed—to think that those old inspired and incorruptible codgers in their deserts had watched the same morning show two and three thousand years ago and drew strength from it, however interpreted, against the sinful cities close by. The very same, unless there should be a little difference from sand instead of water and maybe some modern technological supplement in the atmosphere. Not enough difference to worry about. It was their sun that rose crimson over the mountain, as it had been their stars and storm before, the very same, and everybody's before and since who had the wit to know it, and in some form or other it was everybody's burden that was in the knapsack under Marilyn's arm.

She must have let out an exclamation, whether from that last thought or a vertiginous new surge of color across the sky. Marilyn opened her eyes and said dully, "What?" She wasn't caring about any what, why or whether, but for lack of another answer Dennie gestured with a sweep of the arm to the rampaging palette that was now a total ceiling between them and infinity. Nasturtium, fuchsia, old rose, blood orange combined, separated, swept every which way in a tremolo of shifting intensities, all duplicated in the lake below. Her eyes and Rick's used to mirror each other's just that way, so the twins would hardly know themselves which light from thought or impulse was the original.

"Look."

That was quickly done, and over and done with. "God, how vulgar. Reminds me of Swinburne, or the worst of Victor Hugo . . ." Her eyes were again closed, her voice lifeless. "Grey is the only significant color."

"You don't dress in it."

"It doesn't suit my skin. So I have to put up with what does. That doesn't mean I go for technicolor panoramas. Or hurdy-gurdy art either." She seemed to fall back into her semi-slumber or just the paralyzing clutch of her double suffering.

This was the nearest to conversation between them since the episode in the tent, a few mumblings from Marilyn in the course of the night having had more a sound of delirium.

Dennie dimly recalled that Professor what's-his-name, the guru of the Trojan Hearse—at least that name she did remember—had had a fix on the color grey along with something about triangles. But this was scarcely the time to pursue it. Nor would it ever be.

Marilyn's suffering was in fact more than double, though her physical pain couldn't be mattering much compared to the other two, of humiliation and death. She had a bad gash down her cheek, that had just missed an eye, and probably a broken finger. Dennie's left ankle was swollen and throbbing and beginning to hurt badly. She discovered only then that half her lower lip was hugely swollen too, and numb. Both heads and both bodies in spite of heavy clothes were a mass of welts, bruises and gashes, because they had fallen many times on rock or wood sharp enough to puncture cloth or wound through it. Between them they were such a ludicrous sight, it seemed to her that if only Corky had been there to talk to about it, she'd have been rocking with laughter. At least she could see now that Marilyn's snatches of babble in the night, although really monologues not addressed to anybody, were not so senseless and even bore out some of Dennie's earlier hunches.

———

She didn't remember most of the falls or much else of the actual facts of the night, though a few real scenes and moments stood out from the other kind. In the crash and fierce sporadic glare at the worst of the storm, when the whole sky was slit nearly to their elbows, she knew they had flung themselves under a protruding rock ledge that covered a cave of sorts, out of the deluge; it was the lair or temporary refuge of some large animal, a bobcat most likely; they could sense its breath and presence and in the next flash saw the great eyes upon them very close, so they rolled back fast into the other rage outside and in a further, still more hideous explosion of light saw the man in the boat, not for the first or last time in their flight, braving the storm to prowl just offshore and seek them out. They squatted stock still among some upturned roots; their hands were useless from cold; the dog's body, grown rigid, made a queer shape of the knapsack. They were not yet even at the beaver pond; there should be better footing and more protection beyond it, Marilyn murmured in the uproar. But she was still an automaton, continuing because she had been told to; it was all the same to her if they never got out or the storm never passed.

It seemed to Dennie that really she had been busy dreaming all the way, all the night, through the alternation of falling and crouching and stumbling on. There was a long story, extremely absorbing, of Carter and her father at some kind of large reception or ceremony in a great colonnaded Italianate space which she was excluded from but could view through a clerestory opening above. They were not in black tie or tails though elegantly dressed, her father especially; it must be afternoon. "Leave it to him," a male voice, rather like the Irish priest's, was saying, indicating Carter. "Don't you know he's the most brilliant negotiator we have in the service?" Her father was pulling wires to smuggle an object out of the country, he had it hidden there behind a brocade drapery and drew Carter over to give him a peek; it was Mr. Allen's boat, a valuable antiquity, never mind how he had come by it, a friend of his who was a curator at the Metropolitan Museum was giving him a million dollars for it, naturally to be shared with any accomplices in the deal. In the visitors' gallery alongside Dennie's perch, a bunch of Vermonters surrounded Mr. Allen; they had guns and were very angry. One said, "This country's goin' to the dogs." Her father, getting drunk on *pflümliwasser,* was trying to touch ladies' bosoms and buy people's passports. Carter sent Mario up to the gallery with a written message for the Vermont contingent because they wouldn't have understood his butler's English; they mimicked his fancy manners but quieted down. "He's a good man," Mr. Allen's son said of Carter. "You can trust him. Them Hensleys are smart. He'll find a way to handle it." The crowd below was being imperceptibly ushered to one end of the cherub-ornamented hall. She saw Carter's index finger rise a trifle as from a knife handle, signaling; there was a burst of laughter and a blinding explosion. When the debris had settled, and her father in handcuffs was being led to a paddywagon by two tall carabinieri, the Vermonters were boarding a plane, carrying the boat; they had all forgotten their English but weren't speaking Italian either, although they were uttering sounds with various cryptic expressions.

"Su! coraggio!" she was calling to Marilyn. Her grandfather was picking his way across the beaver dam until a choking fit doubled him over. "Can't you speak English?" he said sternly as soon as he could talk. "And get a move on. What's wrong with you? I'm about fifty years older than you and doing all right. Just a little thunderstorm, I've been out in hundreds of 'em; just don't take shelter under a *tall* tree, that's where you can get hit; pick a little one and you'll be all right." The next second he had fired his pistol from the hip. Thunder boomed right after and in the accompanying flare they saw the man in the boat rapidly paddling to open water, out from the overhanging branches where he had been. Grandpa laughed. "If he'd had a cap on I guess I'd have lifted it off. I did rumple his hair a little, I think. All right, girlies, let's snuggle down here a while till the rain lets up." That was by a huge upturned root system, tilted to give some cover and with no bobcat using it that they could detect. Only Grandpa wasn't there any more. It was she and Marilyn, with a small hairy corpse for their guardian, who were lying tightly embraced, for no reason but to avoid freezing; an impersonal huddle for survival; they could have been any two strangers of either gender, as void of erotic impulse as if both had lacked any such equipment from birth.

At last, when the tempest had waned, they made themselves struggle on once more. It was easier going now; of course they could not actually have crossed the beaver dam, with its crisscross of tooth-sharpened stakes sticking up at all angles, and must have slogged through a mile or so of treacherous swamp around the higher water level the animals had made for themselves. Then they were on higher, rockier ground, sparser in vegetation though still with plenty of deadfall to trip over. Lightning had subsided from bent streaks to pulsings of glow from a distance, and in that light they saw their friend, enemy, lover, in the stolen boat, twice more, once very close to shore, looking for them. They stopped in their tracks, as before, scarcely breathing; he must have heard something, and was not many yards away; a twig crackling could be their end. Dennie thought, "Oh my God, Corky will bark," then remembered and for the first time felt the rock on her heart that for many weeks would roll back to crush it again and again, in a message that came to be inextricable from her mother's death.

It was by starlight, well before dawn, that he gave up the hunt, not without bidding them a whimsical goodbye. Evidently he figured he had been misjudging their strength or will to get over that terrain under such conditions, so had retraced his way and made his salute from quite far back and well offshore, but in the renewed quiet of the night it would have carried much farther than that. He played, as if the excellence of his gift were his soul's entire purpose and baggage, a minute's worth of what might be a Requiem, and then, as if that might be taken as too doleful, a snitch in Papageno vein, prestissimo. It so called for Bravo's and applause, for a second Dennie wasn't far from providing them. After a short interval, when he might indeed have been waiting for that, he betook himself to the entrance end of the lake.

———

Now at sunrise, in the faint surcease from cold if not fatigue or pain, she was lifted to a certainty of surprising love, for her husband, Carter, of all people. The golden billowing conviction therefore entailed an equal certainty of long uphill remorse. She felt equal to that, would even welcome penance; the love was to be won, over and over. The night's delirium had told a truth she seemed to have been yearning for years to have revealed, to allay the injustice of her thoughts of him. Skilled and courageous he was under all the decorum; she knew it well from others, not in the least from any confidence or self-advertisement on his part. He rarely so much as mentioned the tough tangles and battles of his working hours or the varieties of facial expression and tone of voice needed on the job, the calculations that had to lie behind deceit versus straight talk, the daily choices between ugly alternatives. She had granted him almost nothing of all that filled his days; the admiration, almost worshipful in some cases, of people who knew him at work she had put away where it wouldn't interfere with her vital annoyance.

Thank you, Elijah up there in your chariot, and happy landing to you, now and always; thanks, blessed sun in your rising, for letting me see this much, at least. That good and true man, goodlooking too, that I wouldn't hear praises of, my own darling mate, has been the vital one all along, and I the perverse rejector, I the drag, who wouldn't let him show himself to me. May there be time to start our love again. Of course he would contrive to rescue Mr. Allen's outboard, and take no credit for it either; it was just like him.

She spoke with sudden insistence, giving her companion a sharp poke. "Marilyn, are you awake? Listen. That little weapon of yours, with the needles, hatpins, whatever they are—you said you'd used it once in your life and he wasn't any ordinary criminal. Who was it?"

Marilyn was lying on her stomach, head on arms, face turned away, the blood-soaked knapsack close at her side. She just managed a reluctant murmur, still in no mood for talk, of that kind or any. "Oh for God's sake, you know perfectly well who it was. You were right in the next room." A chipmunk chattered very loud, like a Neapolitan street urchin, and skittered away. Dennie didn't speak. "Not that I was wearing the damn thing because of him. Of course not. It was that drunken Hungarian bass-player I was expecting, but your sweetheart got there first. He'd just discovered, or thought he had, who your son's father is." Apparently the silence irked her, and made her grind out a filler for it. "Some little free-lance Italian spy for the Embassy knew somebody who'd seen you checking into a seaside hotel somewhere with a man . . ."

"Viareggio. All right." Dennie's voice had become the more lifeless of the two. "With my brother—Rick."

"He'd taken some kind of compromising pictures of the two of you, through a keyhole I suppose." Marilyn in spite of everything had to laugh at that, to the extent of one harsh squeak, hardly mirthful. "And he'd come to sell them to your husband all those years later. Talk about dogged perseverance."

As if an extraneous point of reason could clarify the whole question, and in fact with a passing sensation that it did so, as a straw might define a brick, Dennie said, "We were off in other posts most of that time—Brazil, Hong Kong . . ."

Marilyn let out another short, withering laugh, with little

interest and less cheer. "You hadn't been able to get pregnant before, is that right? And then you did."

Worse than in her flood of memory the evening before, Dennie felt the dam breaking, demolished under one blow and herself swept along, in a whirl of senseless trash in which no definition of anything was to be sought. "Carter wanted a child so much!" she cried out, as though pleading before a tribunal on high. "So terribly. And Rick was willing. He didn't want me fooling around and risking some awful mess later on. It was all very considerate and quick and didn't mean a thing to either of us except for that purpose, his helping me to save my marriage. He had a girl at the time, an Israeli with a terrible family history in Germany, that he was really in love with. Oh of course way back when we were little we used to show each other our sex organs and play around a little the way children do, maybe a little more than some because we were so close, and I guess it made it more exciting that we looked so much alike in all the other ways, kind of like being one of those sea creatures I forget what it's called that are both sexes in one body, but I swear . . ."

Marilyn interrupted. "I couldn't care less. It's none of my business. Except that your husband was driven berserk enough to try to rape *me*. I suppose you'd call that one of his zany or poetic fits, that you find so appealing."

"Of course it wasn't just once, we had a couple of other flings the same week, to improve the chances." She swallowed with difficulty and felt her face swelling and contorting as from a lifetime of untruth. Her next sentences came tearing out one on top of the other. "I admit it got to be fun, I mean from the risk, all that genetic stuff, it made it exciting in a terrible kind of way. We joked about the pharaohs and two-headed calves, but honestly it felt more like a long purification ceremony . . . Until all of a sudden, it was the third time I guess, it wasn't exciting or monstrous or anything but just boring. Or maybe annoying is the word. We were both eager to be somewhere else, with somebody else."

Marilyn had begun dragging herself up from the ground. They had only about a mile left to go, to the parking place. "But do you honestly mean to say he's never told you to this day that he knew, about you and your brother and your son? Quite a self-possessed gent, I'd say. What *do* you talk about? Well, let's get going."

As for her, the prime mover in all their joint adventure and discoveries, she would not even be satisfied in what Dennie had taken to be the main motive in her sexual acquiescence: the chance for pregnancy, one of her anguished mutterings before dawn having conveyed that the sex act had enraptured her precisely because it was not that conventional. "Said he got the rearview habit in the jug, couldn't even get it up frontwise any more."

Under a windshield wiper they found a note roughly printed on a piece of paper taken from the glove compartment, as the pen had been only that was gone. "Some varmint et 2 of yur tires. No good to me. Lucky fer you. Key back wher it woz. Thanks agen. Yr frend. PS Sory i don't rite so good, never had yur advantidges."

It was true that two tires were flat and the porcupine had left bits of chewed rubber all around. No other car was there. When they had hobbled a few miles in silence, to the end of the grand wilderness avenue and some distance up the county road, a cruising young deputy sheriff heading the other way turned around to give them a lift. Dennie by then was having to lean on Marilyn's shoulder and altogether they must have looked pretty beat up. He knew Marilyn well from his patrol work the last year or two. She told him their canoe had sunk, they'd had to leave their gear, she would go back for it with neighbors. A porcupine had ruined their tires. He said that was some night they'd been out in, wait till he told his wife about that, she'd been scared pink just sitting in a nice warm house. In the same tone of voice he explained that he was going over that way because Jess Allen had gotten worried about his fishing boat, he'd hidden it up the other end of the pond, so he'd made two of his grandsons go and check some time in the evening, in a jeep over the old lumber track up that way, and they'd reported it missing. "And Jess ain't one to tie a boat up so a storm could blow it loose. I tell you, that old man, he's a funny one. He gets a hunch and he's darn near always right. We caught a bunch of housebreakers last month just from one of them ideas of his, what he calls bees in his bonnet." The deputy had waited for daylight to go look around, had been on his way there when he met them; no sense trying to search that pond in the dark.

Had they seen anybody, heard anything all that time? It was Dennie who had to answer. They'd thought they heard something once but with that storm it was hard to tell, and then around three or four in the morning there was music, probably other campers who couldn't sleep and turned a radio on.

"But where's your little dog? Doesn't she always go everywhere with you?"

Marilyn had ridden on the back seat. Now at the path to her house she was standing by the driver's window. She held up the knapsack, from which one rigid paw protruded a little; tears gushed down her face. Dennie explained that they'd heard a sudden awful screaming and scrimmage back in the woods, could tell it was Corky in trouble, and found this; she must have tangled with a bobcat.

He gave a little grimace and grunt of disagreement. "Don't sound like no bobcat to me. Mind if I take a look?" He reached over and gently undid the flap, while Marilyn sobbed. "A mother bear with her cubs it could be. I dunno . . ." Dennie was waiting for him to recognize the work of a knife, but he just made that same skeptical face again and said gee he was sorry, that sure was bum luck, he knew what it felt like losing an animal you cared about like that.

———

"August; with Alan in a beach cottage an hour from Rome; Carter drives out most nights and weekends. I believe he was having a fling with an English girl, a disco singer, while I was over there for the funeral. And for how much more than that! Our stuff has already been shipped, we leave for the new job soon. It will not be like any change of place ever before. I hope I know better now who I am, and where and to what I belong, otherwise there can be no sense to anything. I've lost twenty pounds in two months, or did I say that before?

"I went back to find the Irish priest one day, he wasn't there, a much older American had the English-language booth and practically told me to go to hell. He was obviously sick of confusion, wanted downright sin so I obliged, told him who my son's father was. That perked him up, even if the offense was nearly ten years ago. Not quite in so many words he more or less conveyed that the sin in question wasn't too unusual, in fact under the circumstances had been rather sensible and better than not conceiving at all. Of course some routine penance was in order but he made it clear that a woman who'd waited nine years to feel guilty, and wasn't a communicant anyway, wasn't very promising material. I told the old fool he wasn't hearing me, I had never loved any man but my twin brother in my life. He said in that case I was wasting his and the Church's time, it wasn't in his province to counsel the mentally deranged; disturbed, OK, he'd go that far but no farther. Then judging by what I saw of society he must be idle most of the time, I said and flounced off to my tower and doves so to speak, Hilda all over, halfway between Protestant and atheist and between earth and the moon—that moon beloved of our evil, unanswerable friend.

"Later, I tried the idea out on Carter, about having been in love with nobody but Rick all my life, and he suggested for therapy a mouthwash and three somersaults. I did those last then and there, in front of him, to show off my new figure and agility. He said, 'I suppose we all look for our own image to screw, at least sometimes.' 'Like Marilyn Groves?' I asked him, 'when the gardener's pretty daughter there at the villa was known to be only too willing?' He gave it some thought. 'Yes. I didn't want a willing woman just then but one stuffed with antagonisms, contradictions, unholy ambition. Like me. Me that week anyway.' He said he'd known exactly how grotesque it was, which was exactly what appealed to him, and that it was no more so than Rick and me. I knew that, didn't I? Yes, I did, and do, and Rick and I both knew it a long time ago, how far apart we'd grown, what incompatible people we really were; only as life got more difficult, the road directions in both cases more obscure or lost, we did at moments play a game or fool with the thought of it, about as decisive as parcheesi, with common memories and physical resemblance for the pieces; as if we could both win, both get around the board first, by making ourselves one person again. Carter of course knew perfectly well how critical I was of Rick when he wasn't around charming everybody; he was lazy, never read anything serious, hadn't gotten through any whole book in years, whatever he got worked up about by way of a life commitment would peter out in a few months.

"Carter suggested we both go to a swank American shrink who's acquired a practice and reputation in Rome, and we did, a few sessions apiece. But that was too, I guess the word might be open-ended, for me. Without the thought of perdition I see no way to clarity and couldn't respect it if I did. Corky's little cocoanut shell face and her great black button eyes in the glaze and amazement of death are more instructive than all the professional counselors. There's too much gabble in the world, too much how-to; knowledge must be sacred to be any good. And we acquire that, or glimpses of it, at our peril, nez pah? (This last from you know who.) Assunta knows all this better than anyone and what a laugh she would have at the thought of being paid for it. I drove Alan up to spend a day with her, didn't tell her much, went home with psychic sores nearly healed. She does it with mirrors, that is, a shift of glance, tightening of muscle beside her mouth, certain exchanges of silences, or speech often the far side of words, "Ai!" "Oh . . ." "Ah!", or a dozen intonations of "O Dio!" or "Davvero?" all reeking of wisdom, a long history's worth, and her own.

Then came the notice of Rick's death, somewhere in Cambodia, and it was a full week before it was contradicted—oh yes, mistaken identity, everybody so sorry, the person who would have known better was away that day; some tangled question of i.d. papers lent for a few hours to a fellow relief worker for some reason, probably the obvious one of his needing to pass for American that day. The killing was first attributed to Thai pirates and then, accurately they say, to a gang of American profiteers Rick and some others had got on the track of, who were hijacking relief supplies. One of them could have been the old buddy mentioned by our guest, our nemesis—I know, I should let you forget, as if you could; he said the man was making a mint at it, remember? The location and the phrase stuck in my mind.

"In the course of that week, before the correction came, what we took to be Rick's last letter arrived; it had taken weeks to reach us. It was wanting Carter to work on the State Department, the UN and everything else to get help for those refugees and stop the pirates, it was all too horrible, the holocaust of our decade, why were civilized countries letting it go on, and so forth.

"We had a bitter few days, the worst ever. This was before my visit to Assunta. If you can believe it, or if I can, I accused my husband of, well, not of causing my brother's death exactly but of being party to it, by refraining from doing things that would have forestalled it; he had sat on his ass and let it happen, hoping Rick would be killed, because of our personal imbroglio. Having learned from you to what lengths he could go in madness and also in years of concealment of a crucial truth, I seem to have been ready to believe anything. Or perhaps I wanted discredit to be on his side for a change, as between the two of us. He reminded me, rather too quietly, that Rick's plea had come after the report of his death, and went on, still more quietly, to say that I was right nevertheless, not only for the reasons I'd given in my strange tirade. Not that he mightn't have been up to shooting Rick himself a couple of years ago if he'd been near, and taking the consequences; that would be a crime of passion, rather reputable in this country and at times in ours. But on the main point, every diplomat and every government in the world was guilty of that and all associated cruelties, and there wasn't a day when he wasn't conscious of his share of the blame, there and in fifty other atrocity spots around this wretched globe.

"I believed him. I know his kind of conscience—sick, some would call it; but his quiet was the proverbial one before quite a storm. Of course I'd been outrageous in my accusation and I guess just as much so in telling him a few days before about the extraordinary attraction, to the point of readiness to die, that I'd felt for our killer friend. Just dog-killer, I guess a lawyer would say, sticking to evidence of the senses as if they were such a big deal—the sixth is the one I trust. Well, Carter, the bland, the suave, the so endlessly not to say tiresomely considerate, meaning tentative, was so furious under the shell he was driven again to rape. Of me—his lawful wedded wife. I fought him tooth and nail but hadn't your weapon and the results were, 1) pregnancy, by *him* for a change, and 2) the bliss factor, which I used to think was not for me. So I'll gain back the pounds I've just lost, for a possibly better reason than when they larded me up last winter, and the happy fact is making him a great deal more tender and playful with Alan, I'm not sure why. In short, at the moment we're a family of sorts, such as Assunta and Ottavio created out of their troubles years ago, and I feel you'd forgive me, if you ever knew of it, for not reminding my husband every day how much of this curious development we owe to you. As a matter of fact, the new situation makes him such delightful company I wonder if even you . . . A slip of the keys, ignore it, typewriters getting more irresponsible every day.

"As to the present Hensley ménage, I can see Fred's grin as good as saying What's to make it last? It bothers me that I think of him so often, as you must, for far better or worse reasons. It must be mainly the music. I keep hearing the pieces he played, the tones he could produce on that cheap little pipe, and his face when he was doing it, something like Rick's in the young angel stage. How could such blessed endowment go so wrong?—if it did; oh but it did! What am I saying?—the knife rips the length of Corky's belly over and over, every day. That's his scene, his world, where anything goes and death may be the only good trip. He was right about our advantages. I can see that conscience, Carter's kind or maybe any, is the ultimate bourgeois luxury. I tell myself that that doesn't mean we should give it up, like saints giving up their worldly patrimony to the poor, but it does mean—

"Next day. Crowds and racket on the beach and everywhere here intolerable. We've never had lodgings in such a place in August, never would have but for the move any day now and Alan needing beach and playmates. The human swarm, at its noisiest and perhaps ugliest, in all its frantic seaside garb. No place for a Mozart-lover. It would make Fred change his mind about wanting to see Italy, if he meant that. Or might this be just the Italy for him? Certainly there are plenty of foreigners in this parade, drifters of the world, from young to I'd say upper middle age, those last mostly trying to act younger. Along with varieties of native speech, none very cultivated, you can hear bits from just about any language including Eskimo for all I know, and lots of atrocious bits of pickup Italian. There can hardly be a form of seduction and corruption that I don't see passing this window or on the sand beyond. Some of the participants, in the sex deals and everything, are of course just children, but Alan's in a hyper-athletic phase all of a sudden and seems to be staying clear.

"Well, we're drifters too. I'd hardly say you were in a position to be as rude about it as you were, remarking on our expatriate English etc., but you were right. We've discussed cutting this next tour of duty as short as possible and living in the States, I mean the U.S. afterwards, for good if we could swing it. I've learned how to be homesick; the trip taught me that if nothing else. I want to be where echoes aren't borrowed, where they belong to me as long as any persist anywhere in the

world, and I know there's not much time. The echoes I mean
are dying, dying, to quote one of your most unfavorite poets, for
everyone. How long will there be any lake left that brings my
grandfather's songs to me? My grandmother's house may be a
nursing home now for all I know, with a gas station alongside.
Yesterday the church bell, a few blocks back from here, was
ringing and ringing for a funeral, of an old man of the village I
was told, and I felt like a piece of milkweed fluff in the wind, in
October; I remember the pods opening in the field back of that
house—yes, my grandmother's of course; we never had one of
our own long enough for it to be a basic component of memory,
meaning I suppose an influence of any serious sort . . . What I
think I mean is that nobody is ringing any such bell for any of
us, and therefore I don't understand either Corky's death or my
mother's. I've dreamed about them several times as if they were
one, brought about by a single crime, but I never find anything
to tell the police.

"Nor do I understand, if you'll excuse this . . .

"Oops! interruption. Had to keep Alan company on the
beach for a while and I could have sworn I saw him and that he
recognized me too. Could it possibly be? It's true I don't see
well and this man had a beard with a neat shave all around it,
nothing like our friend's overgrown condition, different color
hair too and much longer but that's easy. He was with a girl
and another couple, in flowered trunks and bikinis and good
quality sandals; the others may not have been Americans, anyhow they were all laughing their heads off at some comic act the
Fred character, or Isaac or Denton or Luigi or Gerhardt, was
putting on so there was no language to hear at the moment. I
could almost swear he was looking at me, in a kind of wild
amusement at the recognition, the coincidence, and the girl
hanging on his arm seemed to be aware of something of the sort
too, because they turned back together and both looked hard in
my direction before heading off from the beach, up toward the
bus stop. Of course I can't be sure. It just did give me a start, as
you can imagine, and has left me wondering off and on: why I

should be conjuring him up so vividly if it wasn't he, and how he should happen on just this spot if it was.

"What I broke off from back then, before that apparition real or fancied on the beach, was my not understanding what came close to happening between you and me. I might be looking at one of those scenes out the window here. Some kind of human alphabet seems to have been left out of my education and it makes me wonder what business I have to be carrying a child again. Not that my mother or grandmother were any better equipped for the role that I can see, and there aren't that many Assuntas among the indigenous mothers I'm hearing on this beach. I say hearing deliberately and would no matter how far-sighted I might be. Yak yank slap and yell—sometimes you'd think the great Italian maternity tableau cherished by the world was a picture indeed, a concoction by early to late Renaissance painters in the pay of the Church and the reality was one long infuriated or not quite so often hilarious earsplitting screech. How a people so musical can produce and tolerate the racket, vocal and mechanical, that distinguishes this peninsula has long been a mystery.

"Not that a lower decibel tolerance makes us any better, of course not. We're all blind as bats, not only in government. Maybe our friend of a night is right and the open-eyed are the killers. That's called despair, the worst of the cardinal sins as I remember from my convent days, and the funny thing about it is that it leads right away to hope and that's a great Christian virtue. Actually I imagine it's just an animal response—abhorrence of the negative, in any living organism. What a mish-mash. Still, it's an improvement over the Dennie Hensley of the last year or two, the one you dragged off from a cemetery in New Hampshire. I suppose you dug Corky a grave somewhere near the house. I know I'll never see it but I think of it, and how she never did catch a salamander for all her waiting and watching, with one delicate little paw poised as though to snatch at her own reflection.

"There I go again. I've got to stop it, for the children's sake.

That sounds queer to me but it's true, it'll be plural soon. I've woken up several times in the night and heard the words 'Louder, I couldn't hear that!' and each time I'm mystified first, until I remember, how he had the knife up at my chest and I was supposed to laugh. As the fellow said about setting the first human foot on the moon, what a giant stride that would be for mankind, if the Freds under whatever name are right. Oh death where is thy sting etc. We may have found the answer at last, after all these bumbling millennia. No savor to life, no loss in death, as simple as that. I wonder if Mummy thought of that in her Terminal Consolation Service; I'm afraid probably not, but our gallant visitor by the campfire was surely of some such persuasion, in what he did to Corky and would have done to us if we hadn't been saved—by a doe and fawn!—as beautiful and ungiven to harm as any of God's creatures. Unless there is something to be learned from this last and the marvel of it, what he intended makes him the avantgarde and us the reactionaries. Old Philosophy can go in the trashcan, no use for it any more, it was only to help us cope with death, wasn't it? (There's no reason why you should know, I majored in Philosophy at Radcliffe, haven't read much of it since.) The immortality bit could go too if it weren't there already. And yet, oh Lord, and yet, old fogey me, in the week before the report about Rick was canceled, I felt sure at moments that somewhere, in thunder or sunrise—technicolor panoramas I grant you—his death would take hold of me and there would be enough of me left to miss him with all his faults, dreadfully, however darkly I may see through the glass. I guess that's what it means to mourn. Am I kidding myself? Can any private sorrow exist in this kind of world?

"By the way, you'd have laughed at the spectacle of me in the plane, with bandages all over and the sprained ankle propped up. It turned out not to be broken but I'm afraid your finger was. In a newspaper I read on the trip there was a story about a penitentiary break in New York State and the last of the fugitives being captured somewhere in Vermont, holding up a

sports store where they sold guns and fishing tackle. The name
was nothing like Fred or Isaac or Denton but of course I wondered; also whether you might have been grilled and had trouble because of what I told that nice young deputy. Will
probably never know. If it was that one, it struck me he'd taken
a marvelous chance leaving the note on your car, either from
some strange genuine friendliness and wanting to communicate
with us once more or because he couldn't resist a final joke,
pretending to be illiterate. The deputy might well have found it
before we did. His farewell serenade to us wasn't very cautious
either. Can there be such an equation as that? However, there
were all those other scenarios and the man in the press story
may have been some other damned soul or victim of social
iniquity or combination thereof. (Perdition again!) In the next
lecture we will consider when, how, to what extent those categories are and are not synonymous. It will be no more boring,
because unanswerable, than any other weighty, I mean bot-
tomline question these days.

"You see, I'm trying to update my English. You and the
fiend/victim (?) between you really made me ashamed of it.

"But you, oh my dear friend and goddess of a moment, if you
only knew . . ."

<hr>

There the letter breaks off. The last entry is dated two days
before the flight from Rome. Marilyn Groves and a new woman
companion were recently reported to be in process of adopting
a baby. She is also said to be working on what she calls a novel,
set in Italy but with a cast of no nationality; having furthermore
neither names, traits nor faces, they must be conceived as something other than characters. According to a professor who was
privileged to read the finished chapters, the single more or less
male figure is somewhat American in speech, has murderous
tendencies and a criminal record and plays a tin flute. Like the
other human adumbrations, he appears as a variegated blob of
grey, in a setting of assorted triangles, said by the professor to

be not so much visible as ideational. Although only half completed, the book has already been sold for an unusually large sum, and expectations for it are of course running high. That could be partly because news of the author's role in this artless document has either leaked or been passed out where it would do the most good.